Mighty One Series:

Their children will be mighty in the land; the generation of the upright will be blessed. Psalm 112:2

Burgundy Gloves
Broken Chain- 11/2017
Black Coat- 1/2018

Escape to an era where true love prevails

Escape with short devotionals and extras at juliadwrites.com

Broken

Chain

A novel by

Julia David

Field Runner Press

*"And this is the secret: Christ lives in you.
This gives you assurance of sharing his glory."
Col 1:27b NLT*

I dedicate this story to my children. Who all have said, "Mom, I'm going on a mission's trip."

Paul: YWAM, Kona Hawaii-Tokyo Japan. Quito Ecuador.
Rebekah: Iris Ministries, Mozambique & Nelspirt, South Africa. San Vicente, Mexico.
Emily-Ann: Shangilia Children's Home, Kisumu, Africa. San Vicente, Mexico.
Chloe: BCS, Nez Paz Mexico.
Sophie: at 13, fulfills a beautiful mission of love to all people & creatures in her path.

To all five of you, being your mom has been my life's greatest adventure.

*"Where Can I Flee from
Your Presence?"
Psalm 139:7 NIV*

1

❧

Southern Wisconsin
Fall 1881

O n a thin cot, Benjamin Graham slept on his belly, his boots dangling off the end. Was his father shouting for him to get up? The familiar echo in his head sounded like his father reminding him that he'd never accomplish anything in this life by sleeping past dawn. Pulling up, he sucked in a rapid breath. Someone was pounding his skull while holding him under water. His heavy eyes peeled open as he ran his hand down his wet face. Sitting up on one elbow, he saw the deputy standing behind the looming thick bars. *Oh, yeah.* He held his head, fighting the fog. *I'm in jail.* The empty cup in the deputy's hand probably explained why his face was dripping wet. And the pounding that came from inside his skull was from one too many pints last night.

"Wake up, boy," the bushy-haired deputy barked.

"No need to yell." Ben swung his long legs forward and held his hand out toward the man's booming voice to deflect the pain reverberating in his head. His stomach picked the same moment to roll up to the top of his throat.

"Oh, Lord." Ben rolled back to his prone position.

"Don't make me come in there and dump you out of that bed." The deputy banged the tin cup against the bars holding Ben captive.

"No. No, sir. I'm getting up. Just didn't want to lose my victuals on the floor of this fine establishment." Ben tried to sit up slowly. "I beg you...the noise. My head..."

The deputy, with a patronizing huff, rattled the tin cup harder against the bars.

Walking down the empty wooden sidewalk, Ben winced as the deputy jabbed him in the back with his rifle. Still confused by his surroundings, he tried to remember the name of this one-horse town. *Bucksville...nah, that's not it. Buckboard Holler? Bucking Squalor? That would be a suitable name.* He glanced up to see the early rays of morning held back by a thin layer of clouds. Thank goodness—nothing too bright and cheery. The fresh morning air felt good in his lungs, while the rest of his body cried out in pain. He caught sight of the reason for his sore ribs and imprisonment. The apple cart still rested in a broken storefront window. He looked side to side, thankful no one was around to see him work off his debt to society.

"You know I only destroyed the cart and window last night, right?" They stopped in front of the store. "No fruit was harmed. Not one peach lost its fuzz." Ben waited to see if the deputy would appreciate his humor.

"Just clean it up." The deputy poked his rifle toward the mess.

Ben pulled the broken cart from where it had slammed into the window. Last night was a bit of a blur. The smoky saloon was the last of his full recollections. Looking at the shards of glass dangling from the window frame, he realized it was better he had landed on the apple cart, Without it, his own body flying into that window might have required a few stitches; as it was, a pounding headache felt bad enough. A brown and white alley cat sauntered around the corner and rubbed against his ankles, distracting him from his work. "Oh, friend," Ben bent to rub the cat's neck, seeing missing chunks of fur. "You're worse off than me. Take my advice, this isn't a good place to call home." The deputy slammed his foot on the wooden sidewalk, scaring the cat off.

"Okay, okay." Ben met the crossed bushy eyebrows. "That lasted about as long as most my relationships," he mumbled. "Do you have a broom for all this small glass?"

"No. Use your hands."

Ben knelt and placed the specks of glass in his hand. He noticed a shiny chain with a little trinket of some kind under the glass. It probably fell out of the store display. He picked it up and held the gold chain with a small cross. It was maybe something his ma would like.

A wave of guilt ran across his chest and squeezed his torso. He wished the sour pain was nothing more than a simple bellyache. How could his family be miles away, yet he still felt like a child under the weight of their disapproval?

The proverbial wanderer, his parents called him. The son without direction. The one who just roams from thing to thing. He dropped the necklace in his pocket. Why just be the drifter of the family? Might as well be a thief, too.

"Wake up, boy!"

Ben rolled his eyes. Nothing like being a six-foot three-inch man with hair everywhere, and still being called a boy. *I probably deserve it.*

"Yes, sir." Ben hoped cooperation would get him a ticket out of this cell.

"Mr. Long said the clean-up is fine, but you owe him seven bucks for a new window."

Ben held his eyes closed. Might as well be seventy bucks. He had no money.

The deputy came over and unlocked the cell and opened the door. Ben looked around, uneasy. Truth be told, he had a cot and hot meals here. He stepped out, second-guessing his release into the free world.

"Unless you got some sweet grannie coming to pay your debt, my guess is you'll be starting work down at the rock quarry. They pay a dollar a day, minus two bits for food and a quarter for a bunk."

Ben added and subtracted quickly in his head, looked at the deputy and walked back into the cell.

"Get back out here, lazy boy."

Longing for another nap, Ben tried to pull his mind into action. "Sir, the problem is…I already have a job. I was on my way to it before that little mishap in front of the store." He prayed under his breath for mercy. "I'm worried they'll think I'm not coming if I don't get there soon. I can make arrangements with my employer to send the seven dollars to Mr. Long."

"Oh, I'm sure I can count on that." The deputy took a seat behind his desk and put his feet up. "Like snow in July."

Ben sat down across from the deputy's desk. He considered throwing his long legs on the desk, too, but decided not to push his luck.

"Where's this job you're in such a hurry to get to?" The deputy threw his hat on the desk.

"I think about fifty miles or so from here, in Elbert County. My family is longtime friends with the Von Kellers. They own a dairy farm there."

"Going off into the big world to be a milkmaid?" The deputy laughed.

Ben felt the sting of the very truth he wanted to avoid. "Beats pounding rock."

"Well, seeing what a hurry you're in to get on to this new job, I'll have Milton at the livery sell your horse and settle it with Mr. Long."

Ben glared up at the ceiling. "How'm I supposed to get there without my horse?" The once communicative deputy leaned forward, with fire and disdain in his eyes. Ben pulled back.

"My brother was about your age when he lost his foot." His voice dripped with sarcasm. "No…no…that's not right. His whole leg got blown off at the Battle of Fredericksburg." Ben swallowed hard and glanced at the door.

"His stump just rotted away, poisoning his whole body. Suffering every day until he died an excruciating death." The deputy's nostrils flared. "But you were just a pup, cuddled up close to your mama. You wouldn't know about real hardship now, would ya? Had enough money to get drunk last night."

Ben's heart pounded in his chest. He knew enough not to answer that.

The deputy leaned back in his chair. "And you got two legs and some decent boots. Head south to Elbert County. There's the door. Get out."

My boots were decent a week ago. Ben sulked, looking down as he walked. Two days of walking had made a mess of his feet and his boots. Blisters and hot sweaty feet did not bode well inside the stiff leather. *Dang, I miss my horse.* He'd worked for two months for his elderly friends, Ray and Thelma. He'd chopped eight cords of wood, hunted weekly for game for them and even held the hot steamer full of canning jars for Thelma. The horse they gave him was a good-natured animal. *All that work, for what?* He groaned. *Just to lose the only possession I've ever had of value.* The heat of the day was causing him to huff, and he needed water. Following a small trail around the overgrown brush, he was pleased to find a small creek. He sat in the grass and pulled his boots off. Tugging off his stockings, he winced as the wool pulled a bleeding blister apart. He held his red and pink feet out and barely allowed them to touch the water. Gritting his teeth, he finally dropped them under.

Growling, he closed his eyes, wishing he was back home in Sault Creek. He and his older brother Levi would have already been fully wet, probably holding each other under. He leaned forward and cupped a drink of water. Sharp pains stabbed at his gut; he shouldn't have eaten those last ten crab apples. He laid back in the grass, clutching his belly. *Oh, for one of Ma's biscuits with jam and freshly churned butter.*

If he were home now, he would never complain again. He had taken for granted a roof over his head and plenty of food on the table. He exhaled wearily, missing them all. He wondered what had really happened between the young woman Levi had rescued, Allison, and his stiff-necked brother. She had soft blue eyes, pretty little thing. Of course, Levi had feelings for her. Levi could try and hide it all he wanted, but since he practically kicked Ben out of his cabin, he must have felt something. Levi had always been his protector, his go-between. Never in a lifetime did he think his older brother would choose a stranger over him. It still felt like a punch to the gut. *Family.*

Ben shook his head and dropped his arm over his eyes. It never really bothered him that his pa rarely spoke a kind word; he was just trying to turn boys into men, but being so far from home when he heard of his father's passing was cause for regret. The thought of his family, mourning together without him darkened his mood. Pulling out a long piece of grass, he stuck it in his mouth and chewed. He had learned to stay clear of his pa, because he had his older brothers. They always protected him, which was not hard when he was always following Levi's footsteps. Levi taught him how to trap and hunt, and they did everything together. But now Levi had made it clear he wasn't welcome anymore.

Truth be told, he didn't want to stay. He was itching to make his own way, and Levi's cabin, far from everything, held little appeal. Ben smelled something rancid and pulled his shirt up to his nose. Yep, it was him. How long since he'd had a bar of soap in his hand? At least there was no one around him to complain. He thought of a good dunk back at Sault Creek, clean clothes, something sizzling on the spit. Who was he kidding? The traveler's life was incredibly lonely, and he'd found out the hard way that going to saloons wasn't going to solve anything. Next time he saw Levi, he was going to get an ear full. Just because they had lost their brother Daniel in a drowning, Levi must have thought his only job was to keep him as his shadow. Well, you can't keep your shadow one minute and push him away the next. It's just not right.

Benjamin's stomach pinched, interrupting his thoughts. He had to get to that dairy. He pulled his feet out of the creek and hugged his knees to his chest. He needed money. With it, he could buy a new horse, which could help him get home. Traveling from place to place seemed like a grand adventure, but now it pained him, like this bellyache and blistered feet. If he went home, he could help his ma, maybe go work in the mines like his pa did, prove himself stable, reliable. He remembered the Von Kellers from years ago. They were decent people, and at least they would feed him. Maybe he'd like being a milkmaid, but the deputy's words still stung.

Shoving on his stockings and boots, he stood. *Pray for me Ma, I'm like the prodigal son in that Bible story. He was welcomed home, and they threw a party when he returned. Doubt anyone would come to a party if I came home, but one of your cakes would be nice.*

2

Nadine Von Keller sat at breakfast, eating her toast and jam, her Ridley and Sons fashion catalog posed perfectly next to the country rose china.

"Frau Edda, more coffee, please." Nadine carefully moved her catalog to avoid even one wayward drop to come near it. "Thank you, Edda." Her parents loved having a German-speaking maid. Nadine tried to ignore anything German. For heaven's sake, they were all Americans. At least she and her two sisters were born here. Her parents wanted to hold on to the old stiff and staunch ways, which irritated her constantly. She carefully resumed her study of the winter fashions.

"Mother." Nadine finally looked up. "You said the alterations on the green gown would be done yesterday. I didn't see a delivery. Maybe we are to pick it up?"

Helga Von Keller shook her head toward her beautiful daughter. "Nadine, you know perfectly well the challenges of living in this county. Everything takes longer. If we don't see it today…"

"I have a book to return." Nadine cut her off. "I'll check on it when I go into town."

"Nadine, you have no patience. Really, you find an excuse to go to town every day. It's not proper. We have help to run our errands. I don't like thinking of you flitting around town," Helga said harshly. "You have the Literary Society coming here on Thursday; certainly that is entertaining enough."

"And I would like to have the gown to wear by Thursday." Nadine got up and left the table.

She took a deep breath as she climbed the stairs of her family's two-story brick colonial. *I never really agreed not to go to town.* Her mother expected her to sit around and do needlepoint all day. One more afternoon of flower arranging or tutoring her younger sister Minna might just send her off the edge. Her mother had never been able to stop any of her daughters from doing what they wanted. For goodness sake, her older sister Margaret pushed her way out the door all the way to Northwestern University. Their mother had had the vapors for a week. Her sister wanted a college paper saying she had a degree in Applied Christianity. What a tale. She could attend the university, Nadine shrugged, but she had no desire for any more boring classes. The piano was the only thing she enjoyed.

Nadine approached her large room with champagne pink draperies and bedding. She checked her appearance, admiring the two stately hair rolls positioned high atop her head. Smoothing each one, she looked side to side in the mirror. As long as they were perfect, who knows who one might meet in town?

An hour later, Nadine walked through the small county library. Her window seat was empty and provided the perfect view of the only thing stimulating in this entire town. She glanced down at the book she held and shrugged. Nothing was as interesting as a conversation between her and her hero, Marcus. And he was real. The problem was, he worked at the hotel and saloon across from the library. Her mother would never approve. But their one encounter had sent her over the moon for days. Now, she waited to see if she could arrange another chance meeting. She entertained her favorite memory—that fateful day her champion had rescued her from a horse trying to trample her. She had memorized everything about him, the way his hand caught hers and pulled her to himself, the way he smelled. She remembered a mixture of whiskey and soap. No page could adequately describe those stormy gray eyes. His smile so inviting. Every feature so perfectly placed on his face. Not a flaw to be found. His words ground into her mind. "Your misfortune has become my favorite moment." Did he hold her as long as she remembered? Was it as improper as she liked to let herself think? Her stomach did a flip. How could another human being leave her dizzy, body and soul?

Nadine stirred from her favorite daydream. The wagon rolling into town looked a lot like their wagon from the dairy. She panicked a moment to think they might be coming to find her, but the wagon rolled past her and stopped abruptly in front of the doctor's office. Nadine rose and set the book aside. It looked like Frau Edda's husband, Carl, jumping down. She jerked back, startled. Her father was being helped from the back of the wagon. She quickly made her way from the library and raced into the dirt-packed street. Running up to Carl, she gasped to see her father writhing in pain.

"Father! What has happened?"

"My leg." He could barely talk. "Go inside daughter, find the doctor."

An hour later, Nadine held a tight arm around her shaking mother.

"You can take him home," the doctor said to them. "I've set the bone and wrapped it as tightly as I can, but he needs to stay in bed for at least six weeks. Mix some of this powder in a cup of tea. It should help the pain."

Nadine waited for her mother to respond.

"Thank you, sir," she said, hoping her mother wasn't going to start crying again.

Frau Edda and Carl helped carry Otto Von Keller to the extra downstairs room.

"Be ready to brew more tea for his powders, *ja*." Helga snapped at Edda and tried to prop a pillow under her husband's leg.

"*Nein!*" He cried out in pain.

"Oh, Mother." Nadine stepped in. "Here, Father, is that better?" Nadine gently moved the pillow.

"*Ja,*" she heard her father whisper as he laid back.

Nadine watched her mother chewing her knuckles. "Don't worry, Mother, we'll manage." She led her out the door.

Helga stiffened. "You sound so sure. Where were you today when that heifer fell on your father's leg? I couldn't find you anywhere. Who will run the dairy? Who will keep track of the workers? Are you going to put the rubber boots on and go milk the cows?"

"Mother, now you sound hysterical." Nadine wanted her to calm down. "We have workers to run the dairy. They haven't gone anywhere."

"Well, I have the house and you and Minna to care for. I can't run the dairy. I wish our boy had lived." Helga started to sniffle.

"Mama, please…" Nadine pulled her hankie free and gave it to her mother.

Helga blew hard and wiped her tears. "I'm writing Margaret this very evening. I've had enough of her independent streak. This is a perfect time to put an end to the university. She needs to get home. The family is in calamity. She needs to be here."

"Hmm, maybe so." Nadine rubbed her mother's back. Any plan to get the focus off her was a welcome one.

3

"Minna!" Nadine shouted, as her unpredictable thirteen-year-old sister ran past. "Get your hair done, now! Your teacher will be here any moment." She shook her head to the empty hallway. *That girl needs to be on a chain.* She gritted her teeth. It had only been four days since her father's injury, and she was ready to lock Minna away in a boarding school. How hard could it be to get her to comply? Nadine walked into Minna's room and looked around. Feeling a prickle of hope, she picked up her younger sister's beloved scrapbook. "You have just become mine," she said, smiling as she carried it into her room and stuffed it under her mattress.

Nadine strolled into the extra room they used for music and school. She took a piece of chalk and contemplated how to leverage the item for her best uses.

Someone has stolen your scrapbook, she wrote on the chalkboard. *It will only be returned when Minna obeys Nadine. Until then, it will be kept in a soiled and smelly place.* Nadine stood back with a tight smile. *That should do it.*

She descended the stairs and checked out the front window to see if the teacher had arrived. Thankfully, he was not early, and if her sister's hair looked like a tousled mess, so be it. Shoulders dropping, she could hear her mother complaining to Frau Edda. Once again, everything was Frau Edda's fault. Father did not like the soup. The window lets in too much air. The tea was cold. Nadine wanted to intervene. Her worst nightmare will be if Frau Edda quit. No one would work for Helga Von Keller. Not in this crisis, anyway. Sighing, she turned the corner to try to console her mother when she heard a scream from upstairs.

"Minna! What has happened?" her mother called, coming around the staircase. Nadine tried to hold back a smile and put her hands up to stop her mother. "I know why she's screaming, Mother. Please, don't mediate. She's just getting ready for lessons."

"Nadine. I can't have this. You said you would be of help. You are responsible for Minna. I cannot…" Another high-pitched shriek came from upstairs. Helga shook her head and covered her ears.

"I am helping," Nadine said. "Go up and lie down, Mother. You look like you're going to fall over." They jumped as someone knocked on the door. "Go, Mother. It's just the teacher." Nadine waited until her mother started up the stairs, still clutching her ears. Just as she reached to open the door, she heard Minna crying and complaining to her mother. She held the doorknob, in hopes that the closed door would prevent the teacher from hearing the ranting.

"Minna! The teacher is here!" she yelled up the staircase. "Leave Mother be and get ready." Another repeat of her younger sister's victim performance. Clenching her teeth, she turned and drew in a much-needed breath. Opening the door, she saw a tall, scruffy vagabond.

"Oh, for heaven's sake!" Nadine couldn't take anymore. "We don't have any jobs. We don't have any extra food. Just get off the stoop and be on your way." Waving him off, she shut the door. She turned to look at the top of the stairs. "Mother, no." Her mother held the weeping performer. "Don't listen to her. She hasn't done one thing I've asked all day." Nadine heard another knock on the door. She flung it open in pure frustration. "I said get out!" Nadine slapped her hand over her mouth. "I'm so sorry, Mr. Peabody. I thought you were someone else. Won't you please come in?" She straightened her back, afraid to look to the stairs.

"Welcome, Mr. Peabody." Her mother's voice rang calmly down the stairs. "Minna will meet you in the schoolroom. Won't you come on up?"

Nadine stood frozen, as an air of calm and civility seemed to magically appear. Mr. Peabody walked by her as if nothing was amiss. *Why try?* She rolled her eyes as he ascended the stairs. *They're all fine as daisies, and I just want to punch something. I need out of here.* She groaned, shaking her head.

Walking south from the smelly dairy, she spouted off to the swaying branches of the tall trees. At least the air couldn't talk back. "I'm young and beautiful...please, someone please get me out of this madhouse. Why should I have to take care of everyone? It's not fair!"

"No, it's not," someone said.

Her heart slammed against her chest, and she looked down to see the vagabond sitting under a tree, chewing on a piece of long grass.

"How dare you scare me like that?" She glanced at the house, gauging how far she might have to run.

"I just answered your question." He scratched his back against the tree, long legs extended. "You're right, you're much too pretty to scrape and scour, taking care of everyone."

Nadine's instinctive caution seemed to fade a bit. "I thought I told you to get out of here." He was younger than she first thought. His eyes were a soft warm brown, but his clothes were worn and dirty. Loose waves of brown hair were tucked behind his ears, highlighting a scruffy face.

"Are you Nadine?" he said.

Nadine startled, her eyes wide. "How do you know my name? I'm sure we've never met. Announce yourself at once!"

"Is your older sister Maggie? I think I used to call her Mags or was it Miss Mags?"

"Sir, please identify yourself at once!" Nadine felt her mind racing. Where could such a vagrant know of her? Is he a worker from the dairy? From town? They had never been allowed to go to the school in town.

"Maybe I should have asked if you were, Na-Na, Nadine." He winked.

Nadine felt her childhood shame burn in her throat, her face searing with embarrassment and pain. Who would know she often stuttered as a child? As a daughter of an overbearing mother who could never get a word in without distress, it was a malady that had taken her years to conquer.

*   *   *

Nadine staggered back, her tongue touching her top lip. Were those tears forming in her eyes?

"Blast it." Ben rose up quickly. "I didn't mean anything by that. I thought it was cute. It was one of the things I remember about you. And your braids down your back. You used to have those little strings…"

"Ribbons?" Nadine snapped, her hands clutching her waist.

"Yeah…those were nice." Ben flipped his hat on, then pulled it back off. Twirling it in his hands, he looked out to the left and tried to find a way to redeem himself.

"Benny, Bens…go ahead, I deserve it. But I'd like to be called Ben now." Her motionless stare unnerved him. "Your folks and mine were friends. We all lived outside of Ready Springs. We played after church. The Grahams."

"Yes, I remember your family, vaguely. You're just a bit taller than I remember."

He shot her a large thankful smile. "Yeah, but I think I'm done growing."

"How wonderful for you," she scowled.

Ben scratched behind his ear and scrunched his face. Why had she gone sour? "Anyway, you didn't give me time at the door to explain."

"We're in the midst of a challenging time," Nadine said, "as you can guess by my rudeness at the door."

"Whew." He wiped his sleeve along his brow. "I worried if that's how you greeted everyone."

"No, of course not." Her nostrils flared. "But this is not the best time for a social visit. Are you traveling with your parents? Maybe you can leave us some communication for another time."

Ben clamped his lips together. This was now the second quick brush-off she had rudely given him. "So sorry to hear things are…challenging." *What a snoot.* He shook his head. *My pa is dead, and I didn't even get invited to the funeral. I probably wasn't even missed. Now that's a real family challenge.* He contemplated just walking away, but the stupid letter tried to burn a hole in his shirt. Nothing in his being wanted a job at a dairy—but he was also hungry, broke and desperate.

"I have a letter from your pa. He invited me here. To work, of course." Ben pulled the letter from his pocket and waved it at her.

"Oh, I see." Nadine tapped her finger against her lip.

Ben felt belittled. She acted as if his fate was in her hands. "Can I at least talk to your pa?"

She chewed on a tiny corner of her lip. "My mother still talks so highly of your mother." Her brow wrinkled. "When my brother died, she was greatly comforted by her help. I'm sure she would at least like to hear about your family." She took in a deep breath. "All right." Still holding her breath, she looked back at the house, back to Ben, and let it out. "But I want you to clean up before you see my parents. My father has a broken leg, and my mother can't cope with anything much." She stilled, thinking. "Just follow me."

4

B en followed Nadine across the grass to the back of the house. Lord forgive him, she had a wide bow that swayed to and fro from her hips, and he couldn't help but stare. It was delightfully entertaining. The sky-blue dress with a line of tiny buttons and the curve of her little waist were enchanting. Even the sound of her walking, swishing back and forth, back and forth…He looked up quickly when she spoke.

"Our housemaid is Frau Edda. She can get the tub ready," Nadine said when they reached the top of the back stairs. She pushed open the door. "Do you have a razor?"

Ben took two steps and stroked his patchy thin beard. "Nope." Near where he stood, he saw the pantry, with shelves and shelves of canned foods. Glass jars labeled with vegetables and fruits lined the area. Bins of rice and beans, baskets of potatoes and onions made him wide-eyed. "Before I'm boiled and skinned, can I have something to eat?" When it came to his stomach, he lost all pride.

Nadine seemed to look down her nose at him, even though he towered over him. "I'll let Frau Edda know. She has her hands full, caring for my father."

"I thought you had to take care of everyone." Ben was sorry as soon as it left his mouth. He tried to smile, to see if she would realize he was only teasing.

"Hmph." Nadine walked a few steps into the kitchen. "Try that basket there for leftovers. I'll go find Frau Edda."

As soon as she left, Ben drew his hands down his face. The girl was beautiful, but brittle, dangling far out of reach, like every other confusing thing in his life. Stomach growling, he looked around. He didn't realize how dirty he was until he reached for a piece of bread and saw his hand against the white linen. No wonder he repelled her.

"Sir," Frau Edda said from behind the door from where Ben bathed. "I have left your shirt and pants here. I gave them a press with the hot iron."

"Thanks. Oh, *danke.*" Ben tried to remember if that was the right word in German. He finished his shaving and held the mirror a bit longer. The clean shave helped his appearance tremendously. His hair was squeaky clean, and he pushed it back behind his ears. Nadine was a flower; any man in his right mind would want a pretty girl to think him handsome. He rose from the dirty water and reached for a towel. It was time to see how long he was staying.

Nadine walked into the extra room, thinking it would be safer to approach her father alone.

"Father, we have a guest," she said calmly.

Otto snapped his paper in half and looked up at his daughter at the foot of the bed. "What does he want?"

"It's Benjamin Graham from up north. He said he has a letter about coming to work here."

Otto looked surprised. "James and Laura's boy? The youngest one?"

"Yes," Nadine said. "That's the one."

"I wrote that letter over six months ago. Ha! And now he shows up? Maybe God's timing, *ja?*" Otto winced, trying to arrange his leg on the pillow.

Nadine gave her father a weak smile. "I wouldn't know about that. Would you like to see him, or should I send him away?"

"*Nein.* Don't send him away. I will at least talk to him." He pulled himself up against the headboard.

Ben dressed and wandered around the kitchen. A house this big must have a bottle of wine or ale or something decent to drink. Frau Edda walked in and stopped his search.

"I wash your other clothes. Those were in your bag. Just needed a press."

"*Danke.*" Ben gave a quick bow. He was just about to ask her what spirits were in the house when Nadine walked in.

Nadine stopped cold and looked at Edda. "Frau Edda, what did you do with the young man I left with you? Did he leave?"

Edda looked at Ben, then Nadine and back to Ben. She finally broke into a wide grin. "Oh, now, Nadine. He looks *gut, ja?*"

"*Ja*, very *gut.*" Nadine imitated her strong accent while looking up and down at the remarkable change.

Ben stood a little taller, something flipping in his gut. Now she found some good will for him? All it took was a bath? He had never understood women, but he flashed her a warm smile anyway.

"Benjamin Graham, my father will talk to you now." She held her hand out to show the way. He walked up to her, enjoying his height advantage. "These are nice." He patted the two perfect rolls of hair sitting atop her head.

Nadine shook her head and gave him a little push down the hallway. "You always were an entertaining boy. You re-membered the ribbons because you were always pulling on them. Seems not much has changed."

He walked forward, turning to look at her. "Things *have* changed," he whispered, casting her a small wink before he turned into the bedroom.

Otto extended his hand toward Ben. "This can't be Benjamin Graham." They shook hands with vigor. "My goodness, you have gotten tall. Did all the Graham boys turn out so tall?"

"No, sir. I got about four inches over my brothers." Otto was just as Ben remembered him, now with a smattering of gray in his hair.

"*Ja, ja*…sit down." Otto pointed to a chair. "Nadine!" he hollered, "You get us something to drink? Some cider, *ja*?"

Ben heard her faint reply from down the hall—something about not being the maid.

"I never knew if you got my letter. And now you can tell I'm laid up." He nodded to his propped-up leg. "This could not be better timing. You are a fast learner?" He didn't give Ben time to respond. "It's not that hard. Carl can show you. You are ready to learn about the dairy?"

Ben hesitated, his motivation lagging for the call to work. Hearing the swishing of Nadine's skirt as she came down the hall with drinks, he faked a smile, "Yes, sir. I'm ready as I'll ever be."

5

❧◦❧

Frau Edda and her husband had a simple two-bedroom cottage behind the two-story Von Keller home. Their sons were long gone, and they seemed happy to have Ben in the extra room. Ben had hoped for a room in the big house, but according to Mrs. Von Keller, it wouldn't be proper with so many daughters living there.

In the past two weeks, he had been invited to supper each night at the long formal table. He heard that the oldest, Margaret, had gone to college, and the youngest, Minna, was only thirteen. Tonight, like each of the other nights, the only female it would be improper to be in the house with was Nadine. He discounted the truth that he was often reckless and immature. But if they made every unmarried man rise before dawn and work as hard as he did, they all would be too tired to worry about anything but sleep. For the last two weeks, he could barely wait for the sun to go down before he fell into bed, dog tired. He stirred around the pale custard and thought about how soft the new bed was compared to sleeping on the ground.

"How do you think it is going, young Ben?" Otto said from the end of the large table.

Ben didn't like the 'young' reference but offered up a quick smile. "Going well, sir. I'm learning a lot." He took a bite of custard. It didn't taste like his ma's. "Certainly I'm used to taking care of livestock and the chores around my folks' place, but we only had one cow."

"Ahh, Benjamin," Helga broke in. "I keep thinking of your *mutter*. How will she manage without her husband? I'm so very sad to hear of your papa's passing. And you being so far away, not being there with your family. *Tsk*."

Ben reached for a drink of water, wishing it had the power to wash her words away. "My brother James and his wife Frieda," Ben swallowed. "They're with her."

"She is such a strong woman, *ja*. I'll never forget the way she came to help me when our boy died." Ben heard the *clink* of Nadine's spoon dropping into her empty bowl. "And you all, in so much grief when you lost one. The way she came to comfort me. I will never forget her kindness."

Just when Ben wanted to watch Nadine, Helga started up again. "And your *mutter* has such strong faith, *ja*? She has great comfort from God."

"The dairy is almost up to speed." Otto reentered the conversation. "You can now have Sundays off. I'm sure your *mutter* would want you in church, and I can give the other workers a full day off, now. Thanks to your help."

Ben nodded. "I appreciate that. I noticed your woodshop is full of cobwebs. If I have some time on Sunday, do you mind if I tinker around in there?"

"*Nein,* it could use some attention, help yourself. Minna, get my crutches." Otto strained to balance the crutches as he stood. "*Ach!* These are determined to break my other leg."

Ben conveyed his thanks and caught Nadine watching him. "It's not quite dark." He kept his eyes on her. "I think I'll take in some fresh air before I turn in."

*   *   *

Nadine waited as long as she could bear it, and finally threw her napkin on the table and made her excuses. She ran up the stairs and tried to look out her window. Which way would he go? She could feel her heart beating erratically. She went to grab her wrap, then put it back. It would be just her luck for Minna to see her and want to tag along. She scurried to her door and looked both ways. The hallway was clear; she just needed to tiptoe down the back staircase and out through the kitchen. How long could she be gone before her family looked for her? Any time away from the house was a pure reprieve. She hiked up the hem of her brown taffeta day dress and ran toward the spot she had first met Ben. She broke out a winded smile when she noticed his long legs in front of the tree. "I thought you were going for a walk." She straightened a loose strand of hair and tried to control her fast breathing.

"I didn't want to go too far. You'd have a hard time finding me." Ben pulled one knee up and dropped his arm on it.

"I'm just out for a stroll myself. I think I might just continue on my way." She started to move as Ben jumped up and grabbed her hand. "Ben…" she said, warning.

He quickly let go of her hand. "I know you've been busy. Your father said you had some ladies' reading club here last week." He stepped back and leaned against the thick tree.

"Yes, I'm the co-chair of the Literary Society. It's very important," she said, patting her hair.

He watched her, waiting.

"We do more than just read books. We helped buy new textbooks for the school. We have one of our largest fundraisers coming up in a few weeks. It's a cotillion."

"A co-what?"

"A cotillion. A dance," she said. "Do you know how to dance?"

"Mmm, no." Ben kicked a rock. "But if I did, would you invite me?"

Nadine stepped past him and looked back over her shoulder. "Anyone can come. You don't have to dance, or be invited."

"But it won't be any fun unless I know someone. And right now, you're the only person I would want to dance with."

"How sad." Nadine pouted. "If only you could dance."

Ben walked circles around her. "It can't be that hard. What if you taught me? I'm a very good student."

She touched her finger to her lip, thinking. This would be a sure way of meeting with him, and sneaking out was so fun. At least her mother would not throw a fit if she explained she was teaching Ben to dance. A suitable cover.

Both Nadine and Ben turned to hear the faint sound of her name coming from the house. Nadine grunted. "That's Minna. On Mondays, I have to help her with the harp before bed. I have to go." She broke from his circling and started toward the house.

"Wait," Ben called. "When's our first lesson?"

"I'll have to think about it." She turned back quickly and kept walking.

He ran up before her and stopped her in her tracks. "I can't go another week trying to get your attention at supper. Meet me here tomorrow night at dark."

She opened her mouth as if she would refuse his suggestion. "I'll try." She smiled wistfully, moving around him.

* * *

Ben, gentlemanly, bowed his thanks to a light, shadowy moon and watched her run to the back steps. *God did a wonderful job on this one.* She was pretty and worth all the effort it took to tease her. He could start to forget everything he'd done wrong and almost believe a young woman as fine as Nadine would have affections for him. So far, he'd found nothing about dairy farming that agreed with him, but this young woman—this he liked.

Stepping carefully through Edda and Carl's dark kitchen, he entered his room. His heart beat fuller and lighter than it had in months. He reached to turn down his bed-side lamp and hesitated. Reaching inside his bag, he pulled out the letter from his father and the gold necklace he'd taken. He held the chain against the light; the little cross was shiny. He let it fall back into his pack. Holding the let-ter to the light, he took a few deep breaths.

The truth was, he hadn't had the courage to read it. He already knew what was expected of the Graham boys. To work hard, be respectful, make him proud. He carefully broke the tightly folded page open and pressed the paper between his fingers. Maybe he should enjoy this lightheart-edness for a while longer, even knowing this paper was once in his father's hands. His father's last words would only up-set him. He could feel the tightness in his throat. *So far, I've been working hard. Haven't fallen down the well yet.* He allowed the folds to press back together. There was a small chance the personal words might bring comfort to his crooked soul, but he strongly doubted it. It was safer to let it slip back into his pack and turn the light out. He wanted a good sleep. Carl would be waking him before the rooster was up.

6

Out of nowhere, a muddy, wet tail smacked Ben in the face. He tried to swipe it away and found foul mud smeared from chin to ear. *Cows.* He could swear that tail hit him on purpose. He heard one of the other workers laugh as they walked by. He'd learned to tie the cow's legs, so as not to get kicked. But nobody said anything about the tail. He leaned his forehead against the cow's large belly and tried to keep his hands on the teats. His eyes were heavy, the air suffocating him in the long cow barn without any breeze. He hated getting up at four in the morning. Maybe he could close his eyes for five minutes. Just five minutes…

Ben jerked as the stool shook underneath him. Someone had kicked it, probably one of the workers snickering at the other side of the barn. He looked down at a tipped over bucket of milk. Did he do that when he jerked awake? Or did the kicker of the stool knock it over? A fly picked the wrong time to buzz up his nose. He snorted hard and grabbed the bucket, then stood up and threw it down the dirt corridor where he thought the other workers were taunting him. He marched down to them. "He finally kicked the bucket," he heard one say, and more snickering erupted. Balling his fists, Ben had a split second to go after one of them or walk out. He kept walking.

He'd been in plenty of worse scrapes with his brothers. Sucking in a deep breath, he knew he wasn't afraid of a good fight. Glancing back at the smelly barn, he contemplated a good fist fight to get some restlessness out. He looked up to the road that fronted the Von Keller's home. If they kicked him out, he'd be walking another long walk out of respectability. He'd never been as reckless as he was in that last hole of a town.

Ben pounded the tall grass as he stalked around the large oak trees. Just one drink. His body yearned for a distraction. He'd gone through every nook and cranny of Edda's and Carl's home. Not one drop of anything. Showing up to supper early at the big house, he waited until Edda was serving and looked through the cupboards. Nothing.

Maybe he should have stayed with the rock quarry? At least he'd have a horse. The sun broke through the branches, blinding him. He moved into the shade and looked around. How long would it take him to walk into town— and what would he do without money? His search for booze had revealed a small canister in the back of Frau Edda's cupboard. It was just pocket change. By the time he got paid, he could replace the money, and they'd never know it was gone. Suddenly riled, he gripped his hands together. He'd rip his hair out if he had to sit on that stool for one more minute. He looked left and right and entered the kitchen. Sanity and survival were at stake. One small drink would patch him right up.

Ben walked onto the shady boardwalk. How could early fall be so hot? Before he even saw the sign, his skin got goosebumps. Maybe he could smell the aroma. The saloon was waiting with open arms. It looked so good. He closed his eyes for a moment and smelled the combination of furniture wax and alcohol. He tried to calm himself. One beer. One slow romantic dance across his lips, that's all. Scanning the almost empty room, he walked up to the bar. Frau Edda's money burned like depravity in the palm of his hand.

"A pint, please." Finally wrapping his hand across a precious cool glass, he found a quiet corner to pull out a seat. His body sank into the hardwood like a feather bed. Nothing brought relief to his body, mind, and soul like that first swallow.

"Hate to see a strong strapping fella falling asleep in here."

Ben looked up wearily to see who was talking.

"I got a couple poker games I could get you started in. And if ya need a good rest, I've got just the gal to help ya... sleep." The man smiled with perfect white teeth.

Ben sat up and smiled back. "No, no...I gotta get going."

"My name's Marcus Monroe. My father owns the place, but I'm the manager." He stuck his hand out, and Ben shook it. "You new around here? Don't think I've seen you in here before."

"Been here less than a month." Ben looked down at the four tall empty glasses and had the strangest urge to hide them. "I've been working at the Von Kellers…it's a dairy farm."

"Really." Marcus's brow crinkled. "Are you family?"

"Ahh, no, not really. My parents and the Von Kellers were friends, years ago. They had three daughters. We have three boys." Ben wasn't sure why that mattered.

"Oh, I get it. You here to marry one and take over the business?" Marcus squinted.

Why does this guy sound so insulted? "I need to get back." Ben stood, wavering.

"Hold on a second." Marcus walked back over to the bar, then turned and grabbed a glass. "This oughta help." He dropped two more quick shots into the glass.

"Thanks, but I'm out of money." He raised his hand as he headed for the door.

"Hold on." Marcus called him back. "It's on the house. For all first time customers. I've never made this one before, so you can be the one to name it." He slid it across the wooden bar.

Ben licked his lips and turned to the waiting liquid. His hand slowly reached the drink. There wasn't even much in the glass. He could amuse the manager. He took the first drink and tried to hide the shock of the fire burning down his throat. He followed with a second larger gulp. Now his bravado had to come through. He needed to gather his senses to get the last swallow down. He forced it down and looked up to Marcus with glazed eyes.

"Did you like it? What do you want to call it?"

Ben wiped his nose, wondering if it was bleeding. "I don't know." He really couldn't think of anything. He thought the room tilted for a minute. He shook his head at the man waiting.

"Fine...I'll name it for you." Marcus paused, acting like he was in deep thought. "Let's call it...The Nadine."

7

Carl and Edda drank another cup of coffee at their small square table, staring out into the morning sky. "I should be waking him up about now. But I don't think he ever came home."

"You sure he's not already out in the barn?" Edda searched out the window.

"I didn't ask Mr. Von Keller if he wanted to give Ben a day off. I think he just might have taken one for himself."

"*Ja.*" Edda chewed a hangnail.

"He couldn't have gone far. All his things are still in the room." Carl stood up and reached for the cupboard. He reached behind the box of cornmeal and pulled out their money tin. He let out a long sigh as he held it upside down, to show Edda.

"Oh, no."

"I'm going to go looking for him. I think his days at the dairy are over."

"Ahh, Papa." Edda touched his arm. "Let him explain. He showed up here with many miles on him. He looks so different, all cleaned up. Maybe the Von Kellers want to give him a second chance, *ja?*"

Carl's eyes narrowed as he headed out the door. Only about a mile from the house, he saw a man asleep on the ground. He walked up and took a long look at Ben. No cuts or bruises. *Gut,* Carl frowned. *He can pay back my money before Mr. Von Keller sends him packing.* He gave him a firm kick in the butt.

∗ ∗ ∗

"Levi!" Ben yelled out, batting the air. He sat up, noticing the crack of sunlight coming across the Von Keller property. "Oh…Carl." Ben rubbed the dirt out of his eyes. "I thought you were my brother."

"*Nein.*" Carl pierced him with a stare.

Ben stood up, wobbling, and tried to shake off the leaves and twigs. His mind and belly were twirling. "I wanted to go hunting, but I… got lost. Then I didn't want to come in late and wake anyone."

"Hunting, *ja?* Hard to do with your rifle under your bed."

Ben tried to avoid eye contact and walked toward the cottage.

"You think you can walk away from me?" Carl said, low and threatening, balling his fists. "You tell me lies and steal our money."

Ben stopped, wincing. Carl was going to beat the stuffing out of him. He wouldn't fight back; he respected Carl too much.

"Carl, when do the workers get paid?" Ben asked.

"Next Friday," Carl said.

"You can have all my wages. I need to pay you back and pay you for room and board. Then I'll be on my way. You can hold my gun. It's yours if I don't keep my word." Ben waited as Carl thought about it. At least he wasn't swinging at him.

"*Ja*, I'll take your gun till then." Carl nodded to their cottage. Ben walked in front, feeling like the sheriff was following him...again.

Ben cleaned up after an uneventful day working at the dairy. Every smell was intensified, making him nauseated, but he never let on. He avoided the other workers, and they avoided him. Every time he saw a shadow, he tensed, thinking Carl was coming to fire him. He knew by this time that Carl and Edda were working in the big house. He shook his head, defeated. If they wanted, certainly they had every right to tell the family what he had done. He walked slowly up the back step. Hunger was winning the battle over hiding. And maybe Nadine would meet him tonight. Did the bartender know her, or had he just imagined that? It didn't seem possible. He rounded the corner into the dining room just as Mrs. Von Keller threw some paper on her empty plate.

"This was written over a month ago! Otto, do you hear me?"

Mr. Von Keller nodded as Ben sat down. "Yes, dear, but there's not much we can do about that now."

Delighted, Ben leaned back in his chair. Whatever was in that letter was keeping their attention from him. Maybe Carl hadn't said anything yet.

"She's going to teach the Indians! Did you hear that?" Mrs. Von Keller let out a puff and stood up.

"Mother, sit down," Nadine demanded, her presence filling the room.

Nadine glowed. Never a hair out of place. Her skin was so white and pure that something in him sank in despair. She was far too fine to ever want his affections. She shot him an angry look, and he frowned back, intending to ask her what was wrong.

"Otto!" Mrs. Von Keller paced in front of her chair. "First, we allow this notion of going to a university. She says 'many ladies are there, *Mutter*.' Why does that make it acceptable? Then she writes, not about her classes, but all about Frances Willard. That woman has the nerve to make our Margaret into a temperance worker! Each letter is about the cause. The cause to stop this alcohol. The cause for the poor. This is not our problem!"

Ben jumped as if she was raging at him. He wiped his sweaty hands across the lace tablecloth.

"Mother, please, can't we just eat in peace?" Nadine sighed.

Frau Edda put a large hot plate of food on the table. "I hate pot roast," Minna whined.

Mrs. Von Keller turned on her daughters, finger wagging.

"You two listen to me well." Her voice was low. "You will not ever go off to university. You will not ever join any

41

Women's Christian Temperance Union. It is not our job to help evil people. Your sister has been deceived by this place. She thinks she needs to go teach these savages about God. It says so right here." She shook the paper. "What kind of madness is this?"

"Helga," Otto said, sounding calm. "She has always had deep convictions. Let me find out more about this mission." He reached out for the letter. "We will get some understanding on it."

"I told her to come home! That's all she needs to hear. She thinks she can make war on alcohol? What kind of absurdity…" Helga finally pulled out her chair.

Ben tried to fork some pot roast. His hand showed a bit of tremor. The evil, vile alcohol was sitting right here, inside him, at Mrs. Von Keller's table.

Later, while the Von Kellers fretted more about poor Margaret, Ben could finally get a whisper out to Nadine. "Tonight," he said while nodding toward the outside door. She shrugged at him.

"What?" he said softly. 'What's wrong?"

She jutted her perfect pointy chin up in the air. "I'll think about it." She got up from the table. "Hurry up, Minna, tonight is violin practice."

"I won't tell anyone where you are if you let me skip violin." Minna raised her eyebrows.

"I wish I could believe that." Nadine scowled, checking to see if her parents had overheard.

"I didn't say where you went…"

Nadine quickly slapped a hand over Minna's mouth.

Ben jerked back. *What was that about?* Nadine quickly took Minna from the room.

Water dripped down Ben's trouser leg as he ladled a drink in the dark. He waited an hour for Nadine. Frustrated and tired, he headed toward the smaller house. Suddenly she appeared, walking toward the tree. He let out a thankful sigh and ran up behind her. "I didn't think you were coming."

Nadine grabbed her chest and swung around. "Stop scaring me," she said, wide-eyed.

Ben gave her his best contrite smile. "Sorry." They stared at each other, each waiting for the other to speak. "You had to do violin with your sister?" He was hoping she was in a good mood.

"Yes, and then another half an hour at the piano." She inhaled and let out a ragged breath.

"I think I did something wrong. You wouldn't talk to me at dinner." He gave her a curious look.

"Did you or did you not ask about a dance lesson?"

"I did…" Ben still could not account for her scowl.

"I thought we were meeting here last night. At dinner, no one had any idea where you went. I waited, only to find you must have forgotten."

Ben scrambled for a reasonable excuse. "Ahhh, I did. I'm so sorry." He ran his hands through his hair. "I went hunting and came back late." The lie slipped from his lips with ease. "If I was sure I was going to be receiving lessons from you, I never would have missed it." He waited, disappointed when she didn't make eye contact.

"Truth is, I'm just not that excited anymore. It's just been one problem after another." She crossed her arms firmly over her chest.

"Like what?" he asked.

"Two of the ladies I put in charge of decorations made these awful flowerets. Beige and pale yellow. How boring. If they don't possess an ounce of creativity, why didn't they ask for help?" Her arms flapped up and down. "And the mayor already had the hall chairs spoken for, so there aren't any chairs available that night." She shook her head.

"Do you need chairs if everyone is dancing?"

"Have you ever been to a dance, Ben?"

"No, I've seen them. Ready Springs had a little shindig on Founders' Day with a fiddle and such."

Nadine rolled her eyes. "People sit and visit. It's the social part many come out for. And the tickets are twenty cents. They expect nice decorations, punch and cake, and a seat if they get tired."

"I could make you some simple benches to line the walls."

"How would you do that?" Nadine scowled.

"You take wood, and a hammer, and a nail…"

Nadine swung at him when she realized he was teasing her.

"Ladies getting splinters in their…" she smiled, and Ben laughed. "In their *dresses*. No, thanks."

"I'll make them as smooth as your mother's fine china."

He could see he had broken through. "But I'll still need those dance lessons. It'll be a trade. And I need you to get permission for me to use the boards on the side of the barn."

"All right. Can you start tomorrow? The dance is in four days."

"Ask your father first," Ben said again. She didn't know that he might be packing his bags any moment. Maybe Carl would have overlooked his delinquency?

"You'll have his permission." A soft smile graced her lips. "I have my ways." She turned and headed for the house.

"That you do," he said, with the crickets singing. "That you do."

The next day, with permission granted, Ben found himself flying through his duties at the dairy. Carl even refused to take all of his wages. Ben profusely apologized for touching their money, but the way Carl squinted, Ben knew he was still on thin ice with him.

Ben whistled a happy tune, feeling the joy of lumber in his hands. Many of the tools in the tool shed were nicer ones than he'd ever used. He made a simple pattern, adjusted the sawhorses to the best level, and began working. He enjoyed building things almost as much as seeing Nadine....oh, blast it. He had missed supper. He ran out and quickly washed his hands in the pump, then ran up the back stairs and into Frau Edda, doing the dishes. He smiled his best sheepish smile and was delighted to see her pull a plate off the stove. She slid it over to him, and he stood at the counter and ate. "Nadine told the family you were helping her with some benches for her party."

"Thank you for the plate of food, Frau Edda." After Carl had allowed him to stay, he wanted to give her his thanks. "I certainly don't deserve your kindness. If my ma were here, she would say I'm not the young man she raised."

"*Ja*, so stealing is not who you are? You just made a mistake?"

Ben could feel his food sticking in his throat. "I'm not sure how to answer that." He reached for the glass of milk she had put next to his plate. For some reason, the little gold necklace from the store front popped into his mind. He looked up over the rim of his glass, hoping she wasn't still expecting an answer.

"Well, your *Mutter* did not raise you to take other people's money...*ja*?"

"No, ma'am."

"You must have made a mistake?"

"I did. Yes." Two more bites and he could be gone.

"Our Lord Jesus did not come to condemn people. He knew we would all make mistakes."

Ben chewed faster.

"When we realize what happened to our Savior on the cross, the terrible whipping and pain he went through so we could find help with our mistakes, then how could we ever want to hurt others by stealing or lying or cheating? Do we not take seriously what our Savior went through? Do we not believe He can bring us up from our sins?"

Ben walked his plate over to the sudsy water and washed and rinsed it.

"Can He do that for you, young man?" Helga said.

Ben nodded respectfully as he dried the plate and fork. He knew everything she said was true. But he had been called irresponsible all his days. He wished he knew how to break out of that role. It seemed it had followed him here to Elbert County. He had no Levi keeping him safe and nowhere to hide from himself.

"Thank you for saving supper. I know what you're saying…" He didn't know what else to say to her motherly expression. "I need to think of that more." He turned quickly and headed out the back door.

8

Ben ran his hand across the smooth wood. It had been another twenty-four hours, and he found himself thankful he still had a job.

"Frau Edda asked me to bring this to you."

Ben looked up into the face of an angel. Nadine, in a beautiful soft pink dress, holding a plate of food. He felt his breath catch in his throat. She was stunning, standing there surrounded by the soft glow of dusk.

"Sorry I missed supper again." He found his voice. "I need this time to work on your benches." He felt his heartbeat quicken as Nadine entered his area and set the plate down on the work table.

"I don't think I've ever been in this building before." She clasped her hands, looking around.

"I would imagine not." Ben returned to sanding the wood.

"Is that the bench for the cotillion?"

"Yes, ma'am." He quickly flipped it off the saw horses and onto the ground. "Here, try it out. See if you get any splinters."

She squinted with a crooked grin and sat down. Straightening her back like a ruler, she moved her hand carefully across the wood. "Maybe not quite like china, but they seem quite safe." She smiled her approval.

"I have four done, and I'm making you four more." He sat down next to her. "I'd like to give them a dark stain. But I don't want people thinking you stole them from the church."

She tilted her head at him, a soft smile appearing on sweet pink lips. For a moment, the air seemed to get thick. They were so close…Nadine jumped up.

"It doesn't seem like we've left much time for dance lessons." She walked back toward the open door.

Ben attempted to gather his wits. Good Lord, he almost kissed her. "Can you stay and talk to me while I work?"

"No, I have a literary meeting in town. Carl is driving me." She looked outside and turned away.

"Wait. I wanted to show you what I made for Minna."

"Minna?" Her voice dropped. "I can't imagine."

"Right here." Ben showed her a large flat board with thick ropes knotted at each end. "It's going in the big oak in the yard."

"A swing?" She frowned. "Isn't she a bit old for that?"

"Does your sister still run in the house?"

"Yes."

"Does she still pound up and down the stairs?"

"Yes." Nadine rolled her eyes.

"This will help with all that. She needs to do something big. She needs some wide-open space. Trust me, I know what I'm talking about. She needs to soar."

"Soar, like a bird?"

"Yep. Let her out, like recess, to swing for twenty minutes or so every day."

"Hmm. You might be right." Nadine tapped her lip. "Thank you, Ben." She started to leave.

"Can you come back when it's over?" Ben moved to follow her. "Besides your family's dinner conversations, I'd like to hear more about you."

"More about me?" She stared at him, confused.

"Yeah, you. What are your hopes, your dreams?"

She squinted at him as if he had offended her. A crow's caw broke the long silence.

"What I want is…out." Her face was stoic, almost pained.

"Out. Out of town?" he asked carefully. "Out of the house? Maybe out to dinner?" He waggled his eyebrows to see if he could get her to brighten up.

"I've got to go." She turned on her heel.

"Wait! I've got it. I don't know why I didn't think of it before. Out, as in outdoors. You want to go hunting with me?" Smiling, he raised his hands. "We could find you some canvas coveralls and a good pair of boots." Looking for a smile, he got another frown. "Outdoors is not what you meant?"

She shook her head. Were those tears glistening in her eyes? She pulled up on her thick skirt and walked across the grass.

"Well, come back after your meeting. I'll wait up. We can talk more."

"I…I'm not sure." She barely turned. "I'll try if I can."

Ben stopped walking after her. "I'll be here."

A few hours later, Ben looked up to see the Von Keller's carriage pull in. He dusted off the wood shavings and stood at the door as Nadine entered her home. He waited, watching Carl take care of the horses. *Probably too late.*

He wanted to see her again. She was so different, so enticing, desirable, yet distant. He was the fish caught with a steel hook, reeled in by her, inch by inch. Leaning against the heavy wood door, he looked from the oil-lit work bench back to the shadows of the two-story home. He knew his feelings for her were real. His gut started to flip every time he saw her, and he thought about her constantly. But he had felt just the same at Sault Creek when he first met Allison. When do you know if a gal feels the same way? How would he ever know if he had a chance? He tried to picture asking Mr. Von Keller's permission to court Nadine. His mind flashed to Mrs. Von Keller yelling and throwing things at him. He looked back at his woodwork. Maybe the Von Kellers would take a shine to him for his doing this for Nadine. Maybe he needed to find ways to be more like a son, someone they would want to stay around.

He saw the faint lights of the house go dark.

The next morning, Ben ate his usual eggs and biscuits with Carl and Edda. He was tired from working late on the benches. For his whole life, dark had meant sleep, and light meant awake. He guessed no one had ever taught that to the cows. Certainty the smells were not as strong in the early hours. He yawned and nodded thanks to Edda for pouring more coffee.

"You about done with those benches?" Carl said, chewing.

"Yes. I have just a few things to finish. Can I take the buckboard and deliver them tomorrow, after I'm done in the barn?"

"*Ja*, as long as it is just to deliver, and you come right back." Carl gave him a stern look.

"Yes, sir." Ben swallowed hard and turned to Edda. "I noticed there was a suit of some kind in the wardrobe. Is that Carl's or your son's?"

"*Ja*, it was Carl's, but our son wore it, too."

"Do you think it might fit me? Could I borrow it for a few hours?" He shot a quick glance at Carl. "I'll be very careful."

Edda set her dish towel down and walked into Ben's room, coming out with the brown woolen suit.

"I try to keep the mothballs in there." She held it up by the hanger and looked it over. "I see a couple of holes down here at the bottom. We can air it out, and I can try to let out the pants, *ja?*" She picked up the hem of the brown trousers and looked inside. "May not be enough fabric." She gave Ben a sad smile. "Your legs are very long."

"Whatever you can do." He looked back and forth between them. "Nadine invited me to her cotillion, probably just because I've helped her with those benches." Ben imagined Carl would be questioning his intentions. "I figured I needed something besides these work duds if I was to show up."

Carl kept eating, not looking up.

"*Ja, ja,* you should go. I'm sure there will be lots of young people. I heard Mrs. Von Keller say they wouldn't be attending, so Miss Nadine might need a ride back-"

Carl suddenly cleared his throat, and she stopped talking.

"Well, *ja.*" She set the suit over the chair. "I'll see what I can do with this."

"*Danke.*" Ben nodded at her as he rose and pushed in his chair.

Shoving a large white and black cow back into place, he plopped onto the small stool. All day, Carl's disapproval had burned a hole in his gut. He didn't need to be reminded he was a nobody. Maybe Carl had forgotten the Grahams were friends with the Von Kellers. Nadine had said to his face that anyone could come. He had a mind to walk in and ask Mr. Von Keller if he could escort Nadine to the dance. He looked down the row of ten more cows he had to milk. As soon as he finished them, he only had to separate the cream, put it up, refill the hay troughs, wash up, finish those benches, and hang the swing.

Ben had a much better attitude as he took the back stairs two at a time. He walked past Frau Edda working in the kitchen. "Supper smells wonderful."

He rounded the corner into the main hallway and listened. No screaming. Everyone must be having a good day. He was about to step toward Mr. Von Keller's downstairs room when he saw Nadine at the top of the stairs. He was so pleased with his idea that he wanted to tell her first. Stopping at the end of the staircase, he smiled up at her. He thought she was about to greet him when Minna ran into her with a stack of papers. Nadine didn't have time to grab them before Minna raced down the stairs. "Minna, you stop this instant!" Nadine tried to gather the papers flying around her feet.

"I'm d-o-n- e," she squealed as she darted around Ben.

"Can I help you?" Ben started up the stairs.

"No, my mother won't want you up here." She waved him off. "I've got to put these back in order for the teacher tomorrow. I'll see you at dinner."

"I finished the benches," Ben called after her as she walked away.

"Thank you," he thought he heard as she disappeared into the schoolroom.

He went back to his original idea and tapped softly on Mr. Von Keller's door.

"Come in." Mr. Von Keller sat in a chair.

"Good to see you doing better," Ben said.

Otto let out a groan. "Helga insisted I stay an invalid for six weeks. She frets and worries like cows give milk." Ben stood back as Otto carefully tried to set the crutches under his arms. "Tell me, how it is going out in the dairy?"

"Good, good." Ben lied. It's not like Otto didn't know what getting up at four in the morning was like. He'd come from another country and made something out of nothing. Reassurance came to Ben. Why did he let Carl make him feel like an underling? Otto, of all people, could understand him.

"You hear anything from your *Mutter?*"

"No, sir. She knows I'm here. I just haven't taken the time to write her."

"Don't let Helga hear you say that. She will put you to task. She thinks highly of your *Mutter.*"

"Yes, I need to do that soon." Ben reached out as Mr. Von Keller wavered backward. He kept his hand near his back as he regained his balance. He cleared his throat to speak when Edda came in to set the table.

"Here, ma'am, I'll do that. I know you're busy in the kitchen." Edda froze and reluctantly allowed Ben to take the stack of plates, napkins, and silverware.

He took a deep breath and tried to remember where all these things went on the table. "While I have you alone, sir, I did want to ask you about tomorrow night." He started to put the fork on the left of the plate and hesitated. "I…ah…understand why you and Mrs. Von Keller can't attend Nadine's dance. I was wondering if…" Ben winced as one of the knives dropped onto the china. "If I could be of help and…" Good Lord, why was his hand shaking? "…escort her there and back. Back home…this home." Of course he would bring her back to her own home. What a lame thing to say.

"Well, that would save Carl the trouble. We've heard you are helping her out by building some benches." Otto replied, gently lowering into his place at the table.

"Yes, I finished them this afternoon." Ben looked up to see Nadine swish into the dining room. She looked cross at him as he tried to finish setting the table. He couldn't help but smile as she looked at his attempt at place settings and began putting them in proper order. "I don't want my mother yelling at poor Frau Edda."

"No, we don't want that." He couldn't help but watch her; she captivated him.

"Ben would like to give you a ride to your event and back," Otto said.

Did I say 'ride?' Ben thought. *I meant to say 'escort.' I did say 'escort.'*

"Oh." Nadine stopped straightening the table and seemed to be looking for the right words. "I need to arrive much too early for Ben. I'm sure he'll still be working at the dairy." Ben's jaw locked like the wood in a vise. "I have so much to do beforehand." She finally looked at him. "Perhaps if you don't mind waiting until after the cleanup, we could ride home together?"

"Of course. I can help you clean up." That sounded acceptable in front of her father. A ride alone with her, sitting next to him shoulder to shoulder. His eyes shot up, pursuing hers. Good Lord, his heart was going to pound out of his chest.

9

B en rubbed up and down the sleeves of his lightweight flannel shirt and blew warmth into his cupped hands. He could see his breath as he entered the lamp-lit dairy barn. He actually didn't feel any resentment this morning as he worked through his tasks. An hour later, the sun had finally joined the day and added to his rising mood. He was young and working a job. He slept in a bed that was warm and dry. His belly was full of coffee and oatmeal. He wished his family could see him. Tonight he would wear some nice duds and be part of something that was very important to Nadine. To be in her world, without her parents or Minna interrupting. Maybe he would kiss her tonight.

He ran a hand through his thick wavy hair and down his patchy stubble. He remembered a look into Edda's small mirror he had used the first day he arrived. Cleaned up, he wasn't half bad to look at. How would he know when? Should he try to hold her hand first? Does a gentleman ask permission? He gripped his neck and tried to work out the knots. For once, he wished his brother Levi was here. Levi had no problem setting Ben on the right track.

By late afternoon, Ben had all the benches loaded. He heard something unusual and came around the barn. Minna was swinging up to incredible heights, flying like a giant pendulum. Her weight carried her much higher than he thought possible. Minna saw him walking toward her, and she smiled ear to ear, twisting in the seat and waving with one hand.

"Whoa…!" She cried out, swinging crooked while she tried to grip the rope again.

"Minna! Hang on!" he yelled. "Don't get near the tree!"

She gripped the rope back, but it swung closer to the large oak tree. Quickly she flew past him. "Slow it down, girl." He jumped in her path and was finally able to grab the ropes and bring her to the ground. "Hey," he said, still gripping the ropes. "You about scared the breakfast out of me." He pulled the ropes out front with straight arms, looking at her as she dangled in front of him. "I'm serious, Minna, if you fall out of this and break your leg, your ma will boil me alive."

Minna smiled. "That would be fun to watch."

"All right, I'm taking it down." He pulled her off to stand.

"No! I'll be careful. I'm sorry. I just don't think I've ever had so much fun. Did you see how high I was?"

"Yes, and I thought that at your age, you wouldn't be reckless."

"I won't, Ben. I promise. No twisting, I'll keep both hands on the ropes at all times."

He stood a few feet from her, assessing her believability. "If I see you going crazy on it or I hear you're giving

Nadine a hard time at home, you're going to come out and find a little piece of twine hanging from that baby tree over there."

Minna looked over to the sapling in the yard and back to Ben. She clasped her hands together quickly. "Okay, it's a deal. Now, can you push me?"

Ben snapped the horses forward and headed onto the dirt lane out of the Von Keller's property. The day just couldn't get any prettier. The deep fall colors were making an appearance with the colder mornings, and Wisconsin was a beautiful land. Everything around here was so much livelier than Ready Springs. Approaching town, he nodded at folks walking to and fro. He slowed the wagon as some children ran home from school. His eyes wanted to bore into the saloon. He had his own money, and one quick drink wouldn't hurt anything.

Looking around, Ben chided himself. It wasn't as if Carl had followed him. The distraction he needed appeared when he spied Nadine outside the decorated town hall. She pointed in the air, forcing some poor man on a ladder to reach new heights to get the decorations hung. Ben pulled up in front and jumped down.

"Your benches, ma'am," he called out to her.

"Just put them along the wall for now." She never looked at him. "George, can you please try to drape that evenly? See how that one is too long?"

Ben looked at George's work while he grabbed a bench. He didn't see anything uneven. He walked into the long hall, where large windows on both sides allowed light and color into the room. He noticed the band chairs up on the stage and decided to line the benches away from the music. If Nadine said people socialize, they probably didn't want to be seated next to some loud piano. Some gals in pretty dresses smiled at him. Nadine was still busy with George, and he caught the attention of one of the other ladies as she walked by.

"I can move these benches anywhere you ladies want."

"No, that seems fine to me," she said, batting her green eyes, never looking at the benches. "Mrs. Borden is in charge of setting up today." She smiled. "But Miss Von Keller, outside..." She nodded toward the door, still staring at him. "She'll rearrange it all her way, anyway."

"Okay." Ben chuckled. That sounded like the Miss Von Keller he knew. He headed back outside and waited until Nadine looked at him.

"Oh, Ben, nothing is turning out right." She squeezed her hands together.

"It looks real nice to me."

Nadine rolled her eyes.

"Tell me what you want to be done, I'll help."

"No, no, I'm just going to have to walk away. I didn't count on being here all day, and now I'm hot and sweaty. The bass player can't make it. Some of the ladies who are supposed to be here left, just because their children were out of school."

"Then come on, let's get you home." Ben pointed to the wagon. "You can cool off before you have to come back."

"No, you go ahead. I already made plans to get ready with a friend." Nadine frowned. "I am sorry about the dance lessons. I didn't keep my part. I don't blame you for not coming."

"Oh, I'm coming." He smiled. "Got my twenty cents and a nice smooth bench to sit on. I'm okay watching everyone else dance."

"And you said you would take me home after the dance?" Nadine glanced over at the young ladies watching them.

A large smile broke across his face. He clamped it shut and rearranged his hat on his head. "That, I am looking forward to." He looked long at her. She was the prettiest girl in town. Fighting the urge to reach out and squeeze her hand, he bit back another smile.

"I look forward to it, too." She nodded and turned quickly back into the hall.

Ben stood a few seconds doing his favorite thing—watching her.

"No, no, Frau Edda, you did your best." Ben looked down at the space between his boots and the hem of the brown trousers.

"I took it all the way out. There is no hem. I just did a little stitch around the bottom so they wouldn't fray." She frowned.

"I see." Ben sat in the kitchen chair and looked down. Since he had committed to bench sitting, maybe it wouldn't be so bad. He felt his hope dropping, though—the pants hiked up so far that the tops of his boots and his stockings were visible.

"I have another idea. Stand up." She pulled on his arm. "Let these suspenders out like this…" She pulled the clasps loose and Ben hung onto the pants as they descended. "Now that looks better, *ja?*"

"This might work, I'll wear the jacket and no one can see how low the waist is." He pulled on the suit jacket and exhaled. The cuffs stopped in the middle of his forearm. He held them both out front. This was a disaster. He looked like a scarecrow. He pulled the jacket off and draped it over the kitchen chair.

"I can try to take the lining out of the cuffs and see." Edda picked it up.

"No, no, Edda. You have done enough. You were kind to try." Ben walked into his room and shut the door. Sitting on the bed, he unlaced his boots and carefully took off the borrowed pants. He had another clean pair of his pants he pulled on. Drawing his hands down the stiff clean cotton, he noticed how kind Edda was to iron his one good shirt.

The sun was gone, and he looked out the window to the blue-black sky, letting out a long sigh. Turning, he leaned back on the bed, clasping his hands behind his head. Damp hair intertwined with his fingers; Edda had even given him a nice haircut. The flame flickering from his lamp almost lulled him to sleep. *Blast it, to think I was nervous about this all day.* Maybe he would go into town and just wait. He sat up quickly. These clothes looked fine to help clean up. And he could still give her a ride home.

As crowded as the hall was, Nadine had yet to make sight of Ben. Something must be wrong at home. Had her father taken a fall? Maybe her mother had forbidden Ben to pick her up. She looked around at the result of months and months of effort. People were dancing. The band sounded fine. Maybe someone should open another window. She turned to find a strikingly handsome man, her knight, stretching his hand out toward her.

*   *   *

Ben pulled the family carriage into town. He wasn't sure how long these socials lasted, but the music was easily heard permeating the town all the way down Main Street. Most likely when the band stopped, it was over. The saloon had a large group of men hanging out front, probably all the non-dancers. Stepping down, he slowly came around the horse and tried to look into the saloon. It looked crowded with people, but he'd passed it by earlier today—certainly he could refrain again. The tug inside him started in, then tingling in his throat, a dryness craving to find relief. He never had free time on his hands. There was no one looking over his shoulder, judging him. He'd worked hard all week, even found forbearance from Edda and Carl. Well, Edda anyway.

He came around the horse again, patting the mare's mane. He didn't get to be part of Nadine's night. All day he'd looked forward to talking with her, watching the townsfolk. Not being near her was the worst of his spoiled plans. He'd have to wait somewhere. Just one pint wouldn't hurt anything.

Why wouldn't anyone ask the piano player to quit pounding the keys? The same stupid song over and over? Ben tried to shake away the ringing in his ears. He couldn't hear the band down the street, and he stood up quickly. The room began to spin, and he grabbed a railing to steady himself. He set his sights on the door and made it out.

The fresh cool air hit him, and he tried to straighten up. Where did the hall go? It was completely dark to the left and completely dark to the right. This didn't make sense. The shindig was here just a minute ago. Where did all the people go? He saw some familiar decorations and walked toward them. What time was it? Why was everyone gone? He tried to step up onto the sidewalk and hit the wood with his foot, falling forward. He caught his weight with his hands and turned around and fell on his back on the side-walk. Pointing up to the yellow curtain swags, he mumbled, "George, I think this one is crooked, too."

Ben awoke in his bed, with drool leaking onto his pil-low. He listened for Carl or Edda and heard nothing. If they hadn't awakened him, it must be Saturday or Carl would be waiting outside the door to kick him out. Ben pulled the soft blue window curtain back. The horse he had taken was out in the pasture. The carriage was where it belonged. Thank heavens everything was in one piece… except Nadine. He never brought Nadine home. He swung his legs to the ground and tried to hold his head on his shoulders. It didn't matter how bad he felt, he had to know how she got home. Certainly one of her friends or…good Lord, now she had every right to distrust him.

Ben swallowed the lukewarm coffee and tried to rehearse his story. The first part was true, then he could say he accidentally fell asleep. No, he had to find something better than that. Disgusted with himself, he shook his head. He was only in the saloon for a minute. How could he have lost track of time? He gripped his hands over his hair, wanting to rip it out. He had to find her. Beg for her forgiveness.

Walking gently to counter the pain in his head, Ben went from barn to woodshop, cleaning up and doing the daily chores. The Von Keller property was eerily quiet. What kind of coward was he? He had yet to check on Nadine. Seeing Edda bringing in a basket of vegetables from the garden, he ran to cut her off before she went up the back stairs.

"What's going on? Is everyone okay?" He winced at his own question.

"*Nein, nicht gut.* The Von Kellers are very upset."

Ben's stomach rolled up to his throat. Edda handed him the heavy basket and headed up the back stairs. Looking at the back door and the basket of vegetables, Ben thought, *this doesn't make sense.* Edda, of all people, would give him a warning if he was about to be hung from a tree. He swallowed hard. If he was ever going to be the man he was supposed to be, he would have to face this head on.

"Bring them to the tub." Edda started pumping some water. She took a few vegetables at a time, rinsing off the dirt. Ben liked Edda, but how could she be so indifferent to his plight?

He rubbed his temple. "Can you tell me what they're upset about?"

"A wire came from Miss Margaret's missionary group." She dropped a scrubbed potato. "I couldn't hear all the details, Mrs. Von Keller was shouting and crying. Hard to understand her when she gets like that." She shook her head. "They are upset about Margaret's missionary trip to help the Indians."

Ben looked to the ceiling, casting God a shocked look. "And so…"

"I think Carl is still in with Mr. Von Keller. Helga is insisting they go get her. Here, pat these dry with that towel."

Shaking his head, Ben dried the carrots and lettuce leaves. Maybe God hadn't shunned him as he thought. Just when he finally allowed himself to relax, Nadine walked into the kitchen.

"Hello, Miss." Edda smiled. "Did you get to sleep in after your big party?"

"Yes, thank you, Frau Edda. May I have this roll here?" She took the roll and waited while Edda poured her some milk. Nadine reached for the glass, ignoring Ben.

He waited while she ate. "Can I talk to you? Outside." Ben said quietly.

Nadine finally looked at him, and he nodded toward the back door.

Ben heard a door slam somewhere down the hallway. Edda shook her head, chopping vegetables. Nadine put her glass down and walked through the pantry and down the steps.

"I wanted to say I'm sorry about last night." He looked down at the ground. "It's embarrassing, but I didn't have anything to wear and…" Ben shifted his feet.

"Don't worry." Nadine cut him off. "Most of the husbands stayed and cleaned up, and I got a ride from a friend."

"How do you think it went? You were worried when I saw you earlier."

She shrugged.

"I'm really confused right now, so I'm going to say it straight out. I really wanted to go. I really wanted to give you a ride home. I'm hoping you're mad at me, because if you're mad at me, then maybe I let you down. If I let you down, it's because you wanted me to take you home."

"I thought you were going to say it straight out".

"Okay." Ben cleared his throat. "I really, really care about you, Nadine. You are so beautiful. I think about you all the time because milking cows gives me a lot of time to think, and…"

Nadine covered her mouth, giggling. "Really, Ben?"

"I'm not joking. Please don't laugh…you're squashing my soul."

"Your soul?" she snickered.

"Yes, my soul. Listen. I know I have a ways to go to become…"

Edda suddenly opened the back door, and Ben wished they had walked away from the house. He closed his eyes and pinched the bridge of his nose.

"Mr. Von Keller and Otto want to talk to you," Edda said.

His hand dropped quickly from his face. "Me?" *Otto and Carl want to see me? Is that what Edda just said?*

10

Ben stepped around Nadine on the back steps. He paused, waiting for Edda to go inside. "Did you tell your father I didn't bring you home last night?" he said, breathing rapidly.

"No, he thinks you did. Whatever you do," she whispered only a few inches away. "Tell him you brought me home."

Ben nodded as he reached for the back door. He had just laid his heart open for Nadine, but it sounded as if she wanted to cover for him. Knowing she held the power to chop it to bits or protect it, she'd chosen to protect him. He watched her walk in and felt his shoulders relax.

"Come in and sit down, Ben." Otto sat at the head of the table with his foot propped up. Carl stood by the large window, looking out to the barns.

"We seem to have a family crisis, and we're looking to see if you can help." Otto sounded fine, but Ben wondered why Carl wouldn't join the conversation. "You know our eldest, Margaret?"

Ben nodded.

Otto cleared his throat. "She has been attending Northwestern University in Chicago. She led us to believe she was part of a school-sponsored trip, some evangelical outreach to the Indians. Maybe part of her teaching school. But we have finally received a letter from the university. It is not a school-sponsored activity, but in fact, it is part of the Temperance Union that Margaret is so passionate about. Her mother and I are very disappointed, as you can imagine. We feel misled and dishonored as her parents. The university did give us the information they had, and we feel it is time to bring our daughter home. As her father, it is my responsibly to go after her. But as you know, I have trouble leaving this house. Carl has graciously agreed to make the trip, but I am concerned about the dairy. Without someone here with the workers, I feel they might not stay on task. And as you know, everything in the dairy must be accomplished in an orderly and timely fashion, *ja?*"

Ben nodded again.

"I propose for you to go after her and bring her home. Carl does not think that is wise." Carl finally glanced over his shoulder at Ben. Ben wondered what kind of vise he was about to be caught in. "First, I can only ask you if you are willing. You came here to work the dairy, not travel across Wisconsin. We are desperate, though. Mrs. Von Keller is distraught about our Margaret, her choices so pitiful. I have decided to take the money I had set aside for her dowry, and we will just have to use it for train and horses. That is her loss. I am sorry to have to be so harsh. We can only pray that one day, once she is away from those crusader influences, she will find our forgiveness for making her family suffer so."

Ben blinked, trying to comprehend why she would have to earn their forgiveness.

"What do you think?" Otto broke in.

"Yes, sir. Of course, I'll do whatever I can do to help the family." Ben looked straight to his boots, trying to swallow past his tight throat. The air was ripe for Carl to mention his dishonest ways. Surely, if Carl had known that Ben forgot to bring one of their daughters home, just from town, this conversation wouldn't be happening.

Ben sat quietly at supper, wondering what Nadine's response would be to the news. Otto began to explain it would take him a few days to map out the journey and get train routes. Ben didn't want to interject that he traveled all the time without maps and plans. But if this helped him get there and back faster, so be it. Chewing a bite of carrots, he almost smiled. The benches seemed a good tally mark for him. Now bringing the wayward sister home would hopefully put him in their good graces.

He looked across the table to Nadine. She seemed agreeable enough tonight, probably because her mother was too worn out to attend dinner. The meal did have a calm to it that Ben rarely experienced. He finally caught Nadine's eye and gave her a tiny nod to the back door. She looked away. What did that mean? Was she upset he was leaving?

Before he could say anything, Mr. Von Keller called him to sit next to him. An hour had passed while Otto showed Ben the best routes to this Indian reservation. Unfortunately, Nadine had long left the room.

He waited outside by their tree until he couldn't keep his eyes open and his head bobbed forward. Standing up, he jumped back, startled. Carl was the last person Ben expected.

"Carl. I didn't see you walk up." Ben rubbed his eyes, trying to see in the dark.

"*Ja.* I'm not sure why I find you asleep outside?"

"Just the cool of the evening."

"Hmmph," Carl said. "You need to listen to me, and listen *gut.*"

Ben tried to straighten up. "Yes, sir, I'm listening."

"The only reason you are here is that I let Edda bend my ear. The Von Kellers have a *gut* dairy."

"Yes, yes they do." Ben tucked his thumbs in his pockets. *Especially if you're a cow.*

"I don't trust you." Carl's brows creased.

"I know I've made some mistakes."

"They give you this money, you are to bring their daughter home. And that's all. If you don't, I will come find you myself. Are you understanding me?"

"Yes, sir." Ben nodded, knowing what Carl thought of him. But Carl had no idea that every bit of his hope was riding on this good deed. He would not mess up. He would be the family hero. How could Nadine and her parents question his honorable sacrifice for the family?

The next day, Carl called him in early from the dairy. "Edda has some things for you, for your trip, she wants you to try them on…after you clean up. We are taking Otto and the missus to the doctor for a checkup today. You need to start to pack for tomorrow."

Ben followed him from the barn and went to wash. Entering his room, he looked on the bed. Edda had sewn him two new shirts. She must have been working on them for weeks. He could hear the carriage rolling out, as he slipped off his old shirt and pulled on the new cream-colored one. This was too nice for work. He held his arms out and smiled at her kindness. She had left the arms extra long. They had no cuffs or buttons and almost covered his hands. She would probably want to pin them.

A small red and white-checked bag with a leather handle lay on the bed. She was doing her best to make him into a gentleman. He walked out of the cottage with his new shirt. She was probably in the kitchen and could pin it now. As soon as he entered the back door, he heard someone screaming. It sounded like Nadine calling after Minna. What had that girl done now? He looked for Edda and walked through the kitchen, stopping at the bottom of the wide staircase.

"Please…help!" Nadine cried out.

Ben took the stairs three at a time and quickly found the room Nadine was in. He stopped cold to see her standing up on her stepstool, facing her large canopy bed. One bare arm and hand stood straight up in the air, while her two perfectly formed hair rolls were all that showed from where her head was trapped inside a large green dress.

"Minna! I can't breathe!" She struggled to get free.

Ben quietly came up behind her and pulled up on the fabric. It finally released her other arm, and he was able to lift it straight up. With both arms above her, the dress slid down past her shoulders. He was about to announce himself when he saw a red mark on her neck.

"Oh, dear Lord, Ben. You scared me." Nadine clutched the dress to her chest, panting.

"But this time I saved your life," he teased. Standing right behind her, he blocked her ability to back off the stool, and his body and feet refused to move. Her beautiful white shoulders were only a breath away. Three small strands of soft brown hair had come loose. Standing on the footstool, she was eye level for all kinds of admiration.

"You have a mark on the back of your neck." He couldn't help himself—he lightly touched the curve of her neck.

She clutched her dress with one hand and tried to smooth her loose hair back up with the other. "I...I burned it on the hot iron."

The way her voice still came out in short, breathless words was making his head spin.

"I think if I could just undo these small buttons back here, you'll be able to get out of this." Ben slowly unfastened three little pearl buttons on the back of her dress.

There was a loud ticking from a clock somewhere in the room. Ben realized she wasn't moving, wasn't talking. What he was feeling, she must be feeling. The house was as quiet as the forest after snow. Those same strands of hair fell back down like feathers. He lightly traced his finger down where they landed and a little farther to the center of her back. An intoxicating heat rose over all his being. Just like trying to stop at one pint, his resolve wavered. With a yearning for more, he carefully brought his lips to touch the perfection of her skin. She was so close, so accessible. Another small kiss a few inches away, and then another. He felt her shudder. Was he mistaken, was she leaning back into him? A gentle kiss behind her ear, then slowly and patiently around to her cheek. "I don't want to leave you," he whispered gently, setting his hands on her hips.

A small cry came from her mouth. He pulled her around and found her lips; they were everything he had dreamed of and more. More exhilarating, more intoxicating, more desirable than he'd ever known. She was still gripping her dress when he picked her up and laid her on the bed. He kissed her fervently while he pulled her arms up over her head, holding them down with one hand.

"Nadine!" Minna's voice shook the room.

Ben pushed back, feet finally finding the floor.

"Get out!" Nadine screamed back at Minna, as she scrambled from the bed and shoved her arms into her sleeves. Minna was gone before Nadine could pull her herself together.

"Ben, g…get out," she stuttered. "You never s…should have been in here." She paced back and forth, and Ben wondered if she was getting enough air.

"Please get out!" She grabbed his frozen frame and pushed him toward the door.

Ben was in shock, wondering if this was what a heart attack felt like. He took a few steps away from her door and turned back. "Don't worry, Nadine. She won't tell."

"Oh no, oh no…" He heard Nadine moan as she grabbed the door and slammed it shut.

11

The roosters didn't need to bother—Ben was awake most of the night. He could hear Edda making coffee. He wanted to wait until Carl left for the dairy. His things fit fine in his own pack, but he wanted to take the small case Edda had left for him. A long glass bottle, full of something that would dull his stupidity, would be nice.

Edda interrupted his dizzying thoughts of saying goodbye to Nadine. "I go get their breakfast on the table, you come over and say goodbye, *ja?*

"Yes." He nodded, pulling his hands through his hair. He leaned his chair back, and Edda laid her hand on his shoulder. He brought the wooden chair back to all fours. "I will pray for you, young Ben." She squeezed his shoulders.

He barely smiled, nodding at her kindheartedness. "I'll be in shortly."

Going back to his room and looking at his things, he felt edgy. Could he get in a word with Nadine? Should he even try? He needed to apologize. Sitting on the bed, he dropped his head into his hands. *I think she kissed me back.* He'd been up half the night trying to figure it all out. Everything was more confusing in the morning light. How did things go from a kiss on the shoulder to pulling her onto her bed? Did Minna think he was attacking her sister? He would never do anything to hurt Nadine. He gripped his hair until it hurt. Did Nadine feel the same passion as he did? Blast it, the last thing on her face was anger. There didn't seem to be any amenable feelings. Ben shook his head and grabbed his gun and belongings.

Mrs. Von Keller got up from the dining room table and walked quickly to Ben.

"*Danke, danke.*" She grabbed both his hands, and her face and voice contorted. "You are very *gut* to go after..." Her sniffles took over, and she gripped his hands harder. "Please promise me that you will bring her home. Do not let her go back to that university, *ja?*" Ben agreed before she cut off the circulation in his hands.

Nadine approached, pulling Minna by the hand. "Have a pleasant trip." Nadine nodded at him quickly, pulling Minna next to her. "Yes, have a pleasant trip," Minna repeated with a hint of sarcasm. They both hastily walked out. Ben was about to follow when Otto called him over.

"Here is the money and routes we talked about. Please wire us if anything changes." Helga blew her nose into her hankie. "Godspeed, Ben. Bring our child home."

Ben rubbed the top of his head. It was becoming sore from hitting it on the ceiling of the bumpy stagecoach. There was only an elderly couple riding along, but Ben felt trapped in the small box. No wonder he liked having a horse. He looked at Mr. Von Keller's plan and tried to gauge how soon the next town was. As soon as he got to the second stop, he was supposed to find a hotel for the night. He chewed his bottom lip, looking out the small window. At least he had a bed and a hot meal to look forward to.

The apple pie wasn't as good as his ma's, but it hit the spot. Traveling had helped him to keep his mind off Nadine's curt goodbye. The way she had Minna by the hand meant something. He left the money for the waitress and walked around the corner to the bar area. It wasn't a full saloon, just four or five tables with men sipping their drinks. A respectable place to make a purchase. He walked up to the counter and asked for a bottle of whiskey. While the barkeep eyed him, Ben laid the money on the counter. No one questioned him, no one picked on his youth. He climbed the stairs to his room, ready for a soft bed.

The next morning, Ben found an empty area to sit on the train. He'd never been on a train. The air and windows all around agreed with him. The people were spread out, and he could easily drop his head to the side and take advantage of a few more hours of sleep.

His body jerked forward as the train pulled to a stop. He glanced down at Mr. Von Keller's map. This was as far as he could go without a horse. He started wondering what kind of women's group would make this trip. It was a bit far to talk to the Indians about giving up the devil's alcohol. The way Mrs. Von Keller pleaded with him, you would think it might be hard to get Margaret to return with him. What would he do if she refused? The train came to a complete stop, and people stood and gathered their things. He really didn't know her; they were all children last time he saw her, but he would find a way to convince her. He would do this right, for once.

Early the next morning, he had his two needed purchases: a beautiful blonde mare named Sandy and a small flask that fit perfectly into his jacket pocket. He laid the new saddle on the horse and let the stirrups down as far as they would go. The sky was clear except for a few white cotton clouds. He brought Sandy around to the fence. "Well, it's you and me from here on out. I don't know much about Indians, and we have to find them on the reservation. Really, we're after a girl. We don't want any Indian trouble." Sandy pulled her face up, bumping Ben. "Good, we understand each other. Just get the girl and get out."

As Ben mounted and rode out, he eyed the beautiful Mississippi River. Why wouldn't the Indians be located by the river? Who would put them on a reservation in the middle of nowhere?

That night Ben rode into a small town and saw a church, a hotel, and a saloon. His backside was sore and weary, and he headed for the hotel. A little bell on the door went off as he walked in. A sweet young woman greeted him and showed him the small dining area and where his room would be.

"Are you familiar with the Ho-Chunk Indian reservation?" he asked her later as she came by with coffee.

"Which one?" she asked.

"North of here."

"They're all north of here."

Ben ran his hand across his day of stubble. "Ahh, more than one." He took out his directions and laid them out on the table. She sat the pot aside and pulled up a chair next to him.

"You aren't from around here?" She smiled.

"No. I'm from Michigan." Ben felt a pang of guilt. He really wasn't from anywhere.

"I'd say your map will get you where you can ask more questions." She circled her finger around the area where he planned to travel. "This is where they're supposed to be. But they don't stay on the reservations."

Ben looked confused. "Then where do they stay?"

"No, I mean they move. The land doesn't support them. Would you want to be told where to live? Where to hunt?"

Ben nodded. She made a good point. "I thought they had to stay on the reservations."

"It is illegal to be off. Some of them are caught and sent off to Kansas."

"Kansas?" That seemed strange.

Where would Margaret and her missionaries go? Ben looked back down at the map. This was going to take longer than he thought. He paid the young woman and left for his room.

Entering his room, he stepped over his saddle and things, opening a drawer to a small desk. Taking out some paper, he jotted a note to the Von Kellers. Who knows when he'd be able to mail something again? He related that the travels were going well, but finding the exact Indian reservation Margaret was in would take some tracking. He folded the letter and put it in an envelope, then fingered another sheet of paper. He'd been away from home a while, and it was past time to let his ma back in on his life.

Dear Ma,

I'm sitting somewhere in western Wisconsin. You know I've been working at the Von Keller's dairy farm. It's been going well. Mr. Von Keller broke his leg and I believe my help has been appreciated. Right now, I'm on the road to bring Margaret back home. She decided to go help the Indians in this area. Only problem was the Von Kellers aren't in favor of it. So my new job for them is to find her and bring her back. I write this so you'll know I'm well. I'm sorry I haven't been home in a while. I still feel like I'm trying to find my way. I know you're praying for me. In many things I've seen God's providence, too many to list. Give my love to the family. The Von Kellers have asked me many times to send their regards.

Your loving son, Benjamin

Ben looked back at his things on the floor. He wanted to finish off the bottle of whiskey he'd bought a few days ago. Rising from the hard chair, he stared at the checkered bag. His ma had no idea how much he drank. Or when he drank, or why he drank. He unbuttoned his new shirt and threw it on the pile. She didn't know anything more than what he told her. He pulled off his boots and pants, kicking them onto the pile. Maybe someday he would tell her. By then he might know for himself.

12

For all the years he'd trailed behind Levi as he hunted and tracked, Ben wished he'd paid more attention. The obvious road had become a small trail, which stopped at a fair-sized river. He got off Sandy and stretched his legs. He pulled his hat back and looked into the overhead sun. A swim and some fishing seemed in order.

Body refreshed, Ben flashed one of his quirky smiles to the blue sky. Besides the swim, he'd taken the time to wash some of his clothes, and his things hung over the shrubs by the bank. Breathing in another draw of fresh air, he closed his eyes; he hadn't enjoyed a day like this in a long, long time. His stick pole bounced abruptly in his hand, and he was rewarded with a nice trout to eat later.

After Sandy grazed her full, Ben pulled his things back together and headed northeast. By early evening, the terrain was flat enough to make out a homestead and some outbuildings. He approached slowly and was greeted by a barking gray dog. A man with a shotgun in his hand came out from the barn.

"What can I help you with?" he said gruffly.

"I'm looking for the Ho-Chuck Indian reservation."

The man nodded. "Just on the other side of that ridge. Stay to the east, should take you a couple more hours."

Ben tipped his head in thanks and rode away. He said a silent prayer that he could find Margaret and not a passel of braves around that ridge.

The sun had long set, and Ben wondered about making camp and trying again in the morning. Why hadn't he seen anything? Surely the missionaries had wagons, and the reservation was marked with shelters and horses and people. He scanned for a place that would provide him safety as he slept. Something moved in the corner of his eye, and he kicked Sandy forward. Tall reeds moved around a creek. Were his eyes playing tricks in the dark? It looked like a child running away. He squinted through the dark and made out a wigwam. He must be on the reservation and didn't know it. Everyone must be spread out. At least he didn't have to worry about an ambush.

The child stopped and saw Ben. His eyes and mouth grew wide, and he ran into the wigwam. Ben dismounted and grabbed his shotgun. He moved slowly, anticipating someone would be coming out any minute. Hearing a woman's voice, he released his finger from the trigger. Someone short lifted the flap and walked out.

"*Carranonda...carranonda*" An older, bent-over woman kept saying. She shooed Ben with her hands. The little boy peeked around her tattered skirt.

"She wants you to go. There is sickness here," the boy said. Ben guessed him to be around six or seven.

"All right, all right." Ben took a step back. "Could you ask her if she's seen any missionaries?" Ben shook his head in frustration. "People with...ah...Bibles?" He rested his gun on his shoulder and made a motion with his hands like someone praying. The little boy and the old woman seemed to be discussing it.

"Cheeksonna." The old woman motioned Ben to come near. Ben looked to the little boy. "She wants you to come here," the boy said.

"But I thought there was sickness here."

The little boy nodded. "Missionary sick."

"Oh." Ben didn't move. "I'm only looking for a lady missionary."

The boy opened the flap and motioned for Ben to come in. Hesitantly, he tied Sandy up and looked around. The boy and the old woman he could handle, but if four or five warriors jumped him, he wouldn't stand a chance.

There was a small fire burning in the center of the wigwam. The smell of dried meat and herbs was harsh and pungent. Ben cautiously took a step in. He squatted down and pulled his hat off. A woman was lying silently on a blanket. For a moment, he wasn't sure what to make of the thin face that caught the shadowy light of the flames, but it looked like she could be Margaret. Why hadn't he thought to look at a photograph? It had been years since he saw her.

His heart began to pound in his chest. No, it couldn't be her. The Margaret he remembered was nothing like this poor woman. This woman was frail and thin. He could see her bones in her hands, and her face was sunken, with parched lips. The unfortunate woman was dying. Just when he was ready to turn and get out, the little boy came and touched her shoulder. The woman slowly opened her eyes. Her lashes fluttered, and she reached her thin fingers up. Ben leaned over in the wigwam and without realizing it, he found himself bent down closer to her.

"Hello." Pity filled him.

"Are you an angel?" she whispered.

"No." He gave her a small smile, shaking his head. "I'm just Ben."

"Benjamin…Graham…" she said softly.

Ben's jaw dropped. "Are you Margaret Von Keller?"

She smiled weakly, her eyes closing. "Mags to you, Bens."

Ben froze. Could it be? The childhood names they had called each other. He turned to the old woman, wide-eyed. "This is the woman I'm looking for." He turned to the boy. "How long has she been here? Do you know what's wrong with her?

"It's typhoid," Margaret whispered.

"Dear God." Ben turned to face her. "Where are the others? Are they dead? Have they gone for help?"

"No." She pulled in a ragged sip of air and opened her eyes for another moment. "It doesn't matter. I'm going to… heaven… soon."

"No, you're not, Mags. I promised your parents I would bring you home."

"Oh, Bens." She gave him a sleepy glance. "You're here to tell… my parents what… happened to me. It will…comfort them…this…this is the providence of God."

"No…no." He ran his tongue under his lip. That would be the last thing to comfort them. "I can get you to a doctor." He waited to hear her response, but she fell silent. Panicking, he leaned closer, watching for her chest to rise and fall. She finally moved a bit, and he rubbed his forehead in relief. Standing but still hunched over, he looked back at the woman and little boy. "I'll be outside."

Sunrise peeked over the barren land. Between the cold ground and the shock of finding Margaret Von Keller, Ben had wrestled all night. Everything was out of his control. Margaret was dying. The Von Kellers would be beyond devastated. They had already lost a son, but what could he do? Whiskey would have helped to unravel the knot in his gut, but it was gone, along with every other option. He couldn't stop a woman from dying. He thought it might be hard to convince her to come home. What would happen if he came home with her coffin?

Ben pushed off his knee and stood, feeling the ache all over his body. He looked up to the new rays of light and shook his head. *God, are you real? Does the earth really rotate at Your word? Do you see what is happening here?* Without thinking, he fell on his knees and dropped his face into his hands. *Dear God, I shouldn't be asking you for any favors. I know I don't deserve any. But for Margaret, God, for her family…could you heal her? Please…* He stayed on his knees, rehearsing some of his childhood Bible verses. He tried to remember the Bible stories he'd heard at his mother's table. Many of the people in the Bible had made mistakes.

David killed a man and God still called him a man after his own heart. Ben knew he hadn't killed anyone, but he also hadn't sought God with his whole heart in a long time.

The little boy had gone back to the creek for water. He stood up, watching him. "What is your name?" Ben asked as the boy walked near.

"Henry," he said, looking at the ground.

Ben noticed he had strange coloring. He seemed darker than he thought Indians would be. When the boy glanced up, Ben noticed the soft round curve to his eyes. "Is the woman…awake?" Ben held his breath.

"Yes." Henry led him to the flap.

Ben entered, nodding to the old woman, who was stirring something in a small bowl. He knelt next to Margaret. Wearing a different cotton gown, she looked flushed with fever this morning. He saw a cloth and motioned to Henry for some water. This wasn't likely proper, but he didn't care. He took the wet rag and held it next to her cheek, gently dabbing the perspiration away.

Her eyelids slowly lifted. She just stared at him, with an almost peaceful glow about her. "God is so… good." Breathy words escaped. "Bens…so…good."

Ben rested the cloth between her chin and neck. It was like speaking to an angel. "Tell me about that," he said, with a sad smile.

"I know I'm leaving this earth." She lightly breathed in. "I'll be with Him soon. But He brought you here…just to be with me…He is so good." Her eyes closed.

Ben dipped more cool water onto the cloth.

"How is my...family...? My father's leg..." Her eyes were still closed.

"Your father is getting around with a pair of crutches that make him miserable. Your mother is well." He couldn't seem to find adequate words. The dairy seemed like another lifetime.

"Nadine and Minna?" she whispered.

"They're well." The old woman held out a cup of water to Ben. "I'm going to lift your head so you can drink." Ben carefully put his hand behind her head. Margaret let out a sigh and rose up on one arm. The front of her gown fell forward, and Ben saw that there was a rash of small red bumps covering her skin. She put her hand to the cup, touching his fingers. "Thank you, Bens," she said, swallowing.

As she laid back down, Ben looked at his fingers where she had touched him.

"How do you know its typhoid? How did you get it?" He rubbed his hand against his pants.

"Reverend and Mrs. Michaels have seen it before. There were only a few of us sick. So they encouraged the tribe to move on."

"What happened to the other missionaries?"

"Not... sure. They were going to keep traveling up... north, I believe...to check on the other... tribes." She winced in pain as she put her hand on her belly.

"How could they leave you like this?" he said, nostrils flaring.

"Jesus said unless you are willing..." There was a long pause. "...To leave your father, mother for the sake of the gospel..."

"Horse crap." The words flew out of Ben's mouth before he could catch them.

Margaret let out a weak giggle. "I'm so glad you're here...I always loved you." She gripped her belly again. "Ben...please leave me...I need Chowwena..."

"Yes." He stood up. "I'll be right outside."

Ben went over to untether Sandy and take her for a walk. He found some grass for her and leaned his body and head against her back. Why hadn't these people taken Margaret to a doctor? Now look at her, skin and bones. He rested his forehead against the mare's coarse hair. Young, caring Margaret. She was always the one holding a younger child by the hand. Nadine was the one crying or pouting over the games, while Margaret always smoothed everything over. She loved on all the children, and truth be known, Ben was a favorite. He knew it back then. It really was a painful fluke that he was the one here with her in her last hour.

Sandy headed toward the creek for a drink. Ben joined her, bending down on a knee to splash water on his face. There was something under the water; he jumped back so hard that he landed on his rump. Even Sandy snorted and moved back. Ben felt a shiver run up and down his spine as he got up and looked again, "Good Lord." Whatever it was had two eyes staring at him. He grimaced and looked away, then grabbed a large tree branch and carefully poked the stick at the revolting thing. He pushed harder until the emaciated face and body came up. It looked like a calf had been butchered and left in the water. He squinted, shaking his head. If it was killed by another animal, they wouldn't leave it in the water. Even the birds would have a chance with the carcass. What idiot would leave it in the water, where it could contaminate the whole village? Ben froze. The old woman and the boy...the typhoid. But then, why weren't they sick?

Ben grabbed Sandy's rope and went back to the wigwam. He came up short and stared. A man was digging a hole about twenty feet away. Another horse grazed nearby. Now what was going on?

13

Mouth gone dry as paper, Ben stiffened as he approached the wigwam. "Henry!"

Henry came out. "What?"

Ben glared at the man shoveling out a deep hole. "What's going on? Who is that? Why's he digging a hole?"

Henry looked back and forth between the two men. "For the sick lady."

Ben almost fell forward. "Is she dead?"

"Not yet, but the old woman can't dig it. So Yellow Bull is helping her."

Ben pulled his hat off and slapped it against his leg. "The water is poisoned!"

The man finally stopped digging. *"Chuhcoo?"*

Ben assumed Henry repeated what he had just told him. He sneered, spat on the ground and kept digging.

"Lord Almighty!" He flung his arms out, then stomped back to the creekside where he had seen the calf. He took the stick again and jammed the calf in the rib cage. He dragged the carcass out of the water and along the ground. Pulling the wet mass that had gathered dirt and leaves, he dragged it past the wigwam and over to Yellow Bull. "See this! This is poisoning the water!" Knowing the man probably couldn't understand him, Ben pulled the carcass into the newly dug hole. He grabbed the shovel from the man's hand and began to bury the calf. The man began to yell and charged for the shovel. Ben pushed him away, and he tumbled back. There was a glimpse of red in his eyes right before he jumped up, knocking Ben to the ground. Swinging arms and legs kicked up the dirt and dust everywhere. At one point, Yellow Bull rose up, the blade of his knife inches from Ben's face as he heard someone screaming. Yellow Bull paused over Ben as the old woman pulled on his back. She bellowed something at him, and he decided to listen. He moved off Ben, with the knife still drawn. Ben was still red hot with energy for more, but he swiped the blood and dirt off his face. The man began to rant to the old woman as Ben looked to Henry for help. Henry tried to help pull Ben up. "They're going to leave. Yellow Bull is angry for allowing his mother to care for the white woman. She will have to obey."

"Good," Ben said, spitting blood. "They are the reason she's sick." Ben stood back as the woman began to gather her things. The son was pulling at the large ropes holding the wigwam together. "They're taking the shelter?"

"Yes." Henry pulled on Ben's arm to get him to move. "You need to get her out."

Ben rotated his throbbing jaw and ducked inside. "Margaret...I'm so sorry." He began to lift her in his arms. "They're moving on...and I'm getting you to a doctor." He turned to Henry as he eased her out the flap. "Can you bring me a blanket?" Henry scurried in and dragged out a heavy blanket.

Finding some shade, Ben gently laid her down. "Can you bring me any of her things?" He looked to Henry and back to Margaret.

"Ben…what…what's happening?" Her voice rose barely above a whisper. "What was all the yelling about?" Why is Yellow Bull taking the wigwam apart?

"They're going on…"

Margaret reached out and held Ben's sleeve. "Ben, please…don't do this. I need her…her help."

"I'll help you," Ben said curtly, watching them.

"No…no…please."

Ben swung to face her. She sounded so much like Nadine. "I will," he tried to say kindly.

"Typhoid is a horrid…" Her eyes rolled back, struggling. "She helps me with the chamber… pot."

"Henry!" Ben yelled. "Grab the chamber pot."

Henry made a pile of Margaret's things.

"Thank you, Henry, for all your help." The boy stood next to Ben and as they watched Yellow Bull and Chowwena tie everything to the poles behind the white and black pony. He wondered why Henry wasn't helping them. There was something unusual in how Henry rubbed his hand up and down his tattered pants. Looking down at Margaret, his throat constricted with panic. Could he do this? Thankfully, she seemed to be sleeping peacefully again. The old woman chattered on to Henry and started to walk away. Ben patted Henry on the top of his dark, wild-haired head. "Thanks again. You better be going. They're leaving without you."

Henry looked up at Ben, and Ben saw the confusion on his face. "I'm staying with you. The sick lady told me she'd take me to a school, school with other children."

It finally registered to Ben why the others were walking away without him. "They aren't your family?"

"No." Henry shook his head. "I don't have a father and my mother left me a few years ago. Chowwena would feed me for help with work." He chewed on his lip. "I'll help you now. Will you feed me?"

"Yes, of course." Ben wondered if this simple trip could get any more complicated. Why hadn't it occurred to him that Henry didn't seem like an Indian name? He looked closer and reached for the boy's hand, still rubbing on his trousers leg.

Ben held up Henry's hand and saw that it had a sixth finger. "If that don't beat all." He shook his head, staring at it. "I've seen some animals with some extra parts, but I've never seen anyone with six fingers on one hand."

Henry pulled it back. "It is because I'm cursed. I have too many mixed bloods in me."

"Who told you that? It wasn't those missionaries, was it?" He licked the crack on his lip. "They'd better pray hard before they come across me any day soon." He clutched his hands, surprised he was so riled. "You are not cursed," he exclaimed, gently squeezing Henry's shoulder.

"Is she cursed?" Henry looked down to Margaret.

"Oh, no." Ben frowned. "She's a perfect soul in an imperfect world."

"She wants to go to her God. She smiles when she talks about him."

Ben nodded at Henry's observation. "That she does."

As the sun set, Ben came and sat next to Margaret. She looked different out of the dark wigwam. Her skin was still pale, and her expression pained. He lightly touched her hair, and her groggy eyes opened.

"Why can't you be...an angel?" She exhaled softly.

Ben smiled at her. If she only knew that was the question he'd asked himself a hundred times. Her hair was the same color as Nadine's, but it was soft and loose around her sweet face. For some reason, it begged to be touched. "No, no angel." His throat was dry, and he wanted a drink badly. But he wanted her to live even more. There was a dampness in her hair as he brushed his finger across it.

"We made it through today," she whispered. "But I need you to do me a favor."

"Anything." Ben was also glad for every hour she hung on.

She lifted a weak hand toward her brown case. "There are some papers I've written. If I don't make it back to Chicago...please promise me...you will mail them to the Women's... Christian...Temperance Union."

"I can do that." Ben wanted to talk about something more pressing. "You know Henry is here with us?"

"Mmm, yes. I suppose I didn't know that... the others would be... leaving." She blinked, heavy-lidded. "I'm sorry to… leave him with you." Her voice struggled between breaths. "But there's a good school…an orphanage, really. I teach there when they need me. There's a letter I started to them before I got sick. The address, the headmistress, everything… in the case."

"All right." Ben tried to smile over his desperation. "This may be uncomfortable, but after I watched how quickly they broke down the wigwam, I built a travois for you this afternoon. I want to take you to the next town. I think we can make it in a couple of days, traveling slowly."

"I…trust you…Ben." She squinted at him with glossy eyes. "Your face looks…like…something has happened."

He rubbed his fingers over his cut lip and bruised cheek. "I've had worse."

"I know…your heart is…good." Her eyes slid closed.

Ben wondered if she was delirious. No one should trust him. His heart was rarely good.

"I guess it doesn't matter if I die here or…" her voice was barely a whisper, "out there."

14

The next day, Henry sat like a perched bird on a bouncy limb in the wind. While Ben led Sandy on the smoothest path, Henry sat on the travois up near Margaret's head, hanging onto Sandy's tail. Ben was thankful to have the extra eyes. Margaret had groaned off and on all night. Her fever would come and go. But in the morning, she took a few sips from a cup of clean water. She even smiled as he lifted her on to her traveling bed. *Lord,* he whispered, *please... please let her live.*

He looked back and noticed Henry had taken off his shirt. He held it out to keep the sun off Margaret's face. Ben was softened by the skinny, unwanted, six-fingered, mixed child, holding a horse's tail with one hand and holding his other arm protectively over Margaret. He wanted her alive as badly as Ben did. Ben wanted the Von Keller's praise. Henry just wanted food and to learn to read and write. This beautiful, frail woman was Henry's only hope. He wondered what God thought, looking down on this strange traveling group. *Please, Lord, give me the strength to do right by all of them.* Ben felt something expand in his chest. He wanted to take care of others, do more than just see to his own needs. These two might be a good place to start.

Later in the day, they found a grove of trees to camp in. When they had Margaret comfortable, Ben collected Sandy and rode out. He remembered this area. The last place he had asked for directions was just around the bend. He rode up to the same fence and watched as the familiar gray dog came out to bark at him. This time the owner and his wife came out the front door.

"I was here a few days ago, and you gave me directions to the reservation." Ben stayed saddled.

"Yes." The man shoved his hat on.

"Two more questions, if you don't mind?" Ben began. "First, the nearest town with a doctor? And the second, I have some money. Could I buy a few eggs? Maybe some bread?"

The woman nodded, touching her husband's shoulder, and disappeared into the house.

After Ben took in the directions, the woman came back and handed her husband a canvas bag.

"The missus says it's free. Just don't make a habit out of it." The man handed Ben the bag.

"No, sir. Thank you, ma'am." Ben tipped his hat to her. "Thank you, both."

When he rode up to their camp, Henry ran out to grab Sandy's reins. "What is it?" Ben felt his stomach clench as his feet hit the ground.

"The sick lady fell," Henry mumbled

"What!" Ben had never even seen her sit up before. He ran to her blanket and knelt next to her, trying to get his heartbeat to settle down. Gently touching her face, he saw a small red scratch raised up across her cheek. "Mags...what did you do?"

"My...stomach...I was in so much pain...I needed to be...alone."

Ben flung his hat to the side and raked his hands through his hair. Sitting back on his heels, he took a deep breath. "Please, please...don't try to get up without help. I'll help you."

She rolled away from him, groaning. "I want to go to heaven. Please, Ben, I knew... the old woman... wasn't helping me. I was ready to die. I'm not...afraid...to be gone from here...is to be with the Lord." Sucking for air, she turned to face him.

Ben looked into her pure dark sunken eyes. "Please..." He felt his throat tighten, "Please, Mags." She closed her eyes, her discomfort obvious. *Oh Lord, I've never been so helpless.* He prayed a few moments longer. His eyes stung, and his nose was dripping. He didn't care that tears were running down his face. "Please don't say you want to go to heaven. Please try to live. Mags. You're all that is good in this world. I want to help you. Please..." He choked out the words, knowing she was probably asleep.

Her eyelids slowly opened, fluttering with the effort of keeping them on Ben. Carefully, she reached up and touched his damp cheek. "No one has ever cried for me."

Ben wiped his sleeve across his face. "I think your mother's been doing a bucket of crying."

Margaret finally gave him a weak smile. "Yes, she can cry a bucket."

"And a well and a few waterfalls." Ben felt his emotions settling down, her smile calming everything in him. "I'm taking you home, Mags, but *please* tell me what you need. We can do this together," he said, tucking the blanket around her.

Ben separated their simple meal onto a cloth. Henry's eyes widened as he saw that his bread was stuffed with ham. He bit in so fast that Ben hoped he wouldn't choke. He held a piece of bread out for Margaret. She took it from his fingers and looked at it. Ben had already started eating before he realized she would want to pray. He put his food down and folded his hands. She closed her eyes, and Ben prayed aloud. "Dear Lord, for this provision we are truly thankful." He struggled for the right words. "And for sustaining Margaret, please, God, touch her. You, Lord, are the bread of life, amen." When he opened his eyes, she had fallen asleep, bread untouched.

As the last rays of the warm fall sun went down, Ben pulled his saddle blanket alongside Margaret's spot. He was not too close, but close enough to help her if she tried to get up. Henry had wrapped himself in Ben's jacket and fallen asleep as soon as he was done eating. The stars began to appear, and Ben flopped on his back to watch them. It was the first time he'd thought about the dairy in days. He loved being on his own again. He certainly hadn't anticipated this was the way the trip was going to go. Backward and taxing it could be, but sleeping outside under the stars invigorated his soul. He'd gone soft, sleeping on a bed. He looked to Margaret and saw that she had pushed her blanket off. As he rose on one elbow, he could see beads of sweat on her face. He grabbed the cloth from dinner and began to gently fan her.

"When did you get so tall?" she whispered.

He dabbed her forehead. "Just in the last ten years." Taking her cup, he gave her a few sips of water. "The way you've changed, I didn't know you. How did you know it was me?"

"My mother….wrote to me. She thinks you were a miracle…coming the week of my father's accident."

"Ah." That made sense. She knew he was helping at the dairy. "Trust me, I'm not a miracle. Can you stay awake for some pitiful honesty?"

She opened her tired eyes and looked at him. "I think I would enjoy that."

Ben rolled onto his back and watched the stars. "I hate milking cows."

Margaret sucked in a small laugh.

"I detest getting up at four. Carl hates me, and I don't like him, either. The only reason I showed up when I did was I needed money. My last decent meal was in jail. I don't usually drink, but after leaving Michigan, alcohol seemed to be my only friend. I don't like German food. Every supper, someone gets mad. I feel like I'm a child next in line for a reprimanding. I need to go back to Ready Springs, yet I don't know what I'll do there. I don't know if your mother told you, but my pa passed. I wasn't there. Their excuse was they didn't know where to find me. I don't think anyone tried very hard. It doesn't matter, I don't know how I would have made peace with my pa. Nobody wants to go home just to be reminded the family doesn't approve of drifters. You should have seen Nadine's face when I showed up at your front door. She called me a few things and slammed the door." He laughed, remembering. "That girl…I follow her around like a stray puppy." He stopped up short. He didn't like how much truth was in that last confession. "I do care for her. I don't think…" He shrugged. That night before he left felt shameful and had left him feeling hollow. "I don't think your parents would approve."

He looked over at the older, wiser sister. Right now would be a perfect time for some of her soft, loving words, but she was asleep. Ben covered her with the blanket, regretting how deplorable his confession sounded.

In the middle of the night, Ben opened his eyes. Something had moved. Maybe Margaret needed him? Leaning up on an elbow, he noticed Henry burrowing in the small space between them. *Poor little guy, he has my jacket. Probably still cold,* he guessed, spreading his blanket over the boy.

15

Ben looked up, squinting; dark clouds had been rolling in all morning. They had traveled past a few homesteads, the outskirts of the town appearing ahead. He circled around until he found a tree to rest under. Truth was, he wrestled with coming into town while Margaret was pale and deathly sick on the travois. It would draw attention. Say the word *typhoid* and some folks might not want to help them. He rubbed his temples and slapped his hat back on. "We need to leave the lady here," he said to Henry, as he untied the ropes from the horse. Henry froze, wide-eyed. "I'm coming back. I just need to find if they have a doctor." Henry began to help him lower the travois. Margaret moaned, her eyes closed.

"If it rains, use this to cover her." Ben pulled a blanket free. "I'm sorry, Henry, but I have to leave you in charge again."

Ben rode into the edge of town and asked the first person he saw where the doctor lived. After a few turns, he dismounted in front of a wide porch. There were some boards missing, and Ben wondered if this was the right place, but a sign read *Dr. Ketchum.* He knocked, and a girl opened the door. Ben pulled his hat off. "Hello, miss, I'm looking for the doctor. Is he in?"

"No, he's out checking on a patient. Maybe I can help you?"

Ben chewed on his lower lip. She looked a bit older than Minna, maybe thirteen or fourteen. "Are you the nurse?" He smiled.

"Yes, sir, I am." She stood a little taller.

"Okay. Ahh..." Ben rotated his hat in his hand. "My friend is very sick. She's been helping out on the Indian reservation. And I really need the doctor to see her. The problem is, she's waiting outside of town, and I think it's about to rain."

"You can bring her here." She opened the door to a parlor. Ben peeked in and shook his head. "You have other people you're nursing?"

"Well, if you count my grandmother, yes. And folks come and go all day. But my father keeps three rooms for the sick."

"If she happened to have typhoid, would your father want her here?"

"Oh, no." The girl stepped out and closed the door behind her. "We can't have her here."

"That's what I was afraid of." Ben stepped back and almost stepped into one of the missing planks. He looked out around the town, with a mixture of hopelessness and anger churning inside. If the doctor wouldn't take her in... He started to turn away, then spun around. "Listen, I'm desperate. Can you think of anywhere we could go, just until your father can come see her?"

"We have an old shed," she offered.

"Where is it?" Ben crossed his fingers.

"It's on some property about a mile from here."

"Could we just stay there, until he's free? I have money."

She smiled and stepped into the street. "Go to the end there, where that white house is." She pointed. "And then left, about a mile. There's an old brick well in front. It's not locked, but it's full of old furniture and stuff. People pay my father in some strange ways. He tosses it in there."

"Thank you for your help, miss." He almost wanted to hug her. "What's your name?"

"Carolyn."

"Carolyn Ketchum, you're amazing. And you'll send your pa as soon as he's free?"

"Yes, sir." She blinked quickly and smiled.

"I'm Ben. Ben Graham." He tipped his hat just as the rain started falling.

"Hold the door," Ben ordered Henry as he held Margaret in his arms. He stood, assessing the room. "Put those chairs over there. And see that rug? Grab it and put it here in the middle." Ben was able to gently lay Margaret down. "No more bumpy roads, Mags." He took the blanket off her. She looked pale and gaunt. He grabbed her hand and began to rub it inside his. The rain pounded the roof and Ben closed his eyes with gratitude that they were inside and dry. He glanced up to Henry, sitting on one of the chairs. The child swung his feet back and forth, like a boy on an unfamiliar toy. Ben bent down to her still form. "I think the boy likes chairs," he whispered.

She tried to turn her head to watch Henry. "We...are both...so lucky to have...you."

The rain had almost stopped, and Ben was feeling anxious for the doctor to arrive. His beautiful Mags had held on this long. This had to be a good sign. He looked for the tenth time out the small shed window and finally saw a black buggy coming. Next to the doctor rode his new friend, Carolyn Ketchum.

The doctor introduced himself and gave Carolyn his black derby. She set it on the table and began to pull her father's things out of his case. Ben heard him say *tsk, tsk* under his breath as he knelt down to Margaret.

"How many days?" The doctor pushed on her belly, and Margaret moaned.

"I've only been with her a few days. Henry, how many days was she sick before I came?"

Henry shrugged. "Many days."

"I would guess she's at about week two. Her liver and spleen are enlarged." The doctor stood up and brushed off the dust from his pants. "Many in my profession panic, but I believe if you keep everything clean and wash often, you and the boy will be fine. But you won't be able to leave this shed until she dies...or recovers. He rubbed his hands on a towel and dropped all his things in another cotton bag. "I'm sorry, I know this town. They'll run you out."

"I'm not worried about us. What can be done for her? Is there a medicine?" Ben asked.

Doctor Ketchum looked to Carolyn and sighed.

"Please." Ben would beg if needed. "I have money. There must be some things to try."

Carolyn nodded to her father.

"My daughter will come by in the morning. We have to get more fluids into her."

"Thank you...whatever you can do. And I can pay for the use of your shed."

The doctor scratched his chin. "We may burn it all when she's gone."

The sixth morning, the doctor accompanied Carolyn. Like they would for a general who had arrived for inspection, Ben and Henry stood at attention at the shed's front door. Both of them had followed every order nurse Carolyn had given. The doctor's daughter had faithfully brought a basket of food each day and had patiently fed Margaret spoonfuls of homemade broth. She mixed medicine and teas and saw to Margaret's bathing and laundry. She was the reason they all had survived the last week. When Ben asked her about school, she said she had chosen to study her lessons from home, to give her more time to help her father. She even brought Henry some of her old books, a slate and some clothes from the free box at the church.

"Thank you for coming today, doctor." Ben greeted them as they walked in. Carolyn smiled as she put down the basket. Henry went up to her and received his daily hug.

"I'm here to have a conversation with Margaret." He bent down next to her. "I'm sorry I didn't talk to you last time I was here. You were asleep."

Margaret smiled slowly. "Thank you for your help. You have an amazing young woman here. She has a gift...you know..."

"If we could ask your young men to step outside, I'd like to examine you."

Ben caught Margaret's eye, and he nodded. He led Henry by the shoulder as they walked out. Breathing in the fresh fall air, he plopped down and leaned against the well. Henry sat down next to Ben and rested his head on Ben's arm.

Sweet Henry. It felt as if he'd lived a lifetime with this interesting kid. Margaret only had tidbits into his sad past. He gazed out into the dry, brown grass of the property. He wondered how Henry would do in an orphanage. Would the kids tease him about his extra finger?

"Clouds." Henry pointed to the sky. "C, L, is there a W?"

"No, no W. Remember the two vowels that go together?"

"Like owl?"

"Well, O is the first vowel."

"Okay, C, L, O, U, D!"

"Yes, Henry! Smart man." Ben caught himself sounding like teacher Margaret. Even in her weakness, she found the good in everything. Ben tried to tell Carolyn she didn't need to skip school to be here, but she was probably drawn to Margaret's kindness, too.

The shed door opened and he jumped up. He reached into his pocket and grabbed two important things. "Thank you, Miss Carolyn, for bringing the paper. This is a letter to Margaret's parents. Would you mind mailing it for me?"

"Of course. But my father has some good news."

Ben felt himself gripping Henry's shoulder.

"You can mail it yourself if you want. I'm lifting the quarantine. But please, you must be careful. No talk of typhoid. She's still very sick. No one's paid enough attention to wonder why there are a young man and young woman living in my shed, with an Indian boy to boot. If you go into town, people will ask questions."

Ben handed the letter to Carolyn. "We're going to stay close to home for now." Ben caught his mistake. "Your shed, I mean. Here's the money for this week's food and doctoring." Ben handed Dr. Ketchum the bills.

"Thank you." The doctor nodded. "If it were my loved one, I wouldn't be moving them for another couple of weeks."

Ben nodded. They'd come this far—he wouldn't take any chances with Margaret's health.

16

The evening's red and orange glow shone through the single window of the small square shed.

"Dr. Ketchum thinks you are *my* young man." Margaret smiled and shook her head.

Ben sat at the small table, curiously looking up over his soup bowl. He had found some old cushions on a settee that Margaret could sit up against. She held her bowl out front.

"Young is the key word, isn't it? Does he know our age difference?" Ben lifted his eyebrows. "Younger man, older woman. It's scandalous, Margaret Von Keller, President of the Women's Christian Temperance Union. Oh, the gossip."

"Older...the way you said *older*," she snapped. "I'm not the president, either." She took another small sip of soup.

"You should be. Holy cow, I read those papers you write." He wiped his bread along the bottom of his bowl. "Do you have a young man, other than me?" he teased.

"No," she mumbled.

"Why not?" He licked the sides of the bowl, still hungry.

"Would you like a quote from my mother? 'Why, Margaret, you have grown too tall...'" she used a thick German accent, 'No one wants a wife taller than her husband. *Ja?*'" She rolled her eyes. "As if I could control how tall I am!"

Ben snickered. She sounded so much like Helga. "But you did the right thing, you fought to go to the university. I imagine there were plenty of tall young bachelors looking for a beautiful, smart, caring wife."

She tapped her finger on her lips, sighing. "One would think so."

Ben wanted to ask more, but he already had a feeling Margaret's passion for God and her radical views on reforming mankind might be a problem for some men. She was tall, all right, but she was plenty pretty, too.

"I had two invitations in the last two years," she said softly. "Not once, but both times, a nice meal, a nice conversation, and then they would casually slip me a folder."

"A folder?" Ben squinted.

"Yes. The assumption was I would be willing to write their papers for them."

"Oh." He frowned. "Did you?"

"The first one, no." She dropped her head. "The second gentleman...yes."

"Mags! To allow yourself to be used that way! Wanted for only your brain and handwriting." He teased her until he noticed the hurt in her eyes.

She shrugged and set the bowl down. "I think I was meant for more." She squinted, looking out at the fading light from the window. "I've always known it. I tried to be who my mother wanted me to be. I want to be who God wants me to be. But from the first article of Frances Willard's I read, I was hooked. My heart would not stop pounding, like having blind eyes opened. My faith needed a place of expression. I wanted a purpose greater than myself." Her shoulder rose and then dropped. "Her words still make my life fit together. If God can use me to help the Indians to survive or to give aid to the poor people of Chicago, then I want to give my life to that."

"Mags, I can get all that, really, I don't believe women have to be who everyone else wants them to be. But what kind of group would leave you sick and alone, to go on with their cause?"

"Would a man stop fighting a war, just to sit and watch his friend die?" She searched his face.

"A man should get his friend to safety and then go on with the fight." He stood and reached down for her bowl.

She looked away. "Jesus said to let the dead bury the dead."

Ben wondered how tangled her thoughts with this group were.

"But Mags." He touched the sleeve of her cotton gown, trying to give her a tender smile. "You weren't dead."

She blinked and turned to watch Henry as he lay on the floor. He carefully stacked rocks then tossed sticks to knock them over. An awkward silence hung in the air.

Ben didn't want to prove he was right. "I prayed for you to live. You had peace in your heart to say goodbye to this

world. Your friends believe they were doing what God wanted. Maybe we were all right." He took their dishes and went
outside to wash.

The next couple of nights, Ben listened as Henry lay
next to Margaret and she read to him from her Bible. She
was still weak but took the time to make the Bible stories
come alive for Henry. Ben even found himself entertained.
She gave Goliath a low and harsh voice, while she imitated
the *swish* of the rocks flying through the air. He noticed
that she put the Bible down and used both hands to tell the
story better. He had an extreme thankfulness for her and
her strength. He used only to want to make the Von Kellers
happy, but now he had a strange desire to make her happy,
too. Maybe he was just full of himself because it seemed that
God had answered his prayers. No, God answered to save
this loving person. It was wonderful to hear from someone
who had a calling, a conviction of what to do with her life.
Henry yawned and went to get Ben's jacket. He curled up
a few feet from the door and closed his eyes. Ben turned
down the oil lamp. "Do you need anything?" He pushed his
blanket into its usual place.

"No." She set the Bible aside. "You can blow out the
lamp."

Ben was thankful for the large thick braided rug underneath them and stretched out his long legs. The soft blanket turned pillow cradled his head.

"Ben," Margaret whispered.

"Yeah." He popped open his eyes.

"Why do you think every night Henry falls asleep on his own but sometime after we're asleep he comes over and sleeps between us?"

"I don't know. I figured maybe he got cold."

"I wonder if that's where he feels safest. Maybe he doesn't want to risk us telling him he can't...so he comes in while we're asleep."

"Could be." He chewed on a careful way to say something. "No one cares if a little orphan boy sleeps next to you. The problem is me. I have bad nightmares, imagining your mother's reaction to how we managed at night."

"Oh." Margaret shifted underneath her blanket.

"I've known from the beginning that I should be sleeping outside. Especially since you've begun to improve. Henry will tell me if you need anything. This will be the last time. I'll tell Henry why in the morning."

"I'd make my mother understand *you* are the reason I'm alive."

"Umm...more like Carolyn." Ben chuckled. "Oh yeah, God gives and takes away, so let's give Him a bit of credit."

"Yes, let's." Margaret's hand reached for his. He knew that this meant prayer. Her hand was warm and soft against his grip, her voice confident and sincere.

"Lord, thank you for life. Thank you for how you save us. Thank you for sending Ben. Not a day too late. You are so good to us, and we trust you for these next days. Help Ben and I to find the right path for Henry. Please show him your love. A love that will never fail him...Amen," she whispered.

Margaret didn't let go of Ben's hand as it rested in Henry's spot. "I've never known the pain of such sickness... but here I am, laying in a shed on an old wool rug, and I've never known such comfort."

"Umm," he whispered, dozing. "Thank you, Mags for living...Amen."

17

As soon as Carolyn arrived, Ben excused himself to go back to the doctor's office. There had been a burr in his saddle since he first came to town. He walked to the lumber yard and got what he needed, then went into the back of the Ketchum's carriage house and found a saw, a hammer, and some nails. He started working on the doctor's front porch, removing the old rotted wood and replacing it with the new planks he had cut. The front door opened and an older lady peeked out.

"What is all this pounding?" she said sternly.

Ben looked up. "Just replacing a few pieces here, ma'am. Won't take me too much longer."

"I don't remember my son saying a carpenter was coming today."

"Oh, I'm not a carpenter." As soon as the words came out, they sounded incorrect. "By trade, that is." He smiled at her and finished pounding the nails. Later, Ben stood back and admired the repair. He jumped on the porch a few times and found it solid again. He replaced all the items he had borrowed just as the doctor's carriage pulled up. Ben steadied the horse while Dr. Ketchum got out.

"Ben, is everything okay?"

"Yes, sir. I wanted to do something for you, but I might have upset your mother. I just replaced a few boards on your porch. I'm sorry if I kept any of your sick folks awake." Ben began to unharness the doctor's horse.

"You fixed my rotten porch?" The doctor slapped him on the back. "I can't thank you enough."

"Truly, it's me that can't thank you enough." Ben walked the horse into the stall.

"There's one more thing I feel I should ask you about, Ben. Carolyn has been a nuisance about it."

Ben came out of the stall, nervous about what the doctor could want. Probably time to get out of their shed.

"She's taken such a shine to the little Indian boy. I've seen that sixth finger. She wants me to operate on it. She thinks he'll always be treated as an outcast. I guess he told her he wasn't real Ho Chunk and the tribe had rejected him. It would be something I could do here in the office. He might need to spend the night, but Carolyn wouldn't leave his side. I know you and Margaret aren't his parents. But I guess as his guardians, it would be your choice. Maybe talk about it." He walked toward the house. "Thanks for the new porch."

* * *

Carolyn helped Margaret into her blue and brown skirt and light blue blouse. "My, you're so thin, but his brown belt can be adjusted." She helped attach the extra length to the back. "I love this white shawl you have." Carolyn held it up. "Did you buy it in Chicago?"

"No, actually it was my sister's. She didn't like it and was happy to give it to me. Here." Margaret took it from her and placed it around Carolyn's shoulders. "I want you to have it."

"No, I shouldn't."

"Yes, you should." Margaret smiled at her. "I could never repay you for all your help." She turned Carolyn to face her, pulling the shawl snug over the young woman's shoulders. "Please promise me you'll consider going to college. Even if your family only agrees to a ladies' college. You are a gifted healer, Carolyn. For someone so smart and wise…you must see what God has for you."

Carolyn smiled and touched the soft shawl. "I promise to think about it."

Margaret felt a bit dizzy and sat down.

"There's a harvest dance this Friday." Carolyn did a small turn in the room. "I could wear this."

"What's the date today?" Margaret had no idea.

"September twenty-third."

"Oh, that makes this Friday my birthday. Hmm." Margaret shook her head. "Twenty-four. Oh, my."

"We need to have a party. When was the last time you had cake?" Carolyn clapped her hands.

"No, no." Margaret held her hand up. "No cake, no party."

"Then come to the dance." Carolyn's eyes were wide.

"I would probably fall asleep. No, thanks."

"Can I ask Ben?" Carolyn grinned in anticipation. "And Henry, of course."

"That would be up to them." She lifted a half smile. "My, my...to be young again."

When Margaret woke from her nap, Ben was smiling at her. "I have to take you outside." He bent down next to her. She started to rise as he lifted her in his arms.

"Ben, I can walk. You don't have to carry me."

"I know, but it's my way of making sure you're gaining weight." He smiled at her; she smelt like lavender soap. "Henry." He looked up from his book. "Grab Miss Mags' pillow and bring it to the tree."

"So, am I gaining weight?"

"My back is breaking." Ben smiled as he walked her out the door and away from the shed.

Margaret looked around and wondered what he was up to. "Oh, just put me down. "She poked his back.

Ben gently dropped her legs as she stood in front of him. "Wow, you are tall."

"I think we're done." Margaret grimaced and turned away.

"Wait." Ben grabbed her arm and slid it down to hold her hand. "Why are you frowning? Are you mad at me?" He gave her a teasing tug, praying that he hadn't hurt her feelings.

"I just...no. I just don't like to hear how tall...or heavy or old I am."

Ben pressed his lips together and squinted at her. Where was this coming from? "I think...I'm sorry...and I like that blouse." He offered a silly smile, still at a loss to why she was fussing. He squeezed her hand and led her to the tree.

"Would you just sit with me a while? I have something to talk about."

Henry had dropped the pillow and run out to play.

Margaret took a deep breath and let it out. "Yes, I'm sorry. I'm just stir crazy, I guess." She sat on her pillow and leaned back against the tree. Ben sat next to her, their shoulders touching. She moved a bit away, and Ben wondered why she was sore at him. Neither one spoke as Henry ran from weed to dry wildflower, plucking them from the ground. Henry looked up on cue, and they both waved. He ran toward them with his bouquet of weeds. Dirt clumps flying off his pants leg, he stopped in front of Margaret and handed them to her.

"Thank you, kind sir." She smiled, brushing the dirt off her skirt.

Henry bowed like a gentleman and took off skipping.

"Oh my, where did he learn that?" She laughed.

"That boy is very attached to you, Mags." They watched Henry kick an anthill. All the teasing was gone from Ben's face. "You can drop him off in an orphanage?"

Margaret leaned her head back against the tree, staring at the blue and white sky. With her forlorn expression, she looked as if she'd lost her reason for living. What was wrong today? Everything was making her more melancholy.

"I found a few of the tribe members who spoke English. They said his mother abandoned him and no one ever really took him in. My guess would be his father is black, Henry doesn't remember him, and no one seemed too concerned for his welfare. I saw the old woman smack him with a stick and it took everything in me to wait and ask. When I did, she agreed for our group to take him. But then I got so sick." The weight of Henry's story hung thick in the air.

"Carolyn is sweet on you." She changed the subject.

"Carolyn has a family. I can't be her pa. Henry, though, my goodness, Mags."

"Just don't be surprised when she asks you to go to the harvest dance in town," Margaret quipped.

"What? Why would she do that?"

"Because she likes you."

Ben dropped his face into his hands. "Yikes." He shook off the unsettling news. "But I wanted to talk about Henry." He looked around, to make sure Henry couldn't hear. "Dr. Ketchum wants to remove the sixth finger. He said we need to talk about it."

Margaret exhaled, squeezing her arms across her chest. "I don't know. What do you think?"

"We aren't his parents, even though we keep acting like it. It's too big of a decision for me. I have trouble making good choices for myself." He picked up a rock and hurled it out past Henry.

* * *

Margaret let out a quiet sigh. Her prevailing problem was that she loved their little misfit family. So many obstacles had brought them all together, so strangely attached. She didn't mind this storage shed. It was like playing house as a child, except this was more desirable than anything she had ever imagined. She could pretend forever. Henry was happy just to run and kick rocks. *Maybe we could just…*waves of sadness surged through her. What had she prayed a hundred times? That she would give her desires up for His service. For His will only. That she didn't need a husband and children. There were enough poor children just in Chicago to fill her every hour.

But somehow, sitting here next to Ben, watching their little guy run carefree in the dry grass, feeling the fresh air in her lungs, not having any responsibilities besides getting rest—how could it all hold such deep appeal?

She looked over at Ben. He gave her his usual, reassuring wink. Goodness, he had the warmest brown eyes on earth. She loved being this close to his side. He had a handsome profile, but it was his never-ending strength that moved her. The way he carried her when she was so weak, getting her anything she asked for, watching protectively over Henry. Her heart ached with longing for this simple life.

Looking down, she slowly tucked her arm under Ben's. Making this decision about Henry was only pushing her back to her responsibilities. But for this moment, this was contentment. She carefully leaned her head into his shoulder. "I don't know, Ben," she said after a few quiet minutes had passed. "Maybe we should let the doctor take the finger off." She pulled in a ragged breath. "But I don't know if I can let him go. I completely love him."

18

That night as Ben lay under the stars, he wondered if he was living a different life. The moments today under the tree were so satisfying. Were the dairy and Nadine real? What were Nadine's thoughts toward him? He'd started to write her a few times, but threw them all away. There was nothing he wanted to say that he would risk Mrs. Von Keller reading. As the days turned into weeks, his old life had seemed to fade. It really wasn't much of a life. There must be a better way to be a man, than the bravado of his hand on a cold pint. Even the way it felt to kiss Nadine was fading. Maybe it was just an impulse? The night her dress was stuck, her soft shoulders, beauty to his eye, yet it wasn't what he wanted anymore.

He dropped his arms over his face. Being away from the dairy somehow felt renewing. More freedom, yet he had these hard responsibilities. Why did these tasks agree with him? He squeezed his brow. He said he wouldn't mess this up. First things first. Get Margaret home. Nothing else mattered. Carolyn was coming in the morning while he did some hunting. They would talk to her about having her father operate on Henry, and then they needed to get back to Elbert County

Later in the week, Carolyn followed him outside. "Ben, I wanted to talk to you alone." He looked down at her, wondering. "Today is Margaret's birthday," she announced.

"Really?" He scratched his head.

"I have an idea," Carolyn said. "Can I tell you?"

*   *   *

Margaret had taken a damp cloth to Henry's slate. "Two more problems and you can go see what Ben and Carolyn are up to." He did them quickly, and she nodded in approval. He'd had a rough life without a family, but he picked up the Ho-Chunk language and survived their culture. With grit and smarts, he could learn to be anything.

She stood up from the little table and looked out the open door. Carolyn and Ben were chatting away. Maybe something confidential, just between the two of them. She stepped back, embarrassed for watching them. Like a child being overlooked for a game, feeling left out was completely silly. Carolyn was probably just asking him to the town dance. She stared at the floor and over at their tiny living space. They needed to have fun. *What a burden it has been for them to take care of me. All three of them feeding me and tiptoeing around me as I sleep. They've given up so much to care for me.* Why did her chest felt like it was being squeezed? She had renewed her practice of reading scripture every night this week. How could she be anything but thankful? God had spared her life. She could again renew her vision for her work. It was profoundly important work. Alcohol was the devil, coming in to steal the life God wants to give his creation. God's people need to rise up and speak out. She turned and grabbed her case. She would evaluate her scribbled notes and begin to work on next month's letter to the legislators.

* * *

"Frau Edda made me this shirt." Ben put his arms out for Margaret to see.

"Mmm hmm." She barely looked.

"It's almost dusk. Do you have a wrap or something?" he asked.

Margaret finally looked up from her Bible. "I'm not going with you all. I already told Carolyn."

Ben looked to Carolyn and Henry by the door. "Go on ahead. We'll be right there." He bent down and slowly took Margaret's Bible and papers from her hands. "Yes, you are." He grabbed her hand and pulled her up.

"No, really I'm fine. You can have fun with the kids." Margaret subdued a smile, calling Carolyn a kid. Ben needed to be careful with Carolyn's affections.

He pulled on her hand. "You want to walk or be carried?" He slid his other arm around her waist.

Margaret smiled and twisted away from his hold. "I'm not going."

"Yes, you are." His eyes got narrower, like a wolf coming after its prey.

"No." Margaret backed up a few steps. "Why are you being this way? Just go on without me. I'll be fine here. I'd like the quiet for some more writing time."

Ben stepped closer. "No writing. We're going to have some fun. I know it's your birthday," he whispered, leaning in.

Holding both hands, he pulled her out into the middle of the floor. He easily picked her up and spun her in a circle. "That's about all I know about dancing." He gently put her on her feet. "It's Nadine's fault."

"Nadine?"

"Wait." Ben reached into his pocket. "I wanted to give this to you without Henry or Carolyn here." He pulled out the gold chain with a small gold cross hanging from it.

Margaret's throat tightened. "Ben, this is too sweet." She held her hand behind the small cross. When had he had time to go to town and shop? He couldn't have picked out a more perfect gift. "I love it." She held her hair up off her shoulders. Ben carefully opened the clasp and laid it across her neck. She put her hand over it. It felt so personal, so loving. She turned to face him and felt her chin begin to quiver.

"Don't cry, Mags. Goodness, anyone who's been a feather away from the grave has a right to celebrate her birthday."

He was so close, she didn't even need to take a step. She fell into his arms as he held her close. She let the tears fall and suppressed her cries into his shoulder. She knew he didn't understand what birthdays were like for spinsters, and she didn't care. His tall lean body fit perfectly against hers. His arms were hard and strong, but with the perfect pressure to enclose her. He rubbed her back, and it caused her to want his closeness even more. Her chest rose and fell with uneven hiccups. Nothing had felt so safe in all her life. This was the best birthday moment her heart had ever known.

Ben was the one to take a small step back. He looked into her face and wiped off her tears with the cuff of his new shirt. She wondered if the long embrace had made him uneasy. It felt tender and honest, but he looked flushed.

"Now will you come, please?" he said, nodding to the door. "It's a beautiful sunset."

"Yes." She brushed her hand down his shirt. "Thank you for the necklace. It's beautiful."

Margaret grabbed her wrap and walked out with Ben. She looked down the fence and observed some lights ahead. They walked closer, and she saw a mixture of small glass jars with candles burning in them. There were five or six hanging from the tree limbs. Looking closer, she saw one of the tables and chairs from the shed.

"I wondered where you were taking those today." When Margaret realized the cake and fixings were all for her, she closed her hand over her mouth. "Oh my," she murmured, fingering the little lace cloth holding the cake and glass dishes and silverware. Henry ran up to her and thrust a bouquet of real wild flowers into her hands. "Henry." She knelt down and pulled him close. "Thank you." He wiggled out of her embrace and scurried behind Ben's legs.

"Carolyn, what did you do?" Margaret stood, reprimanding her with a smile.

"My grandma baked the cake, and Ben brought the table and hung the lights."

Margaret moved to hug this young woman, embarrassed now for having felt left out.

Ben pulled the chair out for her, and everyone sat down. He lit the candle in the center of the cake. "Make a wish."

Margaret paused and bit her bottom lip, not wanting to cry again. She took a moment to really see each one around this simple table. Their care, their patience—there was so much love and attention, looking back at her. She tried to inhale, waiting for her heart to calm down. Truly, the Lord had immeasurably graced her life. Quickly, she blew out the candle.

They laughed, watching Henry lick his plate clean after three slices of cake.

"Listen." Carolyn sat up. "The band and dance floor are outside. You can hear the music."

They all listened. "Good fiddle player." Ben tapped his hand against the table.

"Ben, you should ask Carolyn for a dance," Margaret urged.

"I should?" He looked wide-eyed.

"She gave up her time there to make this a special night."

"Ahhh…well. You'd have to lead, Carolyn." He stood up and offered his hand. "I really don't dance."

Carolyn took Ben's hands and swung them back and forth. "Now, we're going to kind of just go in a circle and spin once in a while."

"Ahh…" Ben tried to move with her. "Just don't spin me too fast."

Carolyn laughed and kept moving. "I can't spin you! You have to spin me."

"I think I've seen this somewhere." He pulled up his arm and swung her underneath trying not to trip over his clumsy feet.

Henry jumped up and ran in the middle. "Spin me!"

"All right," Ben laughed, "let's see what I can do with you." He grabbed Henry by the fingers and twirled and spun him around. Henry began to squeal and giggle. Carolyn put her hand out to Margaret. "Let's show them how it's done."

"I'll be the man." Margaret laughed, rolling her eyes. Carolyn knew her dance steps, and soon they were doing circles around the rambunctious boys. The music floated on the cool of the evening, and candles illuminated the night with sparkles of white.

"Oh, I love this song. *Twisting Green River.*" Margaret slowed her steps.

Ben led Henry over. "Carolyn, see if you can teach him anything." He handed Henry to the young woman.

Margaret started for the chair when she felt Ben's hand in hers. "I'll be the man."

"Mmm, that you are," she mumbled, facing him.

"What?" he asked.

"Oh, nothing." Her thin body glowed with delight. She was in the arms of a handsome man, taller than herself. Carolyn and Henry giggled, imitating their dance pose.

"Let's all circle around the tree. Then we won't collide." Ben grabbed Margaret tighter and began to lead her smoothly around the tree. "It's a bit like the game we used to play after church as kids—remember? Whip-the-Tail, except with skipping."

Margaret laughed with joy. "You are the best, worst dance partner I've ever had." Carolyn and Henry came up close on their heels. Margaret was soon tired, but the smile and laughter from Ben gave her the strength to go on. He spun her close, arm wrapped around her waist, and gave her a quick wink. Her heart fluttered—surely it must be all the exercise. They finally slowed down and began to come around the table.

"I think I hear my dad. He said he would whistle for me." Carolyn said.

"Let me walk you." Ben let go of Margaret's hand, and she leaned against the table.

"Thank you, Carolyn." Margaret gave a breathy curtsy. "You are a wonderful dancer."

"Yes, I agree." Ben patted Carolyn on the back. "Shall we go?"

Margaret took the flowers from her chair and sat down. "Henry, I love these flowers."

He sat and dropped his face onto his arm. She wondered why her compliments were embarrassing him.

"Someday when you're older, there will be a sweet girl your age. Her name might be Susan or Katie..." He peeked up. "She'll see how kind you are, and how smart you are. She'll smile just to see your smile."

"Uck." He buried his face again.

"Someday," she said softly, rubbing his back. "You'll have a night as sweet and special as this one. Maybe you'll be the young man to plan it for your sweetheart." Margaret looked at the twinkling lights and listened to the soft melodies still hanging in the air. Her birthday. She had to be honest, she'd been feeling sorry for herself just hours ago. Touching her cross necklace, now had her heart had ever been so completely full?

The music and the crickets seemed to chime in together when Ben walked up. He started to say something when Margaret stood and put her hand out for his. She quietly pulled him behind her and pointed for him to look at Henry. "I think he's fallen asleep," she whispered. "But look, while I thought I was encouraging him in his future romances, he was eating all the frosting off the bottom of the cake. See." She pointed to the missing frosting. He still had a chunk hanging from his finger.

"*It is* good frosting." Ben reached around her and swiped a finger full himself. He stuck his finger in his mouth. "Nothing like the frosting a Granny makes. Mmm, I think it has some cherry cordial in it."

Margaret shook her head. "Goodness no, the frosting is white." Her voice wavered; suddenly feeling trapped between the table and Ben.

Ben took another swipe at the cake and leaned around her, holding his finger out. "Taste it. It has something extra."

She blinked out into the night and back at the frosting, her heart suddenly beating erratically. He was leaning close behind her, his free hand touching her waist. Opening her mouth, she quickly nibbled some frosting off his finger. He plopped the same finger in his mouth, raising his brows and licking his lips. The intimacy was assailing her senses. His brown eyes were warm and inviting, his face so perfectly shaped.

Twisting, she brought her shoulder back against him and gently placed a kiss on his cheek. He smiled and then his face flushed red. She felt his hands grip her waist and he finished turning her to face him. With no space between them, the only movement was the rising and falling of their chests. She waited, her eyelashes fluttering close to his face as her hand came up his sleeve. She felt his hands move up her back as his lips gently found hers. A shudder ran up her body at his slow, mindful kisses. Now his arms pressed their bodies together, his kisses more urgent and wanting, and she could taste the mixture of sugar and desire, hunger meeting hunger.

* * *

To Ben's increasing delight, she responded to the deepening of his kiss. Her eager innocence was making him crazy. The closer he pulled her, the harder she clung to him. He couldn't think, he just wanted to have more. More of her hair in his fingers. More of her lips on his skin, more of his hands on her. Every fiber in him awakened, just like when he had been alone with Na…Ben broke the kiss and stepped back. They both stared at each other, trying to catch their breath. "Mags…I…" He looked up at the stars. "I can't." The next instant, he looked into his greatest fear. She looked as if he had slapped her. "I'm so sorry…" his voice cracked.

Flushed and looking away, she brushed the back of her hand across her mouth. "It wasn't your fault, Benjamin."

Why did she just call me Benjamin?

She held her hand over her chest. "I was so taken by the necklace and the music. And everything was so lovely." She dropped her chin. "I didn't mean lovely. That sounds like a ladies' tea. Certainly, more than a cup of tea…the details, the effort."

Ben could tell she was rattled, too. She ran her hand across her forehead. "My parents picked the most trustworthy, honorable man to come after me. I'm so sorry. It's my fault you feel compromised now." She stepped back, her hands over her red cheeks. "Please, forgive me."

"Mags," he said with gritted teeth. He gripped his hair and stalked in a circle. "Sometimes I wish the ground would just swallow me up," he mumbled. "Trustworthy, honorable…" His laugh was cynical. He'd never been so conflicted. If she only knew the truth. If she knew what he had done. Who he really was. Why he messes everything up. She should despise him. "Can you please blow out the candles?" He couldn't look at her. "I'll carry Henry."

19

Margaret curled up in a ball, watching the first rays of sun hit the wall of the shed. She looked over and noticed that Henry had his thumb hanging from his mouth. She knew he was too old to be sucking his thumb, but didn't have the heart to correct him. They hadn't even found the words to tell him about his finger operation. She had tossed and turned with God for most of the night. She waited and prayed, listening for God's correction. It was the strangest thing, but she didn't feel sinful. How can love be a sin? Certainly, it was a sin for the unmarried if taken too far into bed. Maybe it was a sin to provoke a young man who hasn't made a declaration. Who by the look on his face doesn't want to.

Margaret let out a long sigh. *I am twenty-four years old, and I kissed someone I care deeply about. So what?* Her stomach did another flip. *What about the way he kissed me back, though? Oh, my. I had no idea.* Squeezing her eyes shut, she prayed for forgiveness, just in case. She surrendered her life again to His will. Now to the harder part of the day—how to make amends with Ben. She rose up and carefully pulled the door to the shed open, not wanting to wake Henry. Ben lay a few feet away, curled up under a blanket. Looking to the sky for strength, she looked down and noticed an empty bottle next to him. She picked it up and smelled the strong odor. She knew it was the despicable alcohol. But how did it get here?

"Ben," she said lightly. He didn't move. "Ben." She tried again. He pulled the blanket over his head.

"What?"

"Can you wake up?"

"Not until you turn the sun down." He sounded sick.

"What did you say? Are you ill?" Something dawned on her. "Did you drink from this bottle? Is this bottle yours?"

Ben finally pulled the blanket down and saw her through squinted eyes. "Yes."

"How? I mean, why would you buy alcohol?"

"I can see you're as smart as your sister," he glared, voice mocking. "First you walk in, you put down the money, take the bottle, and walk out." He rolled away from her. "And drink it."

Margaret stepped back, shocked and insulted. She looked up, dazed, and walked into the field around the shed. *This is what alcohol does. Why am I shocked?* She began to walk in circles. Why did it have to be Ben? Why would he choose this level of evil? *It's the abhorrent venom.* She felt her eyes fill and her nose begin to run. Why Ben? He knew how she felt about alcohol. She'd only pledged her life to its removal. This was blatant revenge. How could he be so cruel?

Tears began to run down her face. Lust, that's all it was. Her roommates had often talked about the wants of sinful men. He only felt lust. She stopped circling with the shock of her revelation. Her stomach twisted in knots and she raised her hand to swipe at the tears. Even if his heart was not honorably drawn to her, what about his heart before God? Did he care at all about his salvation? Why alcohol? It ruins the best people. She sucked in painful sobs. "Why? Why" she said to the sky.

"Why not?"

Ben stood a few feet away, blinking slowly. "Don't you think I tried? Don't you think I knew I would disappoint you?" His voice was raspy and angry. "Better now, Margaret. Better find out now. If all it took was being surrounded with love and care, and someone telling me that I'm an honorable man, then I should be a damn saint of something."

"I don't understand," she moaned.

"You don't *know me*. You really don't know me."

"Then tell me." She tried to steady her shaking limbs. "I think I love you. So could you just try to explain to me...?"

"I disappoint people. That's what I do. I am a disappointment. What you are is what you do." He shook his head. "That's why you're crying right now. I let you down. I tried to tell you. I think you'd fallen asleep. I hate the dairy. I chased after Nadine. She's the only reason I stayed there." He swiped the back of his hand across his mouth. "Yes, it's true. I was pretty sure you didn't hear that. I've kissed your sister and not just a peck. I've stolen and lied, and finally, I can say it." He bent over, gripping his thighs. "I drink.

I drink all the time!" He stood up quickly. "There, I said it. That bottle wasn't my first, and it won't be my last." He moaned and tried to walk away, then turned back abruptly. "So don't waste your time loving me." He leaned over, then tried to straighten back up. "Really. Don't."

Margaret stood frozen, only her slow breathing keeping her intact. She tried to blink until her mind would return, but she still didn't understand. He was the lighthearted boy who played tag after church. He was the one who picked her up and carried her from the reservation. He saved her life. She watched him play and care for Henry, sit up with her at night and talk about her writings.

She walked a few feet to where he stood, staring out into the pasture. She cautiously squeezed his arm. "It's the alcohol." Her thin voice choked out the words. "It's telling you lies about yourself."

He moved away breaking her grip on his arm. Turning, he impaled her with red and blurry eyes. "This is the first time I've told you the truth."

20

"Why's everyone so quiet?" Carolyn interrupted the thick silence.

"Just a lot on our minds." Margaret tried to smile, unpacking the basket of food Carolyn had brought. "We have yet to talk to Henry about the operation."

"My dad said I could help." Carolyn sat down. "But I don't think I will. Whenever things have to be sawed off, I get a little sick to my stomach." Margaret looked up to make sure Henry hadn't heard that. "Please, Carolyn, this is very hard for us."

"Oh, I almost forgot, a letter came from your folks." Carolyn pulled the letter from her pocket.

Margaret took it and pressed her lips tight.

"You don't seem too excited," Carolyn observed.

"No. I think I'll read it tonight."

"Where's Ben? I didn't see him outside."

Margaret shrugged. "I wouldn't know."

"Seems like something happened. Did you two have a fight? I mean, he's never just left before, has he? Are you two boyfriend and girlfriend? It's kinda hard to tell."

Margaret turned her back to Carolyn. Maybe if she ignored her, she'd get the hint.

"Hey, Henry," Carolyn called him over. "I've got a piece of candy from the store for after your operation."

Margaret shook her head and approached them. "What Carolyn is saying is that tomorrow morning we're going to see her father, Doctor Ketchum, at his office. It's a nice doctor's office."

"He'll put you to sleep, Henry, you won't feel anything." Carolyn spouted.

"Carolyn! Please!" Margaret said, surprised at her instant anger. Getting down on a knee, she held Henry's hands and took in a deep breath "You know how on everyone else's hands there are only five fingers on each hand? See how mine match? Five and five?"

Henry tried to pull from her touch.

"And mine." Carolyn smiled, holding up her hands.

"We all think you'll have a better life if you just have five and five, like everyone else." Margaret tried to appear happy. "Like Ben."

"Nah." Henry jerked his hands quickly away from Margaret. He started rattling off in the Ho-chunk language.

"What is he saying?" Carolyn asked.

"Well, I don't understand much. But he's informing me that he will not go...umm...oh, my." Margaret couldn't rise fast enough as he flung open the door and took off running.

"You want me to bring him back? I'm pretty fast."

Margaret rubbed her temple. "No, I don't think he'll go far. Let's give him a minute."

Margaret paced out front as the afternoon sun hid behind large clouds. Ben rode in, wondering about the frantic look on her face.

"Have you seen Henry?" she cried.

"I've been in town all day. Why wouldn't he be here with you?" He dismounted, and Margret's shoulders slumped.

"Carolyn and I tried to tell him about the operation." She glanced back out to the field. "Where could he be?" she murmured, giving Ben a weary glare. "Which is tomorrow. Did you remember?"

"Yes, I remembered." Her tone affirmed he was in the ever-familiar manure pile.

"Where were you all day?" She clapped her hand over her mouth and ran inside. She turned as Ben followed her in. "I'm so sorry—I sounded just like my mother. Ahh!" She gazed out the window, watching. "I'm not even a mother, but I just understood why my mother worried and nagged us so much. I feel like my heart is going to fall out of my chest, and I can't do anything about it!" She circled by Ben, and he reached out to grab her arm.

His touch felt like fire, and their eyes locked. "Mags." Her name on his lips was a soft whisper. How could he ever repair the confusion in her eyes? She swallowed and finally looked away. He cleared his throat and let go. "I'll find him."

Swinging a leg up on Sandy, he turned the horse around. Why did his insides feel like mush? *Why did I reach for her? What was that? She should still loathe me. Does she expect an apology? Would she forgive me? Not likely.* Ben gave Sandy a kick. "Let's go find Henry."

He rode for a few minutes before he saw some movement in a tree. Of course, the tree where they had the birthday party. He rode Sandy right up to the limbs. "Hey, Henry. Miss Margaret is really worried."

Henry worked his way up to a higher limb while mumbling something in his native language.

"Henry, come here." Ben reached out toward him. "Tell me what you're saying. I don't understand."

Henry came back down a branch. "Doctor is taking my finger." Ben could see the dirt streaks down Henry's cheeks.

"And you're scared?"

Henry bobbed his head up and down.

"Are you afraid it will hurt?"

He bobbed his head again.

"The doc will put you to sleep. You won't feel or see anything." Henry swung his head back and forth. Ben wondered what to do. "I made something for you today." Henry stilled. "It's right here in my saddle bag." He had the boy's attention. I'd like to give it to you, but I made it to give you tomorrow after you wake up." Ben had no experience with children, but bribery seemed to work with most people.

Henry crawled off the last limb and stepped onto the saddle. Ben settled him in front of him and reached over for the saddle bag. Henry leaned over, trying to get into the bag.

"Wait." Ben held the flap. "I'm going to give you one look and then you can hold it tomorrow, after the operation."

Henry pulled on Ben's hand as he lifted it quickly and then closed it.

"What is it?" Henry asked as Sandy turned toward the shed.

"It's a toy." Ben smiled.

"What's a toy?" Henry asked.

Margaret was still looking out at the pasture, searching back and forth. An evening breeze blew her skirts, and Ben felt his chest swell. Something about seeing her up and out felt like the comfort of home. Like being tired and wet and cold from hunting all day and finally thawing out, warm by the fire. She slowly turned to see them, her eyes filling with complete relief. She smiled when they approached and reached out to take Henry. He fell into her arms and then pushed her away. Her smile turned to a painful frown. Ben couldn't tell if she was just pulling her wind-whipped hair or wiping a tear from her face.

"He's probably just hungry," he said, leading Sandy out to the pasture.

"Thank you for finding him," she called after him.

*　*　*

Margaret stepped in the shed and looked around. "There's a bowl of stew, from Grandma Ketchum." She pointed to the table.

Henry began to shovel the food in his mouth. Ben walked in and closed the door. He walked to Henry and roughed up his hair. "Slow down, boy. You're *not* going anywhere." Ben gripped Henry's head and turned his dirty face up to him. "Right?"

Henry broke free and grabbed a piece of bread. Margaret stood by the window, chewing on her fingernails. Ben grabbed his own bowl and ladled in some stew. "He'll be fine," he said, walking over to her.

"He doesn't like me." She rubbed her temple. "He's always been helpful and obedient." Ben watched her, chewing his stew. "Did we make the right decision?" She sighed. "I mean, what was I thinking, taking him from the tribe. What if he runs away from the orphanage? I shouldn't have tried to help him. What if he won't cooperate for the doctor?"

"Then he has eleven fingers." Ben shrugged. "Don't worry about this one thing." He nodded at Henry. "Can't you see how much weight he's gained? And he's practically reading and writing." Ben took another bite. "And I saw the old Indian lady. She didn't care about him.

She never even looked back." He wiped his mouth. "You've probably done more for him than anyone… humph, just like me," he murmured.

Margaret dipped her head, not wanting Ben to see her watching him. Wishing desperately to have their old life, their old connection. Everything was still upside down since her birthday. She had heartache competing with a headache all day. "The wind has come up. Do you mind if I go for a little walk? I felt so anxious all day."

"No, I don't mind." Ben glanced at her.

* * *

Margaret walked out to the tree. She sat and leaned against it, remembering that chunk of dried weeds Henry was so excited to give her. The sun had already set, but the glow of reds and pinks made a beautiful portrait. Fingering the letter from home, she finally opened it. The small gust of wind matched the churning inside her.

Dearest Margaret,

I write in hopes and prayers that you are feeling better. We were thankful to get your small note in with Ben's letters. Even though it all seems a bit vague, we are so pleased to hear you are feeling better. You are our lovely girl. We know you will soon be home and looking forward to rejoining the family. Your sisters eagerly await your arrival. I've had Edda freshen up your room. Maybe it is time to change the colors? Some new wallpaper would be nice. I will so enjoy your help with the holiday preparations. You don't need to worry about anything. We can send for your things from Chicago soon...

Margaret crumpled the paper and dropped it into her lap. She shook her head, watching the last rays of pink fade. Her chin began to quiver, and she looked back toward her little home, blurry with pooling tears. *I don't want to go home,* she cried. *I want this to be my home.* She covered a cynical laugh with the back of her hand. *I want Ben to be my husband and Henry to be my child. How ridiculous does that sound? Should I write back, that I lost my mind with my illness?* A sob escaped the back of her throat. *What would you say to that, mother?*

21

Doctor Ketchum had asked Margaret to make sure Henry was bathed before they came to his office. He might as well have asked her to rope the wind.

"Henry, please. It's just water," she said after breakfast. "Look at the soap. Here, you do it." She held the soap out to him, and he grabbed it and threw it under the stack of old furniture.

Ben knocked and walked in. He looked at the bucket of water, and Henry backed into the corner in nothing but his drawers.

"I know, don't say it." Margaret held up her hand. "I'm completely frazzled." She went to look for the soap.

"Henry, drop your drawers and get clean or I'm dropping you down the well."

Margaret turned around and whimpered, slowly closing her eyes. When she opened them, Ben was nodding to the door. "I think you need to get out. Even little men need privacy."

She shook her head in defeat, handed him the soap, and walked out. After pacing and trying to pray, she looked up as they came out the door. Henry looked clean. His dark hair had been parted down the middle and combed flat like a little gentleman. She reached out to touch his cheek, but he jerked away from her. She swallowed his rejection and went in to grab her reticule and gloves. It felt like her first day back to civilization. She wanted one look in a mirror but was thankful there was none. Certainly, her sad reflection would only fuel her shaky nerves. Outside, Ben had swung up on Sandy, and reached down to pull Henry up on his lap. She assumed she would be walking. Why was this scene making her heart break anew?

"See that brick on the well." Ben pointed. "Step up on that, then the one on the top." He leaned down, grabbed her hand and brought her over to the well. She finally understood and stepped up as he reached for her and pulled her onto the back of the horse. Why did she feel like a china doll about to be dropped? She grabbed his waist as he led Sandy down the road. What a strange, unstable state she was in.

Margaret was thankful for Carolyn's friendship with Henry; after entering the office, he went to her without any fuss. But what she really wanted was to hold him for a moment before they took him away.

"My father said it will be about an hour." Carolyn closed the door, leaving Ben and Margaret standing alone in the foyer.

Margaret was motionless, staring at the closed door.

"Let's walk down the street. I noticed a bench not too far from here." He lightly touched her elbow.

"How did our mothers do it?" she said dismally, as they walked out. "Your mother lost a son, my mother lost a son. How can a heart beat with that much loss?"

"That's the reason they became friends." Ben led her to the bench.

"I can't understand it," she said. "I never felt such pain as I did from typhoid." She was chatting at the sky. "But this crushing pain is like nothing I've ever known. After our brother died, my mother began to smother us. Nadine hated it and fought her the most."

Ben touched her gloved hand. "I think Henry's going to be fine."

She gave him a tired smile. "He doesn't like me. I must have some crazy notions. How can I rescue someone who doesn't want to be rescued by me?" The silence deepen their distance. "I got a letter from my parents." She pinched the bridge between her eyes. Her mouth was as dry as dirt. Reading her mother's expectations, sitting here next to Ben, worrying about Henry...staring out at the sky again, she mumbled, "I can't do it."

Ben reached around the top of the bench and lightly touched her shoulder.

"I can't go home," she confessed.

"Margaret, you have to go home," Ben said, commanding.

"My mother wants to entice me with new bedding and wallpaper." She squeaked out a sigh. "I live in a simple brownstone in Chicago with other teachers. I like it there. Well, I did." She bit her bottom lip. *Until you, Benjamin Graham came along.* She finally looked over to his hand resting casually on her shoulder, oblivious to her distress. She sucked in a deep breath. "Ben." She barely could make eye contact. "I want you to know how sorry I am about the other night. How embarrassed I am now. You're younger than me. We have always had a brother-sister relationship. I'm so sorry."

"No." Ben squeezed her shoulder and released her quickly. "You're not going to take the blame here. No, no way." He twisted in his seat.

"Just let me finish. I…"

Ben sat back roughly and clutched his hands together, staring into the street.

"I do…maybe I shouldn't say it…have a deep love and respect for you." Her tone sincere.

He raked his hands through his hair and leaned forward, his elbows on his knees.

There was a split second when she knew she would cower or drive ahead. "And…I know what I know. I don't care what you tell yourself. I know what's true. You're smart and caring and good, and any woman…even my sister…" She cleared the tightness in her throat. "…would see that. What shocks me, is you don't see that. Why do you think you're the only one who can't make a mistake? We all disappoint people. I'm about to completely disappoint my parents. No, that's not true. I'm a disappointment because I'm too tall, not married, an overzealous crusader, but somehow until now, I've moved on. I've decided my God is the only one I can get approval from."

"Do you have God's approval? Do you?" Ben squinted at her. "Have you written enough legislators? Have you taught enough Indians? Have you rescued enough orphans?" His voice dropped. "Closed down enough saloons?" She could feel him provoking her.

Margaret pulled on the trim on her sleeves. "I believe what Jesus did for me on the cross was to show me His love and how to live," she said hesitatingly. "Which is to make the world a better place."

"But does He approve of you?" Ben turned to her, red-faced. "If you had never risen from your sick bed? Couldn't make the world a better place. Just you. Margaret Von Keller. Not because of all the things you do," he said rapidly. "Does God approve of you?"

She swallowed hard at his abrupt words. Suddenly it hit her. Was she working for something she already had? A warm fall breeze caressed her face. Margaret tucked a strand of loose hair behind her ear and sensed an unusual stillness. It felt almost like a holy moment. Like taking communion or praying for someone. *Is God trying to show me something?* Her spirit rose with the confident answer. "Yes." She smiled and looked at Ben. "He does approve of me." She stood up quickly in front of the bench and put her hand on her head. "This tall, He approves of me. I haven't worn my hair up in weeks." She ran her fingers through her loose hair. "But I believe He still approves of me." She breathed in and gave him a serious nod. "If I can't do one more thing, for one more person, God still approves of me." She sat down quickly, enjoying the crooked smile on Ben's face.

Moments ticked by as they watched a few townsfolk come and go.

"Let's go check on Henry!" She pulled him off the bench. She tucked her arm inside his, grinning ear to ear. "Because I want to." She tried the phrase again, pulling him forward. "That was a good talk, Bens. It's more joyful to serve God from your heart. I've been serving Him from right and wrong, thinking I should earn what was already given me at salvation. You've given me cause to stop and think. Thank you."

They stood back in the familiar foyer. There were dark, heavy stairs to the right, a hallway in front of them. Ben shuffled his feet, looking a little pale. "If you don't mind, I need some fresh air. I'll be on the porch."

Margaret nodded, smiling inside to think they were taking turns being strong for one another. Instinctively, she touched his blotchy face. He grabbed her gloved hand and kissed the back and walked out.

Oh, Lord. I'm in so much trouble. She rubbed her temple. *I've got Henry enclosed on the right side of my heart and Ben wrapped around the left.*

Ben looked out to the street. The saloon was only half a mile down to the right. His nerves and thirst seemed to be colliding. Leaning his forearms on the sidewalk railing, he dropped his head. It wasn't as if he needed a Bible to drop from the sky. Whenever things were unsettled for him, he reached for the bottle. His problems went away for a while, but problems had no difficulty waiting until he sobered up. If all the time delays and getting Henry through this surgery wasn't enough, Margaret had announced she wasn't going home. That wouldn't work, because he was going to tell her he wasn't, either. He had enough money to pay the doctor today and buy them a train ticket. He needed more time to figure things out.

Every ounce of him was at odds. His mouth was so dry. He wanted to see this through—he would have been the hero if it had gone as planned. Why was she so sweet and loving? The moment she put her head on his shoulder under the tree, something had shifted in him. She leaned on him. She trusted his strength. All those things she said about him were considerable. He wanted to see himself reflected in her eyes. If she saw him as strong and reliable, he really didn't care if anyone else did. Maybe that's what love was like? You want to be all the person sees you to be. And then there was the warmth rising up from his toes when he thought about their kiss. The way she fit perfectly against him. The way he wanted more. Nadine left him wanting, yet unconfident.

The door opened. "They said we can see him." Margaret called him in.

They walked down the hallway until Carolyn showed them the room. There was a table with a cloth covering the doctor's instruments. Ben noticed some blood seeping through the towel. He tried to focus on all the hunting and skinning he had done with Levi. Blood never affected him before. He felt Margaret's ungloved hand slip into his.

"Hello, Henry." She gripped Ben as they leaned toward the sleeping little boy.

"It went well," Doctor Ketchum said, standing up. "I used extra skin to make a flat covering. Only four or five stitches. Unless someone looks close, they'll never know it was there." Ben nodded as he looked to see Henry's hand wrapped in white gauze.

"I'd like him to stay here," the doctor said. "Carolyn has assured me she'll keep him in bed. You can pick him up in the morning. He should be good as gold then."

Margaret chewed her bottom lip. Ben knew she wanted to scoop up the sleeping boy and care for him tonight.

"Is that okay, Margaret?" He squeezed her hand.

"Yes." She glanced at Carolyn. "Will you tell him when he wakes up that we'll be here in the morning?"

"Yes," Carolyn agreed.

"And those muffins you bring, those are his favorite. But no nuts."

"Yes, ma'am."

"She nursed you back from typhoid," Ben whispered in her ear. "Thank you, Carolyn. You've been extremely good to us."

"You're good people," Carolyn said, more mature than her years. "I'll miss all of you."

Margaret rubbed her arm. "And we'll miss you, too."

22

Margaret and Ben stood outside the doctor office as Ben dug into Sandy's saddlebag and pulled out a wooden cup with a handle underneath. A little round wooden ball dangled from a string. He tried to flip the ball up and catch it in the cup. It bounced off each time he tried. "Let's hope Henry is better with this than me."

Margaret came close and touched the smooth wood of the cup and handle. "Where did you buy this?"

"I made it," he answered. "Yesterday."

When he was gone all day. Margaret remembered how annoyed she had been. And he was just working on a toy for Henry. Of course, she thought he was at the saloon. She bit her bottom lip, bothered for being so judgmental. "It's beautiful."

"Speaking of beautiful. You haven't gotten out much. Let's go for a ride. I know a spot where all the leaves have already begun to turn. The colors are amazing." He put the toy back and pulled Sandy around.

Margaret looked back at the Ketchum's office. "Could we circle back here and check on Henry before we go home?" She dropped her chin. "Well, you know what I mean."

* * *

Ben sensed a tingling rising from his belly. "Of course." He had never really been alone with Margaret. Why was the thought of being with her tonight making his mouth go dry? He found himself drawn to her lips again. They were so soft and sweet. He turned and grabbed the saddle horn, quickly swinging up. "Here." He reached down and caught her upper arm. She jumped and slid up behind him, locking her fingers around his waist. This woman, alive and well. Talking, walking, and sharing life. Even offering undeserved forbearance. *I'll be done in, but this is nice.*

The ride was invigorating. Margaret felt more newness of life than she had all week. Fresh air, light conversation about the weather and landscape. The fall colors were like painted layers of gold, copper, and brick red. Ben held his arm out to her and carefully lowered her off Sandy, then swung off and tied Sandy to a branch.

"You know," she started as they walked along the side of a small creek, "I'm pretty much a city girl. I love the dairy, but just for the holidays. I've become accustomed to the noise and smells of the city. Something is being built on every corner. Someone selling something everywhere you look, so much business there. This is good though, too." She pulled a red leaf and twirled it in her fingers. "Listen."

Ben stopped walking and tried to listen. "I don't hear anything."

"I know," she said. "There's no noise." She started walking. "As a man, you're free to live anywhere. Where would you live, Benjamin?"

Ben smiled at her formal question and walked closer to the creek's edge, "I suppose I would need this. I've grown up my whole life hunting, fishing, in the woods." He nodded from where they had ridden. "I wouldn't mind a town like this one. Plenty of wide open space all around. But I don't know how I'd fare in a city. Levi didn't like it." He picked up a rock and threw it down the stream.

"Really, why?"

"He worked on the docks for a few years until he had enough money to buy a cabin by Sault Creek. I guess he didn't know exactly what he was going to do. Trapping is difficult. Living alone isn't easy. He just couldn't take city life." Ben stared off as they walked on in silence

"You're deep in thought." Margaret bent down and let her fingers trail along the cold water.

"It's strange. I always looked up to Levi. He's strong and solid. You remember how he was? But you should have seen him. Meeting Allison and figuring out his life with her. They had a rough go. He definitely fell off his own footing."

"Did it work out?"

"Yes." He smiled at her. "So my ma's letter reports. He left Sault Creek, moved to Madison. So my brother who loves his solitude has found a new way of life. Something I would have never predicted." Margaret saw peacefulness in his eyes. "You're getting to me." He squinted at her.

"How is that?" she asked.

He looked down at his feet, finally looking up. "You said I made you think, but truth be told, you cause me to think. Think hard." He pulled in a deep breath. "You just make me want to be a better person. And I don't really know if I have the ability."

She walked past him. "You're complicated. You're right, I didn't know all your sides." She turned to face him. "Don't you think it's a bit unfair for you to see me in my weakness? To rescue me and help me get well. But I can't see you in yours? You were sent from God, in my opinion. I believe He uses all our imperfections any way He wants."

With strange timing, a breeze came up, and the leaves began to twirl and dance. They smiled at each other. Was there moisture skimming across his eyes? He swallowed hard. The gentleness was there, even with no words to say. She carefully touched the necklace on her neck. Such a fitting gift to touch her heart. Margaret wondered where her defenses had gone as she rubbed the cross between her fingers.

Ben shuffled his feet and looked up through dark lashes. "I've always admired your faith."

Henry was awake and sitting up in bed when they walked in. Ben handed him the new toy and gave Margaret a dismal look. "I forgot he was left handed." Henry didn't seem to mind as he gripped the handle. Tossing the little ball in the air, he tried to catch it in the cup. He even brought his wrapped left hand in to steady it.

"So the old five-finger hand still works?" Ben ruffled his hair. Henry gave him an annoyed look.

"Ben made that toy for you." Margaret tried to chime in.

"Most people are grumpy after their operations." Carolyn took the toy and tried to flip the little ball in the cup.

Henry whined and reached for it.

"Okay, okay." Carolyn handed it back to him.

Henry's dark brown eyes filled up. Margaret had never seen Henry cry, and she pulled on Ben's sleeve, imploring him to help.

"Also, Henry, I made you a sling shot. It's still in my saddle bag."

Henry turned up a crooked little smile.

"But I didn't want you shooting Miss Carolyn. So I'm going to give it to you in the morning."

"He'll be spoiled rotten by the time you pick him up. My grandmother already made him a cake. And I promised him I'd teach him checkers." Carolyn added.

Margaret was just so relieved to see him awake. She had to admit she was starting to feel exhausted.

"I didn't have time to bring food," Carolyn said.

"No, of course not." Ben looked at Carolyn. "I think I'll take Margaret to supper at the café and then we'll get home."

Margaret suddenly felt the impact of those words. Carolyn knew they weren't married. She was young and impressionable. The silence seemed to mark the point.

"And then we'll be here first thing." Margaret knelt by Henry's bed. "Try to hold still." She gave him a sly smile. "Because I'm going to kiss you." She quickly pecked him on the cheek. He rubbed his thick gauzed hand over his cheek. "Ick."

Ben laughed. "Henry, go easy on Carolyn when you beat her in checkers." He winked at Carolyn. "We will be leaving in the morning. Thank you again for all you've done." They bid the children goodbye.

Before they could get to where Sandy was tied, Margaret asked. "We're leaving in the morning?"

Ben nodded. "Yes, I think it's best. If you're feeling strong enough."

Of course not, she wanted to proclaim. *Everything will change all over again.*

Margaret walked quietly next to Ben as he pulled Sandy down the street to the little café. A squeaky old door announced their arrival. A red-haired woman showed them a small table. "Never met you two before." She smiled. "New to town?" She set down two coffee cups.

"We're just on our way home." Ben smiled, looking away.

"Where's home?" she asked, pouring the coffee.

"Elbert."

"Chicago." They said in unison.

"We have family in both places," Ben said, flustered.

"We get around." Margaret smiled.

"It's chicken and dumplings tonight. Two?"

Ben nodded. "Yes, thanks."

"Certainly *I* get around" he grinned. "But you're going home to Elbert."

Margaret's shoulders dropped. "I don't know, Ben. What will my parents say to Henry? If I go back to Chicago, I can get him settled in at the orphanage school, then go home for a visit."

Ben frowned, scratching his neck. "That won't work. They want you home. Honor your mother and father and all that."

"That's a low blow." She squinted at him.

The waitress set their plates down, but neither one moved to eat.

"I'm sorry, Mags," he whispered. "I should never use the Bible against you."

"It just upsets me, because you're right." She picked up the fork and tried a bite.

"I feel like I'm killing your family if I don't deliver you." He took a bite of his buttery roll. "They gave me your dowry. Whatever that is. I feel like I should pay them back or something."

"My dowry?" Margaret sat up straighter.

"It's just money. I have no problem telling them how much I paid the doc and Carolyn for all they did. I know they wouldn't blame me." He swallowed another bite. "We've got enough for train fare. I can work and pay it all back."

"No, I'm glad it's gone," she murmured. "They don't expect me to marry. I'm an old maid."

Ben's cup clanked into the saucer. "Your parents don't know you. Give them a chance."

She rolled her eyes at his words.

"Really, you're strong and beautiful, and they need to see how amazing you are. I have an idea. We both need to face this. I want to run. You want to run. Let's just charge in. It's time they really heard you. *Really* heard you. And if they won't listen, then so what? You go on with your life. At least you can hold your head up high, knowing that you tried. I'm going to go back and get fired like a man." There was a delay of a few seconds before they both laughed at his words. "Does Carl do it, or does your father?"

"My father usually fires the help. But you're like family." She gave him a sly grin.

"So maybe Minna will do it? *Ja?*" They both shook their heads and laughed.

23

Ben walked into the dark shed they called home and lit the lamp. He set the wrapped piece of pie down on the little table. Margaret began to gather Henry's little things and make a stack. "We should take these things back to Carolyn when we pick up Henry." Ben sat at the table and watched her pull several items together. She began to stack the furniture back up into the corner. "Carolyn can use some of these things when she gets married and sets up house."

"I thought you wanted her to go to college." Ben unwrapped his peach pie.

"I do. I just thought...oh, forget it. Did you pay Dr. Ketchum for the operation today?"

"Yeah." He took a bite of pie. "I did some work on his porch, and then I guess your father paid him, too."

"My dowry?" She pressed her lips into a thin line.

Ben wished he'd never mentioned that. It was just money to him.

Margaret brought her hands over her heart. "I'm so thankful for that. Really, it makes my heart sing." She began to stack the few dishes they had. "I was so tired a bit ago. Now I'm wide awake. I'm so glad that money went to help Henry. Probably shouldn't have drunk that last coffee. Have you seen my Bible? Oh, here it is. I should have asked Carolyn for a broom. Little boys sure can track in the dirt."

Ben chewed his pie, watching her flit around. He could always tell when something was on her mind. She put Henry's chalk on the table, and he grabbed her wrist. "It's a shed, Mags. It doesn't need to be spick-and-span." She looked down at him, and her leg brushed against his. He wanted her undivided attention, so he pulled her onto his lap. "Tell me what you're thinking."

"I'm thinking that I shouldn't be sitting with you like this." She tried to get up, and he held her tighter. She fought a smile. "Ben, please." The more she tried to move, the closer he pulled her. "I'm thinking about you and Nadine." His tight grip released her to stand as fast as it came from her mouth. Reaching for Henry's blanket, she went back to being busy.

Ben pushed his chair back off its front legs. He deserved that. They were sisters, and they were opposites. What kind of cracked affections did he possess? What could he say? Each of you is special? Good Lord, that sounded warped. The chair slammed back down.

"Listen, you don't need to explain." She looked out the little window. "I just had a birthday. I'm at the end of suitable marrying age. You're at the beginning. Nadine is, also. I understand why you were attracted to her. I do, she is petite and beautiful. And really, I don't want to know the details. I really don't." She straightened the little window curtains. "I'm just sorry for-"

"Mags..." he sighed. "I hate it when you do that." Leaning back, he squeezed his palms against his head.

"What?" she said, brows crossed.

"You're always saying sorry and taking the blame upon yourself." He rose and faced the window. "This has nothing to do with your age. If I was this short, would you care less for me?" He bent his knees and walked up to her.

She suppressed a laugh and pulled up on his shirt. "Stop it. Of course not."

He stood up and looked down on her. "I've never worried about you being older than me." He lightly touched the back of her arms. "You're the only person who has made me believe I could fill my own man boots." He carefully tucked her hair behind her ear. "The problem is, you spoke to me like your beloved little brother." He winked. "But I've never had sisters. I took everything in. Somewhere it gave me such familiarity with you. You fill my heart. But then, you probably fill everyone's heart." Nadine flashed to his mind. "I want to get back to the dairy, to face things I don't want to face. I need to talk to Nadine. Then I'll know what I can say to you."

Margaret nodded in agreement. There was a strange affection, yet distance between them. His kind words touched her. "I'm sorry I always do that."

Ben groaned and threw his head back. He ran his hands down her sides as he fell to his knees. Reaching to grasp his head, he rolled back onto the rug.

"I surrender." He let his long arms flop out onto the floor.

It had been dark awhile as they talked about their plans to get back to the Von Keller's farm. Ben would sell Sandy at the livery, and the money would get them all on the stage. At the next town, they would catch the train. Margaret asked Ben not to mention typhoid. Certainly, some kind of stomach infection was all she thought her mother could handle. She would stay a week or so and then go back to Chicago with Henry. Ben had long kicked off his boots and folded his blanket under his head. Margaret was tired and blew out the light. It was comforting to be back in their old spots, even without Henry.

"It seems strange. I don't think I realized what a companion Henry has been." She yawned. "I don't know what to do if he doesn't warm back up to me."

In the moon lit room, Ben could see her staring at the ceiling. Her fingers tapped on each other over her stomach. "He's just mad about having his finger cut off." He loved watching her face in the dim light.

Margaret covered a small gasp. "And he blames me?"

"No, no. He's just scared. He'll warm back up."

"It means the world to me that you'll be with us at the dairy," she whispered before the shed fell silent.

Ben looked at her the same time she turned to look at him. "This is our last night," he said, his voice husky. "If I don't have a chance again... come here, Mags." He held his arm out toward her. "I want to whisper in your ear."

Even in the dark shadows, she locked eyes with him. Judging him safe? Allowing her heart to come... how far? He wondered. She wiggled over, filling up the gap. She gently rested her head on his extended forearm, lying still and waiting for the secret message.

Ben rolled toward her, settling his arm around her waist. He nuzzled his face against her ear. "I forgot what I was going to say," he whispered.

"Ben." She laughed and tried to move away.

"Hold on." Pulling her closer, he grabbed her hand. "Feel my heart." He took her hand and pressed it against his shirt. "It's pounding like I just killed my first buck."

Margaret looked up, inches from his face. "Really...killing a deer?"

With a flicker of amusement in her eyes, she allowed Ben to pull her against him. He pressed his cheek against hers. "Being near you is a thousand times better than killing something."

She leaned back and shook her head. "Is that meant to woo me?" She pushed away, rolling to face the other wall.

Ben dropped his hands over his face. "Sorry." He moved over and pulled her body back against his. "Please sleep next to me." He came up on one elbow, looking for permission. He fingered a strand of her hair and brushed it against her cheek. "This will be just one more thing we won't discuss with your parents."

* * *

Margaret pressed her lips tight, repressing her retort. *Ben, oh Bens.* His closeness brought tingling comfort. Locking herself still, she wouldn't look back into those eyes. His kisses would push her over a cliff. She tried to relax as his arm pulled protectively against her waist. She waited, fighting her desires, and finally draped her arm over his. The fascinating feel of warmth. His arm hair and skin next to hers. She squeezed her eyes shut. Feeling his fingers open, her own slowly curled inside his. Overwhelming peace and security flooded her as they closed their fingers together. She waited patiently for something she may never experience again. Lying next to a man and listening as his breathing deepened into sleep.

24

Ben opened his eyes to the new morning, and for the first time in his life, he knew what he wanted. Raising up to press his lips on Margaret's forehead, he felt as if he was finally his own man. Not his brother's shadow. Not his pa's expectations. Just Ben, waking up with the most beautiful, kind creature God had ever made. She believed him worthy. Her soft rhythmical breathing mesmerizing him, and he ran his fingers up and down her arm. She began to stir.

"Oh, my." Her eyes flickered open, and she pushed away.

Ben laid back, folding his hands behind his head. "How did you sleep?" He loved watching her sit up, her cheeks turning red.

"Well." She rubbed her finger under her nose and looked around. They smiled awkwardly at each other, waiting. She began to rise, but Ben reached out and held her down by the folds of her skirt. She struggled a moment, then gave him a questioning look. He didn't want to be away from her. Back in his arms would be ideal.

I love you almost escaped from his lips, but instead, he said, "I liked sleeping next to you."

Trying to pry his hand from her skirt, she shook her head, looking embarrassed but happy.

"You're adorable, you know that? And you smell like flowers." He softly kissed the inside of her wrist. "But the cursing in your sleep. Really Mags, worse than I've ever heard." He shook his head at her.

"What? I cursed in my sleep?" She jerked her arm away, face riddled with anguish.

Rising, he laughed and pulled her up from their sleeping rug.

"Please tell me you're joking."

"I'm kidding. He wrapped her in his arms and dipped her backward.

"Bens…" She pushed on him. "That's not funny." Biting her lip and fighting a laugh, she finally got away.

"Let's go get our boy!" Ben clapped his hands together.

"Boys are active." Dr. Ketchum said, watching Henry bounce up and down on the bed. "But as long as you keep the incision clean, everything should be fine."

"I don't think he's ever slept in a bed," Carolyn said as they all watched him.

"Henry, have you ever slept in a real bed?" Ben asked, the metal springs beginning to squeak louder. Henry swung his head back and forth, trying to jump higher.

"Thank you so much, Doctor, and you too, Carolyn, for all you've done." Margaret squeezed their hands.

Dr. Ketchum gripped her shoulder. "For all the people I've seen pass because of typhoid, it was a mighty good thing to see you recover. God's ways are mysterious." His voice trailed off.

"Your Carolyn is amazing." Margaret embraced the young woman.

Ben stepped up and caught Henry in midair. "Are you ready?" He pulled him close and whispered something in his ear. Henry wiggled free and ran quickly up to Dr. Ketchum and Carolyn.

"Thank you." He barely hugged Carolyn and grabbed Margaret by the hand. "Let's go."

"Okay, then." Margaret was pulled out the door.

"Thank you again, sir, for not giving up on us." Ben shook the doctor's hand and went out.

He grabbed their bags sitting outside the office. "Let's get these to the stage pick up area. Then I'll go settle up for Sandy."

Margaret took Henry's free hand and followed Ben down the dirt street. "I'd like to get a few things for the trip," she said as they approached the stage area. "Do we have time?"

"Yes, go ahead." Ben handed her some money. He watched them as they went down two store fronts and walked in.

Scratching under his jaw, he wondered about a long glass bottle to fill the checkered bag with. The saloon was so close. He waited, staring at the saloon doors. His long list of reasoning didn't seem to flow today. The idea of upsetting Margaret made his feet like boulders. Sandy picked that

Julia David

moment to bump her nose into his back. He turned to greet the faithful horse. "Let's go take care of you." He headed to the livery. "I'm going to miss you, worse than a stiff drink."

"Your father made detailed routes for this trip." Ben pulled the papers from his bag. "But we're a bit off, in time and location." He smiled, pushing the papers back in. "Tonight, we'll spend the night in Black Falls and then we can catch the train from there." He opened the stage door and helped her in. Henry seemed to have a change of heart, and he jumped to sit next to Margaret. Ben took the seat across from them. The stage lurched forward. "How are you feeling?" She seemed a bit pale.

"I'm fine." She flashed him a quick smile. "You just reminded me that my parents are probably worried sick." Watching the landscape, she fingered the cross on the gold chain he had given her. Back and forth, gently. Then back and forth again.

He leaned forward and rubbed her knee. It was much too personal, but he didn't care. "It'll be fine. Remember, we march in together." Henry shot up and flopped over Ben's extended arm.

"Okay, okay." Ben grabbed him and turned him upside down.

"Careful, Ben," Margaret said. Henry's feet were hitting the top of the coach. Ben tickled him while Henry squirmed.

"Our chaperone is back," he said to Margaret, flipping Henry back over.

"What's a chaperone?" Henry asked, pushing free of Ben's long arms.

Ben raised his eyebrows at Margaret, looking for help. "Someone who needs to take a seat." He gave Henry a pretend punch to the gut, pushing him to sit next to Margaret.

Henry landed a punch on Ben's arm.

"Henry, settle down. You're not well enough to wrestle with Ben. And this is not the place, either." Margaret shot Ben a serious look. Ben stiffened and put one arm behind his back. Henry slowly put his recovering hand behind his back. They nodded to each other and then to Margaret. She squinted and scowled at both of them. Henry and Ben reached out quickly, trying to tickle her. A bolt of laughter hit her as she fought to block their hands.

"Stop! Stop…I mean it!" She laughed and squealed.

Ben pulled Henry back. "We don't want her stopping the stage. All that screaming, the driver might think something is wrong." Ben remembered Allison and dunking her in the creek. That didn't go so well.

Margaret panted, pulling her skirt and jacket flat. "This is going to be a long trip."

Margaret and Henry walked around the dusty rest stop while Ben stretched his back side after sitting in the bumpy coach. "I'm missing Sandy, somethin' bad," he said as Margaret approached.

"I'm sorry you had to sell her. I never thought how hard that must be for you." She blocked the sun with her hand while checking on Henry. "How long did you have her?"

Henry began to kick rocks.

"Not that long."

"Did you bring her to the dairy with you?"

"No. I mostly walked." He started back toward the stage. "It's time to go."

"You walked from Ready Springs to Elbert County?" She had to hurry to keep up with him.

Ben took her by the arm and helped her inside. "Henry, let's go." He waited for Henry to climb in. Her expression indicated that she was still waiting for an answer.

"No, I had another horse. I just mostly walked to the dairy." He fell into his seat.

"I don't understand." She shook her head.

"Well…" He bit back the desire to be sarcastic. "When you get thrown in jail and you don't have any money, they can take your horse." She squinted and clutched the seat as the stage rolled forward. Looking out the window, Ben saw the dust and dirt kick up. Henry got out his cup and ball toy and began flipping it. He knew this explanation challenged her virtue.

"What did you do, to get in jail?"

"I robbed a bank and shot the sheriff's cat."

She flattened her hand against her cheek. "You did?"

"No," he said expressionlessly.

"Ben." She relaxed into her seat. "It's not funny."

"What if I told you it was the wicked alcohol? Knowing you, robbery or death of a cat might get me a pardon." He wished he had caught his words before they escaped. Dang it, why did she need to bring this up?

"Can we talk about it, Ben? I feel like you're angry at me."

"All right." He'd give her credit for stating the obvious. "I thought we already talked about this, but I was probably hung over. So here's what I know." He sucked in a deep breath. "You're part of a crusade to rid the world of alcohol. I've read those letters you write. All the scriptures you quote…"

"I've never said anything about ridding the world," she interrupted.

"Okay." He tried to even out his tone. "The state or city then. I can't remember."

"Ben, watch this!" Henry pushed his toy into the middle of their conversation.

"I don't just write about alcohol." Margaret tried to ignore Henry playing. "I've seen firsthand what the whiskey shops do to a city. They break down the family. The men spending their wages on alcohol instead of food. Boys as young as Henry, wanting to be just like their fathers. Women leaving babies alone to find work." She shook her head, turning to the small window. "Poverty and crime are shameful. We don't just preach with our fingers wagging. We pray. We raise money. The ladies have started an orphanage and school. We work, we volunteer selflessly…"

"I know, I know." Ben tried to move Henry aside. "It's your calling. Don't forget the Indians. You'd lay down your life so they can be saved."

"I would," she whispered.

"I swear to you, this day, if I came upon that missionary group that left you, I'd string them up myself. Don't doubt I will."

Margaret was quiet, squeezing her lips in a thin line. "Your parents were such strong Christians. I remember when my brother died. Your mother came to me and wrapped her arms around me. She wiped away my tears and kissed my cheek. She gently told me about a loving God who had prepared a place, a painless place called heaven. I had just watched them lower his body in a box into the ground. She told me he's not in that box. He's in a new, perfect body in heaven. Her soft words on that horrible day have always stayed with me, comforting me."

"That was my mother, not my father."

Ben moved over as Henry came and laid his head on his leg. "My brother James grew up more like my pa. Levi is more like our ma." Ben ran his hand across Henry's dark silky hair. Henry's heavy eyes bobbed closed. "I just need to work out who I am."

25

They all bounced from hitting a rut in the road. "Who do you want to be?" Margaret couldn't help but watch the paradox of Ben gently soothing Henry to sleep. Yet his drinking had landed him in jail. Could both these people live in the same body? Did she just see what she wanted to see? Had she been enamored by his handsome face and strong arms? Hadn't he been trying to tell her all along? Maybe she only heard what she wanted to hear.

"I think I have a plan. It feels good and right. For me, anyway," he mumbled, looking down at Henry.

"As you should." Margaret wondered how the air of indifference seemed to invade the coach. They had agreed to forge into to the Von Keller household together, but suddenly she felt very alone.

"You are young and have many things to look forward to."

"I hope so," he said, eyes slowly closing. He leaned his head against the bumpy seat.

Margaret watched him sleep and wondered about her own choices. Hadn't it been the greatest thing she had fought for? To be her own person? A servant that God could use for His glory. A voice for those who could not speak. She reached into her bag, grabbing her Bible, and flipped the pages open to Psalm 16.

Preserve me, O God: for in thee do I put my trust. O my soul, thou hast said unto the Lord, thou art my Lord; my goodness extendeth not to thee. She dropped the Bible into her lap and chewed her bottom lip. She couldn't live a day without the goodness of God. She pulled her Bible up. *But to the saints that are in the earth, and to the excellent, in whom is all my delight. Their sorrows shall be multiplied that hasten after another god: their drink offerings of blood will I not offer, nor take up their names into my lips.* She remembered when Henry had curled up in Ben's coat. Henry pulled out the silver flask. Of course it held alcohol, but why didn't she confront it back then? Where had Ben hidden it? How many things had she been ignorant of? *The Lord is the portion of mine inheritance and of my cup: thou maintainest my lot. The lines are fallen unto me in pleasant places.* She pressed the Bible against her chest. It wasn't a terribly clear sign with Ben's transgressions. The feelings of love and attention were overwhelming pleasant, for a woman of her age and inexperience. Is that why she had missed them? If it were a blatant disregard, she would have seen it. She read on. *… yea, I have a goodly heritage. I will bless the Lord, who hath given me counsel.* She read the words again. *The Lord is giving me counsel. My reins also instruct me in the night season.* She watched the two sleeping across from her while her finger smoothed over the pages of her Bible. *I have set the Lord* *always before me: because He is at my right hand, I shall not be moved. Thou wilt shew me the path of life..."*

* * *

Ben watched Margaret out of the corner of his eye. He didn't think she was sleeping, more like praying. Her lips moved, and he wondered if she was praying for him. Of course she wanted to hear he'd be a good young man and never take a drink again. What if he couldn't say that? What if he didn't want to? Her eyes opened, flashing onto his. Flinching back, he stilled, with Henry leaning on him.

"You okay?" He studied her for a long moment. "Were you trying to sleep?"

"No, not really." She held his gaze.

Ben watched. There was obviously something she wanted to say.

"Black Falls," came a shout from the driver.

Ben sat up taller. "Henry, wake up. Put your toys back in my bag. It's time to get out."

"Where are we? Are we at my school?" He looked to Margaret, rubbing his eyes

"No dear. This isn't your school. We still have a way to go." Margaret helped him with his things.

"How much farther?" he whined as the stage slowed down.

"It'll take a while, but not today. We'll go on a train tomorrow. You'll like that."

The door swung open, and the driver dropped a step down in the dirt. He held a hand out to Margaret as she stepped out. Ben gathered their things and took in the layout of the simple town. The hotel was down a block, and it looked as if the train station was a couple blocks or so on the right.

"Shall we get a room?" He looked at Margaret and started walking. Margaret stepped up on the wooden walk and tried to match his long strides.

"Ben, you'll ask for two rooms? I can keep Henry with me. It will give you a break." She gave him a weak smile.

He didn't want a break. Something else was going through her head. They'd only lived together for weeks—now she wants her own room? "Sure, that's fine." He nodded at two ladies walking by on the sidewalk. Maybe it had to do with etiquette, something his ma had tried to teach her uninterested sons. They entered through two tall glass doors. The hotel was quiet, but as Ben looked around, he noticed the nice carpet and shiny furnishings and wondered how much two rooms would cost. Margaret took a seat in a red wing-backed chair, and he left their bags with her. He approached the gentleman behind the counter. "Your rooms, sir? How much for one night?"

"Four dollars, just for the room. Meals are a dollar a person." He flipped open his ledger book.

Ben chewed on his bottom lip, knowing the money was getting low. "We need one room, please."

"Would you like to include dinner? They start serving in about an hour."

"Yes, sir, three." Ben counted out seven dollars. He nodded his thanks and grabbed the key. He walked over to Margaret and grabbed their bags. They circled around the nicely-decorated dining area and headed up the staircase.

"They start dinner in about an hour." He took the stairs without facing her. "I could only get one room, it's a bit expensive here." As they reached the second floor, the shuffling steps behind him stopped. He found the door and put the key in to unlock it. Before he stepped in, he looked down the hall to her red face and frozen glare, reminding him of Nadine. He swung the door open and dropped their bags inside. Henry let go of Margaret's hand and raced by him.

"A bed, a bed." Henry chimed.

Ben walked back to where Margaret stood, stoic.

"I'm sorry." He scratched the side of his head. "I think this place is empty, and no one knows us." He wondered why she looked like she was about to cry. "Do you want me to look around? You can have the room. I'll go find something else."

"No," she shot back. "I'll be fine." She walked past him and turned into the room. He followed, wondering what was wrong. The furnishings were freshly polished, and the bed was large with a soft white crocheted covering. A large wardrobe stood next to the window.

Ben stood watching her. Surely this nice room was a good thing. She turned a few times, chewing on her bottom lip. She was probably just tired from being bounced around all day. Henry jumped off the bed and landed with a *thunk* on the ground. "Oww," he whined. "I hit my hand." He cradled the painful gauzed-wrapped hand.

"Oh Lord, Henry," Margaret sucked in a breath, bending down to him.

"Here, let me." Ben reached and swung Henry up. "We're going to take a long walk and see where the train station is." He headed for the door, pushing Henry farther over his shoulder.

"Mags." Ben turned from the door. "You take a bath or nap or whatever you want. We won't be back until supper." Margaret gave him a faraway look again.

"Okay?" he said to Margaret, hoisting Henry up from his back. "You're like carrying a tree around, kid." He shot her a smile and walked out.

"How's the hand?" Ben said as he put Henry down. "We can find a doctor in this town. Maybe have a few more fingers taken off?" They headed down the stairs.

"No!" Henry whined, pulling on Ben's shirt.

"I was just joking. You're going to need all those fingers for the dairy. I'm going to give you some of my duties. Have you ever milked a cow?"

Henry grimaced and shook his head as they walked out of the hotel.

"Did Margaret tell you her folks own a dairy?"

"No." He tried to keep up with Ben. "Is that where my school is?"

Ben pictured the upstairs schoolroom, with piano and violins and a harp. "No. I don't think that will be your school."

"Why not?" Henry sounded disappointed.

"Because that's a girly girl school. You need a man school." The words made him think. *What will they do with Henry in Margaret's orphanage school? He's lived like a scavenger, never having to sit still. Will they hit him with a ruler until they mold him into something he's not?*

"Give me your good hand. We're crossing here to the train station."

"Are you taking me to a doctor?"

Ben laughed. "No, Henry. I promise."

Margaret seemed quiet at dinner, maybe because it was so far from what they were used to.

"Is the food okay?" Ben asked, scraping the last trace of potatoes off his plate.

"Yes, it's good. You must have enjoyed it."

"I did. Henry, are you going to eat those green beans?" Henry made a sour face, shaking his head. Ben stabbed them off his plate.

"Really, Ben, you should make him eat them. They're good for him."

Ben was certain now that her tone was unusually cross. He wondered what was upsetting her.

"What did you do while we were out?" He sipped his coffee.

"Some reading." She shrugged. "And I wrote a few letters. What does the train schedule look like?"

He dropped his cloth napkin on his plate. "It was closed, so I couldn't buy our tickets. But it opens at six. There's a train at seven, but we don't catch ours until ten."

"That's good. We can sleep in and have breakfast." She offered up a smile, one of the only ones all day.

"Listen, Mags, I know the closer we get to Elbert County, the harder it is for you. Please don't worry. There's nothing we can't sort out." He felt more confident as she nodded in agreement.

They slowly walked back down the hallway to their room. Ben wondered if she was uncomfortable with him. The way he pushed his way into her space last night. Maybe she worried he would want something from her tonight? He put the key in the door. "Do you want Henry on the floor with me or sleeping next to you, in the bed?" He looked to the ground as they walked in. He quietly closed the door.

"Henry." Margaret looked down at him. "If you put on your nightshirt and climb up on the bed, I'll read you a story." Henry nodded and started to take off his clothes. Margaret slipped off her boots and climbed up on the bed. "It's like laying on feathers," she said, propping the pillows behind her.

Ben grabbed the quilt for the floor, feeling left out. He helped Henry into his nightshirt and arranged the quilt to sleep on. He laid down as Henry crawled up and leaned into Margaret's pillows. She opened her Bible and thumbed through. "There was a man named Jacob who wrestled with God."

"Yeah, read that one! I like wrestling."

"Hmm," Margaret flipped the pages. "He also had trouble marrying the right sister."

Ben froze. Did she just poke him with a red hot stick?

"There was a girl named Esther. God gave her a job to do, and she saved her nation."

"Nah, I don't want to hear about a girl. Tell the one about the boy and his slingshot."

"All right. Here, pull this blanket over us." Margaret held the Bible open and began to tell the story of David and Goliath. Ben could tell she wasn't reading it, but Henry didn't care. Ben listened, tossing and turning a few times but finally giving up, his eyelids too heavy to keep open.

26

Fighting to stay asleep, Ben felt something tapping on his arm. It was dark outside, with a faint glow of morning coming through the window.

"I have to take Henry to the water closet. Take the bed. It's your turn," he heard Margaret whisper.

Ben rolled up. "I'll take him. You go back to bed."

"No," she pulled him toward the bed. "I can't sleep, you might as well." She made him sit down. "Here, lie back. You need to feel this, it's so comfortable."

"Just wake me up in an hour," he mumbled.

"Mmm, right."

Ben wondered if he should stay awake, but as soon as his body went prone on the bed, he felt as if he might just dissolve into the soft mattress.

It seemed as if she was letting him sleep forever. Had he heard them come back in? He finally cracked his eyes open to the full sunshine coming in the window. What time was it? Had they gone down to breakfast without him? He sat up and pulled the cover back. Looking around, he stretched his back, then suddenly noticed something missing from their things. Her carpetbag and satchel were gone. He raked his hands through his hair, now wide awake. Maybe she was bathing. He pulled on his boots and grabbed his things. Why didn't she leave Henry with him? Something didn't feel right. He plopped his hat on his head and walked out into the hallway, stopping to peek in the bathing room. No one around, not even any sign of water being in the tub. He headed down the stairway and looked around. Maybe she had gone to the store again. Stopping, he asked the clerk the time. *Nine! That late!*

"The woman and the little dark-skinned boy. Did you happen to see them this morning?"

"Yes, sir. They left over two hours ago."

Ben blinked, trying to comprehend those words.

"Two hours? Are you sure?" His heart slammed in his chest. "Did you see which way they went?"

"I believe they headed for the train station."

Ben felt his whole body snap to attention. "Thank you, sir," he said, jerking the hotel door open. He started out walking, but quickly found himself in a hard run. Jumping up onto the top of the train platform, he was certain they must be there waiting. They had to be. As soon as he could find her, he would shake her silly for scaring him like this. No amount of sleep was worth this distress.

Circling the building and every bench within the station, he bit down hard on his lip. Only a few people stood around. What in the world was happening? Where could she have gone? Did she have money to buy her own tickets? Before he could reach the ticket booth, he whipped out his wallet. Inside was a white piece of paper that had never been there before. He didn't want to open it, fear of what it said choking him. Taking a deep breath, he opened the flap and saw the money missing. Stepping backward, he fell back against the station, purposely smacking his head against it. His hat fell forward, and he threw it to the ground. Sliding his back down the rough wood exterior, his knees came up to his chin. *Lord, please help me.* He opened the folded paper.

Dear Wonderful Bens,

 I am a coward to you, but maybe I'm being faithful to my calling. Henry and I are on our way back to Chicago. Please don't follow us. I've prayed and prayed and can't face the wrath and confinement of going home. You must be brave for both of us. You must finish strong. You must ask God about your purpose. I think you're close, but I cannot get in the way of what He is doing in your life.

 Please, please know this is killing me. I hate the idea of hurting you, especially after all you've done for me. If God truly approves of me as you have pointed out, then I must not listen to my condemning heart, but the fact that I am more than my mistakes. I am loved and valued in spite of them.

 Forever yours in heart,
 Mags

Ben knocked his head back against the wooden siding for the second time. He felt numb all over, his racing heart now hardly pumping. He dropped the letter into his lap. Margaret, who was the epitome of trustworthiness, had run off. Left him behind. He shook his head, staring blankly ahead. He didn't even get to say goodbye to Henry. That was just plain cruel. What was so wrong that she couldn't face her family? Now *he* had the sole responsibility to face them. *Her kindness does have a limit. I guess I just found out the hard way.*

The clacking of the train tracks just kept in tune with the rehearsal going on in his head. Didn't he ask her to wake him up? How could she scheme and lie so readily? The way she was curt with him at dinner. Pulling back and forth on the gold necklace, her conscience probably eating at her. Poor Henry, how did she keep him quiet? He'd given her time alone yesterday, and she used it to plan her escape.

Ben felt his fingers forming fists. He tried to watch the other people on the train, but every child made him think about Henry. He wanted to see the excitement on his face over the train ride. He wanted to show him around the dairy, maybe take him fishing after work. A tree in the distant landscape reminded him of the tree where they had sat just last week, watching the sunset and talking.

He cut short his sentimentality and wondered what he would say to the Von Kellers. Right now, he'd like to tell them what a waste of time it had been to send him after her. She wasn't ever going to come home. They could have saved a lot of worry and money. She had a mind of her own. Strong-willed like Helga. Poor Otto, how did he stand a chance? A wife *and* daughters, demanding and self-regarding.

Ben stretched his neck as he noticed a small settlement in the far distance. It looked run down, probably abandoned. *This territory can be hard on folks.* He remembered the dread of finding Margaret so close to death. He should be thankful he wasn't coming home with that message. He tried to draw in some benevolence, but it kept getting trapped next to his anger. She was alive because of him. Well, because of him and God and Carolyn. Maybe he would just march into Chicago and tell her that.

The train made its stop in Joesburg, and after grabbing some food, Ben found a freighter going to Elbert County. When the old man asked Ben what he did there, he never let Ben talk but went on nonstop about the prices of wheat and dairy. Ben barely got a word in, but he didn't mind. He didn't feel like talking.

The freighter slowed to a stop and Ben jumped off the wagon. He grabbed his bag and waved goodbye. He stood for a moment, taking in the surroundings, then looked down the road leading to the dairy. It was late; everyone would be asleep. Rubbing his face, he walked forward, and in just a few feet he reached the steps of the saloon. He ordered a stiff drink and found a chair. He sipped it slowly, allowing the burning to restrict his emotions. Just one more and he might be able to bury this whole trip. Forget Margaret, forget what she did to him. By his third drink, he was thinking about what he would possibly say to appease the forgotten Nadine.

"Haven't seen you in a while."

Ben looked up into the face of the slick saloon manager. What was his name?

"Why aren't you drinking your signature drink?" He flashed a dark smile.

"I'm fine." Ben looked down at his empty glass.

"You don't look fine." The bartender rested his hands on the chair next to Ben, "Must have been a rough trip."

Ben tried to blink back a light fog. Did he tell this guy he was on a trip?

"Do you annoy all your customers?" Ben narrowed his eyes at him.

"Whoa, pal, just trying to be friendly." He took his hands off the chair.

"You can take it somewhere else, whatever your name is." Ben felt the alcohol mixing with his anger. It felt good.

"Fred," the manager boomed back toward the bar, "no more for this guy. He doesn't appreciate our fine hospitality." He kicked a chair back under Ben's table, where it rammed against Ben's knee. Sharp pain awoke his recklessness and Ben flew up, knocking his chair backward. In a split second, his arm flexed, his hand formed a fist and cocked backward. This was going to be good.

27

Sluggishly, Ben tried to open his eyes, but only one eye would cooperate. The other one was swollen shut. That was a good fight, what he could remember of it. He winced, splitting his cracked lip. The steel bars around him looked familiar. He didn't care, as long as it wasn't Carl finding him. He dabbed his bleeding lip on the back of his shirt cuff. A short man with a gray tweed vest looked at Ben through the bars.

"Someone's here for you." He stepped back as Carl stepped up to the bars.

Ben moaned, squeezing his eyes shut.

"Someone from the saloon said he thought he works at the dairy. If you can speak for him, he's all yours."

Carl stared down at Ben. There was no redemption; his unavoidable vengeance had arrived.

"Where is Margaret?" Carl growled low.

"Probably in Chicago by now." Ben held his head, feeling as if a possum had died in his mouth.

Carl glared, waiting for more information. Even with one eye, Ben could see him seething. Carl was probably contemplating if he could beat him up some more.

"He didn't do that much damage to the saloon. The manager lost a tooth. Your worker here can settle up with them."

"Lost a tooth…" Ben mumbled, nodding. "Good."

"Shut up," Carl snapped.

Ben reached into his pocket and pulled out his billfold. "Here, Carl." He stood up, steadying himself. "After doctors and food and train fares, this is all I have left." He pushed it out to Carl. "Margaret left me in Black Falls. I tried to get her to come back, but I failed," he said hoarsely. "Tell the Von Kellers that I'm sorry. I'll move on."

The jailer unlocked the cell.

"*Nein.*" Carl stood back as Ben walked out. "You will tell them. The wagon is out front."

If confrontations weren't bad enough, Ben had to do it with one impaired eye and a pounding headache. Edda had cleaned and wrapped the gouges on Ben's knuckles, but the more he moved around the small cottage, the more new pains appeared.

"The Von Kellers are ready to talk to you," Carl said after walking in the back door.

Ben looked to Edda and then back to Carl. There was little comfort in their eyes. He let out a long groan as he walked out. Even with Edda's care and concern, he knew his life in this place was going to come to an abrupt end. He glanced back at the tree where he and Nadine often met. He would miss her enchanting tough exterior. And the hot meals at the big table—Edda was a true German cook. He walked in the back door of the kitchen, coming in through the familiar pantry. Nadine stood in the large kitchen. He stopped short and thought about hiding next to the shelves. She turned to the sound of the door, and he pulled back into the shadows. His heart did a jump—was she waiting for him?

She walked toward him. "I heard you were back." Her voice was light, like cream with sugar.

"I'm just a little bit worse for wear." He stepped out, and he heard her gasp.

Her hand hovered over her mouth, and she gawked, wide-eyed. "Oh, my goodness. Are you okay?"

Why did she sound so much like Margaret? Ben felt a suffocating lump rising in his throat. He'd convinced himself the sisters were night and day. And day had won his fickle heart. He shuffled his feet and pulled his shirt collar flat. "I'm fine. How have you been?" *Lord have mercy, she's wearing the green dress. Did she do that on purpose?* His mouth went dry with regret, and he looked away. Out of all her dresses, why that one? He glanced back at the back door, wanting to run.

"Oh, you know." She nodded, seemingly out of breath. "My father is walking all over the place now." She looked back, checking the hallway. "But since I don't know much more than my mother's letters, I want to ask you. Whatever has happened, please don't go anywhere." She lightly touched his arm. "Please make sure you stay. Say whatever you need to. Please, Ben, they may rant and rave, but don't leave on account of it. They get over things."

Before he could grasp her strange words, she turned and whisked out of the kitchen. He walked down the hall and found Mr. Von Keller in the parlor. He stepped over the threshold and felt a hand on his back.

"Oh, Benjamin." Mrs. Von Keller was behind him. She stepped back, looking at his face. "Oh my, are you alright?" Maybe his depraved state would work to his advantage.

"What has happened? Our Margaret? She is unharmed? *Ja?*" She grabbed his hands, squeezing them. Ben blinked his eyes at the pain.

"*Mutter,* leave him be and come sit."

She found a chair and sat.

"Benjamin Graham, we can see this was not an agreeable trip. Please sit and tell us what happened." Mr. Von Keller held his hand out to a chair.

"First, Margaret is fine." Ben sat down and felt his bad eye crack open. He blinked a few times. "This," he pointed a finger at himself, "has nothing to do with her."

"Oh, praise be." Mrs. Von Keller held her hands over her chest.

"You know when I found her at the Indian reservation, she had taken sick. So we went on to the next place." He finally glanced up at Mr. Von Keller. "That's where we found a good doctor."

"But you were gone so long." Mrs. Von Keller rocked forward in her seat.

Ben struggled for words. "The doctor said she needed lots of rest and fluids. I didn't want to take a chance."

"*Ja, ja,* of course." Mr. Von Keller nodded at him.

"Then we were able to catch the stage to Black Falls." Ben cleared his throat. "I thought something was bothering her at dinner that night. But she wouldn't say." Ben looked out the lacy curtains to the dairy barns. "The next morning, I went to get them. I mean I went to get her. I couldn't find her anywhere. I thought maybe she was waiting for me at the train station. I asked around, and I believe she took the train to Chicago. It had left at seven. Our train wasn't until ten."

"No note or word?" Mrs. Von Keller asked tearfully.

Ben looked at her, wavering. "Yes, she left a small note. She didn't want me to follow her." He hoped that would suffice. But looking in their eyes, he knew it didn't. He sat back and rubbed the back of his neck. "To be honest, I'm not sure she was ever going to come with me. I mean come home. I'm as confused as you are. I know how important her work is in the city. She has a big heart. She wants to help people." He leaned forward, scratching his head, pulling his scraggly hair behind his ears. "You can't fault her for that." Now he wondered why he was defending her. "She writes these articles, even writes to the legislators. She's found a community of ladies that seem like good Christian women." He stood and looked out the window again, feeling his ire toward her leaving. He wanted to tell them what a wonderful mother and friend she was to their... He turned around to face them. Henry wasn't their... anything.

"I don't know what to think." Mrs. Von Keller stood, walking over to Otto.

"Well, young Ben, we are thankful for your attempt." Otto rubbed his leg. "I'll be able to travel soon, and the holidays are coming. You provided an important service. We're glad you were there to get her to a doctor."

Ben nodded.

"Please take a few days and recover," Mr. Von Keller said, scrutinizing Ben's appearance. We could still use your help at the dairy."

"Yes, sir." Ben nodded and walked out, realizing that went not at all as he expected.

As he entered the kitchen, he could hear someone banging recklessly on the piano upstairs. That was more like what he remembered.

28

Ben heard a noise and sat straight up, but it was only Edda in the kitchen. Smelling coffee, he realized he was back in the small bed. The room was dark, but a rooster reminded him it was time to get up. He slept most of his two days off, but each time he woke up, he wondered where he was. He rolled back down and gently rubbed his eyes. The bruises were still there, but everything was working— except his heart. It must still be bruised, he concluded, pushing his palms against his head. He'd lost his spur, his drive. The rooster went off again. He grabbed the matches and lit his lamp. Margaret's letter was in the top drawer of the nightstand. What did she say? He had read it over and over and still didn't understand.

You must ask God about your purpose. I think you're close, but I cannot get in the way of what He is doing in your life.

Ben remembered waking up one morning with some grandiose ideas. Was it because she was lying next to him? Of course. She had the faith he needed to take on the impossible. He rolled back and forth, covering his face with the letter. It was joyful and easy with her, allowing himself to dream some dreams he would never have. Now it all seemed unimportant. He folded the letter and set it back in the drawer. The smell of bacon pushed him upward. *Just make it through today. Milk the cows, separate the milk, feed the cows, clean the stalls...*

After work, Ben dried his clean hands and looked over to the big house. Edda had told him that morning that the Von Kellers wanted him to join them for dinner. For some reason, the walk across the brown grass looked daunting. He felt like he was about to be trapped under a stack of hay bales, just tolerating a Von Keller dinner. He leaned his head against the pump handle. Just one month, and he'd have the money he needed to move on. He could do this for a month and then he'd have cleared his head of his previous bright ideas and head back to Ready Springs.

He walked into the kitchen as Edda put the touches on the hot food.

"*Grunkohleintopf und Kasespatzle,*" she said, nodding to the steaming dishes. Ben reached for a cloth and took them. "I can bring them to the table, as long as I don't have to pronounce them."

"*Ja,* go on...you are a *gut* boy." She chuckled at him.

He rolled his eyes at her comment and entered the dining room. Putting the dishes down, he nodded to Otto. Nadine came in, complaining, with her mother in tow, but stopped short when she saw him. He wondered if she still thought he looked like a bruised reprobate. She flashed a forced smile. While hiding in his room the last two days, he had wondered what her little speech was about. Part of him wanted to hope it was out of affection for him, but he was no longer looking for her erratic attention. But yet, it sat in his gut as odd. Maybe because his feelings had been twisted in knots. Up from down wasn't clear anymore. They both took their seats and passed the food.

"So what did the other guy look like?" Minna piped in.

"Minna!" Nadine scolded. "Hush and pass the peas. Mother, are you going to be able to be on the bake sale committee?"

"*Nein.*" She shook her head. "Your *Vater* and I are still talking."

A solemn quiet appeared as they ate their food. If Nadine had meant to save him from conversation, he would thank her for that. Taking a drink, he looked over his water glass and saw her watching him. She nodded slightly to the left—their old signal for meeting at the tree. He set the glass down and gave her a small nod in reply.

An hour later, walking out of the house, he pulled his jacket on. The evenings had gotten cold since he left. He found his spot and sat back against the tree. Lifting his collar, he wondered if he could smell the little guy. He checked the pockets—maybe one of Henry's rocks or a half-eaten cookie remained—but they were empty. He looked out at the stars, wondering how Henry was faring in the new school. Did they allow him outside? Did they know he'd probably go crazy inside? What had Margaret explained to Henry? Did he think Ben had just left without saying goodbye?

"Hello, Ben." Nadine's voice startled him, and he jumped up

"Hello, Nadine. I see you were able to break away." He brushed off the dried grass.

The silence was awkward. He knew he should say something, but nothing was coming to him.

"So my sister refused to come home?"

He gave her a small nod. "That's about right."

More silence hung in the air.

"How have you been? You really didn't say, when I saw you in the kitchen." He tried to sound interested.

"Oh, I've been well." She did a little half twirl and faced him again. "Helping Minna with her lessons. I'm still very involved with the Literary Society. Our bake sale is coming up. With the funds, we do food baskets for the needy."

"That's good." His brow furrowed. That sounded like something Margaret would do.

"I have a good heart, too," Nadine said.

Ben's mouth went dry. Had she been listening a few days ago? Did she hear him defending Margaret to her parents?

"Of course, my mother told me of your talk. You did a wonderful job. There wasn't even any ranting and raving. They prefer saving that for me." She twirled again, voice trailing off.

Ben watched her, confused. Why had she said it was important that he stayed? What did that mean? She was so hard to read. But it didn't matter; he needed to get out of here. He didn't want any more sticky attachments. Hopefully, their moment together was already forgotten.

"You're awfully quiet tonight. Too much on your mind?" Her voice hinted of sarcasm.

Ben took a deep breath. Now was as good as time as any. "I never got to say I'm sorry for what happened in your bedroom, with Minna walking in. "

"Probably a good thing she did." She bit her bottom lip and smiled coyly.

"It was hot-headed and you are a perfect young lady. I shouldn't have...well, you know." He gestured helplessly. "You were there." He clamped his mouth shut, looking to the ground. Funny how his feelings had cooled toward her. She still turned his head, though. No one could ignore how pretty she was. He found her watching him carefully.

"Did you miss me?" she asked.

He stilled, weighing his response. "Yes."

"What did you miss?"

"Mmm," Ben tapped his chin. "Let me think. I missed hearing your voice echo through the big house."

"What?" Her nose crinkled.

"When you're screaming at Minna."

"Oh, really?" Her eyes darkened. "That's it?"

He reached out and grabbed her hand. "I'm just teasing." Quickly, he let it drop. "I was going to write you, but there wasn't anything I wanted your mother reading."

"I suppose Margaret and all her ideals were diverting for you."

Ben felt trapped by her question. "She was really, really ill, more than she wanted your parents to know. The doctor thought she had typhoid."

Nadine stepped back and covered her mouth. "For heaven's sake, I'm glad she didn't come here. We all could have gotten it." She shook her head. "My mother is right, she'll probably catch some disease from the slums of Chicago. Or from Indians or drunkards."

"It's not like that. Please don't say anything to your mother." Ben scratched the side of his head. "She knows the risks. Her convictions are just more important, I guess." He suddenly felt tired. "I have to get up early. I'll wait here till you get in."

"Your chivalry knows no end." She turned and stalked away.

Ben waited, wondering if he had just burned the bridge to the only friendship he had.

29

In the cool of the evening, Ben jogged to the big house, wishing he'd grabbed his coat. In the last few weeks, the leaves had fallen off all the surrounding trees, and the crisp layers crunched under his feet. Carl and Otto had been gone all week to purchase more cows. The big house was women only. For some reason, he enjoyed the ease. Last night he'd played checkers with Minna. The night before, Nadine reluctantly agreed to play the piano. She actually smiled when he stood up to give her his applause. Tonight, after he helped Edda with the dishes, Edda agreed to trim up his scraggly brown hair.

Edda looked up when he entered the kitchen. "Ah, young Ben. I want to tell you there is some soup on the stove." Ben wondered why she was folding up her apron. "The tutor came by and picked up Minna and the missus. There is a children's play in town. So…" She clapped her hands together. "I'm going to go home early. You tell Nadine to let me know if she needs anything." Edda already had her coat on.

"My haircut?" Ben asked, pleading.

"Pish." She threw her hands up. "I forgot."

"No, no." He nodded to the door. "You deserve a night off."

"Tomorrow night, *ja?*" She walked past him as he held the door.

Ben went to the warm stove and held his hands over the soup. It smelled wonderful. He wondered if Nadine would want any. He listened, but the house was strangely quiet. He thought he heard something outside, and by the time he looked out the kitchen window, the front door slammed. Steps pounded quickly up the stairs, and another door slammed. It had to be Nadine. What was she doing outside in the dark? Maybe she was looking for him? But why the door slamming? *Maybe it's just a family trait.* He looked at the bowls sitting near the stove, and his stomach growled. Picking up the bowl, he heard something muffled and low. It was Nadine, all right, and now she was yelling. He set the bowl down and listened. Was she breaking furniture? He moaned and headed up the stairs.

"Nadine!" He knocked on the door. "What's wrong? Are you okay?" He knocked again.

"Go away!" Her angry words hit the closed door.

"No. I'm not going anywhere till you tell me what's wrong. Are you hurt?" He placed his hand on the knob.

"Just go away!" she screamed louder.

Ben hesitated, shaking his head. So many things could upset this girl, but this sounded serious.

He carefully opened the door. She sat in a crumpled mess of light blue fabric in the corner of the room. Her little dressing table was overturned. Powder and smelly perfume were spilled all over the floor. She glared at him and buried her face back into her knees. Pounding her fists into her head, she rocked back and forth.

"Nadine, please." Ben put the desk chair upright. "What's wrong?"

"I can't find my hankie," she hissed, "and I have snot all over me."

Ben looked around and found a hankie. He gently laid it on her knee and stepped back, knowing it wasn't the real problem. "Did something happen tonight? I thought I heard something outside."

Dabbing her face and blowing her nose, she ignored him.

"Did you want to go with your mother and Minna to town?"

"Dear God, Ben, please go away. P...please." She dropped her head.

Something in his heart seized up. She was usually such a fighter. To see her so broken and trampled was crushing him. He bent down in front of her and touched her locked hands, gently pulling them apart. Her weeping began again, and he slid next to her on the floor and pulled her over.

"Don't," she choked between sobs. "Don't be good to me."

Ben wrapped both arms around her and pressed her head under his chin. He held her as the tears and pain rolled out. He felt her fingers twist in and out of his shirt.

"Nadine." His voice pleaded, trying to be patient. "You can tell me. Maybe I can help."

"Would you like to h...help, Ben? Really?" Her voice held a sad sarcasm. She began to draw in deep, choking breaths. "Would you like to m...marry me?"

"What?" he mumbled, sure he'd heard wrong.

"Do you like children?" Her voice cracked.

Henry came to mind. "I love children."

Pulling back, she locked her puffy red eyes on him. "Benjamin Graham." The room went silent. "Will you marry me?"

*　*　*

Ben pulled his arm from her back and moved away. "What are you talking about?"

Nadine's chin was still shaking. "Will you m...marry me?" Her stuttering made it difficult to catch, but Ben couldn't hear any humor in them.

"You said you l...loved children. Isn't that what you said?"

"Yes." He held out the word, confused.

"Well, I'm having one, and it needs someone to call father," she said bluntly. Face indignant, she blinked, and the large tears made their way down her blotchy cheeks.

Ben let out a small cough. His lungs had quit working, and he felt dizzy for a moment. His mind tried to reenact the last time he was in this bedroom. He glanced over to her bed. There was passion and kissing, but for heaven's sake, they had all their clothes on. How could this be happening? Nadine was still stiff and frozen, looking at the floor.

"You're having one? You mean you're with child?"

She barely nodded.

Ben scooted away until his back hit the footboard of her bed. "Whose baby is it?"

"Mine." Nadine pulled her knees tighter and rested her head on them.

"Nadine, who else? Who got you with child?"

"Trust me," she murmured, "it's all mine."

He reached out and squeezed her arm. "Were you raped? Did someone do this to you?"

Pulling her arm free, she dropped her forehead to her knees and shook her head.

"This makes no sense." He dropped his head back, looking at the ceiling. "Who would do this to you? A young lady, from a good family. Tell me who it is." He felt the heat rising in his face. "Tell me, and I'll..."

"What? Shoot him? Beat him? Maybe k...knock another tooth out?" Her voice trailed off.

Ben froze. The manager of the saloon. He bolted to his feet. He began to pace and pick up the things spilled all over the floor. He had a vague remembrance of the signature drink he had offered. The Nadine. *That scum.* He picked up her brush and hairpins, setting them on her vanity. He gripped the small chair and picked it straight up and slammed it down hard. A shocking thought hit him. "Do you love him?" The silence was nauseating. "Do you want him left alive?" The words flew from his mouth.

"It sounds as if you want to do something about this." She sucked in a hiccup.

"As I live and breathe, you better believe it." He began to pace again.

She rose off the floor, shaking. Ben held out his hand to steady her. She gripped his arm.

"Then marry me." She looked into his eyes. "Save me."

30

"Lord, what are you doing to me?" Ben started to light his lamp on his small stand, but turned and rolled to his other side instead. The rooster was going to go off before he got a lick of sleep. *Maybe it's not too late to head into town, find which direction this Marcus has fled.* He'd always been a good tracker. Enough people in the saloon probably knew where he was going. He just needed a few leads. He turned and rolled onto his back. *Nadine said it would be useless. Something about going west. His father giving him the money to open another saloon. Probably as far away from Nadine as he could get. What a coward. That worthless slime, all slick hair, and smile.* Ben could only hope he was missing a front tooth.

Just to settle her down, he told her he would think about her proposal. She understood it was a lot to take in. But she had looked so hopeless when he left last night. Two months ago, he would have snapped up her offer. But now she was carrying another man's child. Thoughts of Margaret brought a flood of pain. He dropped his arms over his face. He wasn't over what she did to him. Why did she just up and leave? Probably the thought of coming back with him. His age, his instability, his mistakes—her family wouldn't understand in a million years. Did he need to tell Nadine about what happened? Would he be keeping secrets just like she had kept things from him? The rooster crowed. As he swung his feet to the floor, knocking over his pack, his pa's letter peeked out. Grabbing it, he lit the lamp. *Stop being a coward,* he said to himself as he opened it up.

Dear Benjamin,

Just seeing his pa's crooked handwriting brought tears to his eyes.

There are many things I wished I had sat across from you to say. But since none of us know our days on this earth... Ben slammed his eyes shut, trying to hold back the emotions. He sucked in a deep breath. *I would like to write down a few of my thoughts toward you. I love you, son.* His throat tightened, and a sudden sob tried to escape. He swiped his hand across his wet face to see the rest of the letter. *I wish I had told you that a hundred times. I always wondered if your ma's love and attention would make you boys too soft. How wrong I am. She made you all into the men that you are. All my sons are strong men that work hard and make me proud. Each of you has your own path. I understand that. Yours may always take you further away. That's okay, you'll know when to do the right thing. Thank you for always making your ma smile. You carried such a joy, after so much pain and loss. I know you were a gift from God. By the grace of a loving God who never gives up on us, I've made my peace with Him. I do regret not doing that earlier in my life. But I will never regret being your pa. My family is my greatest blessing.*

Yours truly,

James Graham

Ben hung his head while the tears flowed freely. The letter was a good letter. Why had he waited? Why was he so sure it would be reprimanding him? It was good. Really good! Maybe his pa found God? It sounded like he did. The man just wanted to write his feelings toward him. He believed he would make a good decision, whatever path he was on. Ben raked his hands back and forth through his long hair. *Oh, pa, if you only knew the decision I need to make.*

"Young Ben, you up?" Edda softly rapped on the door.

"Yes, ma'am, getting dressed." He wiped his face again and reached for his clothes. He buttoned his shirt and stared at the crack of dawn out the window. Yes, Margaret had left him, but Nadine was here. She needed him. She wanted him. He wouldn't be the servant-boy anymore. He would be the son-in-law. One day the owner of the dairy. He'd had some other ideas floating around if he was to leave here, but maybe it was time to settle down. His pa believed he'd make the right decision. Maybe this was his purpose. Margaret had even said he was close. Certainly, Margaret had made her choice. Swinging the door open quickly, there was a quickening in his step. This is a future he would be proud to tell his family.

Hours later, he headed up the back steps, but he stopped at the door. He could not live in this house. Where would Nadine want to live? There were so many things they would need to settle. He opened the door and entered the warm kitchen, hoping to see Nadine. Had she thought how her parents would react?

"Mr. Von Keller and Carl are supposed to be back soon. Maybe even tomorrow," Edda said, watching him reach for the coffee pot.

Ben nodded. "That's good. Have you seen Nadine?" He wrapped his cold hands around the cup.

"Let's see, I hear a squeaking violin and a pounding piano. She is probably upstairs. You want that haircut?"

Hair was so far down on Ben's concern list. How interesting—a life can change on a dime. His gut dropped. Is this what he really wanted? He stared into his coffee. Would he be satisfied to give up his dreams to rescue Nadine?

"Young Ben, yoo hoo." Edda waved at him. "Haircut?"

He jerked his thoughts back. He was tired of being *young Ben*. Flighty Ben. Wandering Ben. "Yes, and cut it short."

Minna bounced into the kitchen as Edda was finishing up Ben's hair.

"Can I have some hot cocoa, Frau Edda?"

"*Ja, ja,*" she said, pushing Ben off the stool. "All done with you."

Ben ran his fingers through his short hair. "Thank you, Edda, I'm respectable again."

Minna snorted, almost snarling at Ben.

He came up to where she was standing and looked sideways at her. "Are you still sore about all those checkers games I beat you at?"

"No," she barked.

"Just a bad day, then?" He went to pinch her nose, and she swung at him. "Okay, okay." He moved backward, holding his hands up.

She leaned forward, speaking low. "Maybe I don't like things to change. And ever since you came, Nadine has changed. She's still *my* sister." Ben thought maybe she was going to cry. *Oh, Lord.*

"Hey, Minna." He tried to keep his voice agreeable. "I have older brothers. I know how I felt when they left home, and I didn't like it, either."

She gave him a stare. He tried to give her a humorous stare back.

"Having a stare-down with Ben, Minna?" Nadine walked into the kitchen. "What happened to a quick snack?"

Minna turned away, taking her cup of hot cocoa, and left. Ben watched Nadine. She had returned to her usual self. Prim, proper, not a hair out of place. Her cool, controlled apperance was back.

"May I have a bit of that cocoa?" she said, as she walked over to the stove. He poured some into her cup.

"Short and suitable." She touched the wet sides of his hair, with vacant eyes holding little warmth.

Ben suddenly felt troubled and hesitant, his confidence gone. It was a sickening feeling, something unusual, like being homesick. The letter must have stirred up thoughts of his family. Could he ever see her wanting to live near Ready Springs? She had as a child. It was somehow good enough for her parents back then. But now they had a dairy, a business.

"Ben, can you sit in the parlor for a minute while I drink my cocoa?" Nadine said softly.

He nodded and followed her to the parlor. They sat, and she took a small sip.

Nadine looked back toward the hall and then faced him. "As you can imagine, I'm very nervous about the time we have to make a decision. I've thought it through. If it's soon, no one will question the timing." She looked out the parlor opening again, to make sure no one was listening. "Babies come early all the time. If we could marry very soon, I don't think anyone will not believe this is your baby."

Ben rubbed his knuckles on his chin. "I'd like to talk to my family. Even just Levi. I need to share this with them. I wouldn't be gone long."

"Travel to Ready Springs? Ben, please. Do you care for me at all?" She set her cup down, pressing her hands on her skirt. "You just got back. Could we just marry first and then you could go see them?"

Ben wanted to tell her Levi lived in Madison, but her face was painfully twisting.

"What are you going to tell your parents?" The muscle in his jaw flexed. "They'll wonder about this sudden marriage. Will you tell them the truth?"

"I've thought of that." She stiffened and reached for her cup. "I don't want to upset them. No daughter wants that.

This way, even if they think our marriage is premature, they won't think the worst."

Ben shook his head, looking to the ground. He couldn't seem to think straight. Did he want to take the blame for this?

"Also," she said, "they like you. You've come to their rescue."

"I couldn't get Margaret here," Ben mumbled.

"But you helped my father so much. This dairy would be yours one day."

"I don't know." Ben sat back and rubbed his hands through his short hair. "I could never live in this house with your family."

"I understand completely. We could get a little place closer to town. You could ride back and forth."

"Oh, Nadine, there you are." Mrs. Von Keller stopped in the doorway. "Minna said you haven't gone over her new music." She nodded at Ben. "How nice to see you, Benjamin. Have you heard from your *mutter* lately?"

"No." Ben stood up. His legs felt like lead. Nadine rose and took a step next to him. "Mother, Minna can wait one more minute. I'm just about done with my visit with Ben." Her voice was so syrupy sweet that even Mrs. Von Keller looked confused.

"*Ja.*" Mrs. Von Keller's brows crossed and she turned toward the stairs.

Nadine laid her hand on his back and looked up at him. "I know I haven't had a chance to say the right things." She looked back to the empty hallway. "I sincerely care for you,

Ben. I would be a good wife. I would be faithful to you. I would make a good home for you." Her eyes began to pool. "I can only pray one day you would forgive me for my mistakes."

Ben looked down and carefully swiped a wet tear from her check. "We all make mistakes, Nadine. You don't need forgiveness from me. It's just a simple heart to heart talk with God. That's what you need. Trust me, I have a lot of knowledge on this." He smiled.

She leaned in and wrapped her arms around him. "Thank you, Ben. You can't imagine how much it means to me." He returned her embrace, but something was amiss. He did feel sorry for her, but he quickly broke away, suddenly missing the way Margaret had occupied that space.

31

B en dropped into bed as soon as his feet would get him there. Sleep couldn't come fast enough. It seemed as if only a minute had passed before he heard Carl calling him. His bed shook.

"Get up, Ben." The voice loomed over him in the dark. "We need help getting the cows unloaded." Carl gave his bed another kick.

"In the middle of the night?" Ben tried to find his clothes.

"It's not even ten o'clock. Meet me out by the barns." Carl walked out.

A few minutes later, Ben grabbed his coat by the back door and saw the two big wagons holding the four new cows. Carl moved from wagon to barns.

"Get the planks from the wood shop. Make a ramp for them." Carl said, handing him a lantern. Ben headed out, hoping there was enough wood left from all his projects. Soon Carl and Ben had unloaded the cows, fed, and watered them. "Take care of the horses," Carl barked, walking toward the little house. "The wagons need to be parked over there." Carl pointed to the side of the barn.

"It's just me now," Ben said to the horse, grabbing the bridle of the horse in front of him. "You tell your buddies to cooperate. You'll get some rest, and I'll get some rest." He pulled them forward to park the wagon.

The next morning, Ben walked out to Edda's pre-sunrise breakfast. "Smells wonderful." He sat down. Grabbing his fork, he hesitated, sensing that Edda was watching him. She had grabbed her coat and lantern, ready to go begin the Von Keller's breakfast.

"Have a *gut* day, Benjamin." She squeezed his shoulder, smiling.

Ben nodded. Why had she left off the *young?* For months, all she had ever called him was *young Ben.* As the door closed, he knew what was needed. He dropped his fork and bowed his head.

Lord, is it time? Time to put away childish things? Time to be a man, take care of a wife and baby? Stay put in a job? He paused, waiting for an answer. *Lord, please grant me the grace to do the right thing. Amen…and thank you for this food.*

Ben had finished all his morning chores and was hauling the planks back to the side of the wood shop. He dropped the last load off his shoulder with a crash and walked into the shed. Putting some tools back, he heard a shuffle at the doorway. He looked up to see Margaret watching him.

"Hello, Bens," she said sweetly.

He swallowed hard and blinked a few times. "What are you doing here?"

"I came to see you." She took a step in.

He noticed her blouse and skirt—ones he'd never seen before. Blowing air out his nose, he wondered if she really expected him to jump for joy and open his arms. He looked away. "That's interesting."

"I told you I'd come and make things right with my folks."

He found more things to straighten on the work bench. "I thought we were going to do it together." He didn't look at her, waiting for his heart to stop beating erratically.

"I have no excuse." She shook her head, looking down. "I can't expect you to understand anything I say or do."

"You never let me say goodbye to Henry, Margaret." How he wanted her to feel her mistake.

"I'm sorry, Bens." She bit her bottom lip.

"Don't call me Bens. That's over. You ended it." He looked back to the bench, knocking tools around.

"I didn't want to end it." She took a careful step forward. "I just panicked, I guess. I wanted to see Henry settled. I couldn't find a plan where the three of us showing up here would work. I didn't want them accusing me of more things than they already do." She pulled in a sharp breath. "He likes the school. All the kids are welcoming him. I've started teaching English and math on Tuesdays and Thursdays. Most days I ask to have lunch with him, but he begs off to be with his friends."

"Hmm." Ben shrugged.

"Okay, so here's the important thing, I've rehearsed a hundred times," she murmured.

Ben tilted his head for a moment, watching her. Should he tell her that no excuses really were going to make him feel any different?

"You know how set in my ways I was…I am…about serving God?"

Ben gave her no response.

"I needed to know if my feelings for you were the real thing. I know that's the overthinking, controlling Margaret. It's just that feeling love toward someone is the most important thing in my life. I wanted to know if what we had was just a temporary attachment. I wanted to know how I would I feel when I got back to my old life. My old routine. Away from our little shed. Away from your touch. Away from birthday cakes and dancing in your arms." Ben turned toward the back wall.

"Where would my heart be," she slowed down, "when I wasn't with you? You know I had convinced myself that serving God would be my call. I needed some time with God. I finally had to admit that I had buried my true longings." She paused. "My true desire would be to be married and have children. That it is still noble enough. You were the one who made me take a long look at my motives. I would say with my words that God accepts me as I am, but I didn't live like it." She stilled as he turned slowly to face her.

"So what did you learn?" he said, face stoic.

"That my heart is…"

"Margaret, there you are." Nadine swept into the sunlit wood shop. "Look what the cows brought with them, Ben, a sister arriving with my father in the dead of night." Nadine went to Ben's side and curled her hand around his arm. He looked down at her. She had just staked him through, like a dead animal over the fire pit. A deep sadness flickered in Margaret's eyes. She had fully received Nadine's unspoken message.

"Really, this is the perfect time for a visit." Nadine smiled quickly at Margaret. "I need someone to stand up with me. Ben and I are getting married this Friday. Would you mind? It's going to be a simple affair. Here at the house. I guess the minister is trying to go visit relatives for the holidays. We didn't want to wait for him to get back, so I don't need anything fancy. Whatever is your best dress will be fine." Ben pulled on his arm and felt Nadine squeeze it tighter against her.

"Ben." She looked up at him. "Would you mind having a word with my father before dinner? He just got back, and he doesn't understand about the minister's trip."

"The minister's trip?" Ben finally stepped away from her. Was that even the truth? She gripped his hand.

"Okay, we girls will let you get back to work." She released him and took Margaret by the arm. "I've got my cream taffeta. Let's go see what you have that will look nice with it."

Ben stalked from the wood shop in the opposite direction of the house. If ever there was a good time to pack his things and leave, this was it. Talk to her father? The day Margaret arrives? Did Margaret tell Nadine her feelings?

He slid down the steep bank toward the creek bed. Losing his footing, he fell back, and sharp rocks bit into his hands. *Perfect.* He grabbed a handful and peppered a tree with them. Friday! Nadine wanted to get married Friday. That was only three days away. He couldn't even put his tangled thoughts into a letter to his family in three days, let alone get married. He stomped his boot on an innocent beetle. *I thought you would help me, Lord. But everything just got worse.* The look on Margaret's face. How could he doubt she loved him? If she had kept talking just a few more minutes, he would have pulled her into his arms. He missed her and loved her, too. He even understood why it moved her to make the decisions she did. She was so careful. She wanted to do everything right. Unlike Nadine. He scraped up another handful of rocks, throwing them harder. *What a mess.*

Ben stopped in the kitchen to help Edda with the hot dinner dishes as he usually did.

"No, no." She pushed him away. "You go on in with the family. Everyone's so happy to have Miss Margaret here. I can do this."

Ben took a few steps and stopped. His only ally was pushing him into the lion's den. He got halfway down the hall when Nadine came up and pulled him back toward the downstairs bedroom. He moved away from her grip. "Stop it."

"I know you're mad," she whispered, "but I need to tell you what happened. It's Minna. Something you said upset her. I was trying to calm her down." She looked around, making sure no one was listening. "But she threatened to go to my parents. She said she would tell them you were in my room. That we were on the bed together."

Ben shook his head and looked away. So much deception, even though Minna was telling the truth. Had he compromised Nadine? Could he see himself explaining what had happened? Of course, the Von Kellers would believe Minna. He raised his hand to cover his face, but slammed his fist into the wall instead. "All right. Fine." His mouth was suddenly dry. "I'll talk to your father." Nadine squealed and jumped up and down. She had to pull his arm down to reach a quick kiss to his cheek.

Ben hadn't even entered the dining room when Otto met him in the hallway. "Nadine, you said you wanted to talk to me?"

"Yes." Ben felt as if his blood was forgetting to pump. "Maybe we could talk in the parlor."

"*Ja,* this is *gut.*" Mr. Von Keller sat down, still favoring his leg. "I want to tell you I still appreciate you trying to bring Margaret to us. She explained about the little Indian boy and how attached you were to him. She spoke so highly of your help and concern for her and the boy." Ben wondered if this could get any more difficult. He scratched his head, willing his mouth to open. "I hope you know that I wouldn't do anything to hurt your family."

"*Ja, ja.*" Otto nodded.

"Nadine and I have taken a shine to one another." Ben gulped, like a man who was just about to go under for good. He took one glance out to the stairs that led to Nadine's room. *Why did I ever go up there?*

"I wanted to ask your permission to have her hand in marriage."

32

After dinner, Otto stood, waiting for the family's attention. He held his glass up, and all eyes turned to him.

"I am surprised and pleased to say that Ben has asked to marry Nadine, and I have given my consent."

"What!" Mrs. Von Keller stood. "Nadine and *this* Ben?" Her eyes were bulging.

"*Ja, ja, mutter.* Sit down now. Where is your fan? Your face is bright red." Otto lowered his glass, forgetting the toast.

"How can this be? There has been no proper courtship!" Helga glared at Nadine. "We will have to make something up when people ask. Nadine, why didn't you tell me? The announcement will have to wait. Summer should be sufficient."

Nadine stood, her back straight and strong. "We are getting married this Friday."

"What?" This time both her parents stared at her. "Child, have you lost your good senses?" Helga's mouth gaped open.

"I probably have, Mother." She took in a deep breath. "The minister is leaving for the holidays. We don't want to wait. Ben would like to see his family. Once the weather gets bad, it could be months. Margaret is here to stand up with me. Lord knows how hard it was to get her here. The minister will be here Friday at one."

"No, no, no." Helga stood behind Otto's chair. "This will not do. You must cancel this. There are other ministers in Elbert County. I don't like it at all. People will talk, Nadine." Beads of sweat appeared on Mrs. Von Keller's brow. "I insist you listen to me."

"We are both of age, Mother." Nadine stayed stoic.

"Where are you going to live?" Minna piped up.

"Ben and I are still discussing it."

Minna slammed back in her chair, dropping crossed arms.

"I will still be here to help you," Nadine said.

"I'll do fine without your help, Nadine. I've known something was going on. How many trips to town to return books do you need, considering you're never reading any of them? I like it when you're gone."

"Minna!" Nadine growled. "I've spent hours upon hours helping you with your education and music lessons and never do I get a bit of appreciation. Never! How dare you, you spoiled little imp!"

All eyes watched as Edda set the bread pudding on the table and left in a hurry. Ben knew this wasn't going to be pretty.

Minna glared daggers at Nadine, eyes beginning to pool. She began to bawl. "I hate you, Nadine!" Spit and tears flew out onto the table.

Margaret jumped up and wrapped her arms around Minna. "Shhh, it's going to be fine. She didn't mean it."

"I did mean it, and I don't need your help, Margaret." Nadine seethed. "You seem to conveniently leave to go do whatever you want. When it's my turn, everyone acts like I've fallen off a cliff."

Margaret let go of Minna and stood tall. "It is a bit of a shock, Nadine. You have to take some responsibility for that. Minna is in shock. Mother and Father are in shock. Give your family some time. I'm sure we can find another minister. I'll come back when you have a proper date."

"No, thanks. If you don't want to stand up with me Friday, you don't have to." She squared her shoulders. "I'm sorry if I've shocked you all. Ben has only been sitting at our dinner table for months."

"*Ja, ja,* but we didn't know, Nadine." Helga pleaded. "Otto, did you know?"

Otto shook his head.

"That's because she's so good at sneaking around," Minna whimpered.

Nadine's face turned red and she stalked around the table toward Minna.

"Wait." Ben stood quickly and grabbed Nadine by the arm. "This is going nowhere." Nadine shook loose as Ben moved to block her path. "Please, Nadine, stop it."

"It's just because we all care for you, Nadine," Margaret exhaled. "We all have mixed emotions. Give us time to get used to it."

Nadine, nostrils flaring, slowly returned to her seat. "All right. While the family is taking their time getting used to my announcement, maybe Margaret would take a few moments to fill us in on how she got typhoid."

Helga gasped.

"Typhoid!" Otto exclaimed.

Ben could barely look at Margaret. The betrayal in her eyes would haunt him all his days.

She carefully walked back to her seat. "I was near death when Ben found me at the Ho-Chunk Indian reservation." She sat down calmly.

"Now that is a shock for the family," Nadine interjected.

"I don't understand." Helga blew her nose into her napkin. "You said it was a infection or something." She sat down, shaking her head.

"When Ben found me, I was just skin and bones. I was ready to go to heaven."

Helga let out a whimper.

"He built a travois for his horse and carefully took me to the nearest town. He found the best doctor and nurse. They all worked tirelessly to give me fluids. My nurse's name was Carolyn. She was only a year or so older than you, Minna. She changed my bedding and helped bathe me. She brought us food and supplies. She was an angel from God." Margaret tilted her head at her parents. "That's why it took us so long. I asked Ben not to mention the typhoid. I knew you'd want to send out the cavalry." She smiled. "As soon as the doctor said it was safe to travel, we did. Except..." She blew out a soft sigh. "I had a little Indian boy under my care. His name is Henry. He was orphaned. I made a hasty decision and left Ben early in the morning and took another train to Chicago. I wanted to get Henry settled in the Ladies of Mercy School."

"Oh, dear child." Helga sucked in a deep breath. "We see that you have such an open heart to help others. But this is why you cannot continue. You could have died. We are your parents. We have allowed this too long. We could never live with ourselves if something happened to you. We insist you stop this crusading. With Nadine marrying, we need your help here. I'm sure there is some church work around here you can do. It would be a wonderful way to meet new people."

Nadine covered a crooked smile.

"I'm afraid this bread pudding is getting cold." Ben lifted the glassware. "Mr. Von Keller, would you like a scoop?"

33

Ben squeezed on the teats of the cow, the milk filling the bucket. He pictured his hands squeezing those two rolls atop Nadine's head. Were they pinned too tight? How could she be so cruel? Maybe he should have taken the lead. Sisters can be vicious; the whole dinner was a mud slide before he could get in a word. He dumped the last of the milk into a large tin. Making his way across the grounds, he looked up to the sky. Maybe God had brought him here to rethink his family. His father was stern, but he had never forced them to stay home. He taught them everything they needed and encouraged them to get out. What would his home be like? Would Nadine be like her mother? He slowed his pounding steps when he saw Margaret pushing Minna on the tree swing. Higher and higher, Minna squealed and spun. He was glad to see her laughing and having fun. Minna saw him walking over and dragged her feet in the dirt to stop.

"I'm cold, I'm going in." She jumped off and ran toward the house. He couldn't help but approach Margaret.

"I like your hair down, but it's pretty the way you have it up in that knot thing." He twirled his finger at her head, wondering why he kept thinking of hair.

She looked over her shoulder at him and touched her soft, loose bun, then looked at the ground.

The silence hurt Ben's ears.

"You never finished what you were saying yesterday. In the woodshop."

She raised a sad smile, shaking her head. "It doesn't matter."

His muscles flexed with the desire to touch her arm, her hand, anything. "Mags, I didn't know."

She shot him a quick glare.

He opened his mouth, searching for words. "I thought you didn't want me. I never even thought about you wanting time to sort out your feelings. I guess I was stuck with my head in a bucket. I've been mad and confused. But..."

"Is Nadine pregnant?" she interrupted.

He looked around the yard and met her intent brown eyes. "Yes."

"Is it yours?"

Ben felt his nostrils flare. "No, Margaret, it's not mine."

"Whose is it, then?" she said, bluntly.

"I hope you believe me. It's not mine. I've never lain with Nadine. It seems she had something going on with the saloon manager. His name is Marcus."

"Why isn't he marrying her?"

"According to Nadine, he's left town. I've wanted to do some tracking, find his toothless grin and give him another taste of my fist."

"You already had a fight with him?"

"Yes. It wasn't about Nadine, though. It was about something else."

"What? What did you fight him over?" She let out a tired sigh.

"I can't remember. I had too much to drink, I woke up in jail. Again."

"Oh, Ben." She pivoted in a circle, unable to face him.

Ben knew that kind of talk would rile her. His life was so upside down, why would he try to hide anything now?

She finally stopped circling. "Do you love her? Do you want to marry her?"

"Mags." He rubbed his forehead with the back of his hand. "You of all people should know about this. I'm trying to do the right thing. I'm trying to think of someone else besides myself. She was crying and pitiful." He crossed his arms and let them fling loose, then gripped his head. "I didn't even know about this Friday and the minister until she said that in front of you."

"You never answered me."

"Right now, it's taken every ounce of man in me to stay. I want to run. I don't want to be tied to this place. I'm just trying to grow up. To quit running. You told me I was close to my purpose." He jabbed his cold fingers in his pockets. "I figure God wants me to do this."

"Oh, Ben!" She stepped forward and grabbed his arms. "You sound just like me!" She let go and glared out to the gray sky. Finally, she turned to face him. "God wants people to marry because they love Him and love each other."

He kicked the dirt. "At one time, I told you I did have feelings for Nadine. It was a strong attraction," he said, words dripping with regret.

"You obviously weren't the only one." She slapped a hand over her mouth. "I shouldn't have said that."

They both looked up through the bare branches. Cold ice sprinkles started to fall.

"It's really funny." Her chuckle was disheartening. "I spent all this time in prayer, listening for God's direction." She wiped the cold drops from her face. "I guess I don't listen very well. I wonder how many other things I've done under the disguise of God's will." Her jaw twitched back and forth. She reached to pull her collar closed, then jerked her hand away from her neck. She held out the gold necklace he'd given her. The broken chain dangled through her fingers. "I can't keep this. You understand."

He put out his hand, and she dropped the necklace onto his palm. Watching her walk slowly across the damp brown grass, he felt suspended in some other wretched life.

"Margaret, please wait!" He ran up in front of her. "You left me with a note." His eyes widened, pleading. "I could feel you pulling away on the stage ride." He tried to calm his breathing. "What am I supposed to think? What am I to do now? Tell me. Tell me what to do!" He gripped her arm as she stared at him in silence, the icy rain soaking their hair.

She pulled her shoulder up, trying to release his grip. "Let me go." Her voice shuddered. "This is killing me." She clapped her hand over her mouth as the tears fell. "I...I... did waver. But I had to see you again. I even tried to tell myself—your feelings could have cooled. But what if..." She swallowed a sob. "What if it was real? Would you stop drinking for me?" Her eyes shadowed with anger and pain. "Should I even have to ask you that?"

Ben felt the weight of her question down to his core. He couldn't find anything to say that would change the deep hurt in her eyes. She took a step back, never taking her eyes from him. With each step backward, she took with her all that was right and good, leaving him alone with no one to blame but himself.

Trudging back under the eaves of the wood shop, he looked down at the broken chain and small cross, now wet from the rain. The cross. The sacrifice. Somehow it had new, personal meaning. He closed his eyes and dropped it into his pocket, a cold shiver running down his spine.

34

Edda grabbed a tin can from behind the pickled beets. She brought it over to the small table where Ben sat, picking at his eggs.

"Here," she said, pulling the top loose. "I want you to take this money and go into town. I don't have enough time to sew you some trousers."

Ben looked up, finally following her. "For tomorrow, you mean?"

"*Ja, ja,*" she said, patting him on the back. "Remember what happened when you tried to wear Carl's old suit? You want to look nice, *ja?*"

Ben watched her count out a dollar and some change, handing it to him.

"I don't want your money, Frau Edda." He put it back into the can, closing the lid. "Mr. Von Keller paid me yesterday."

"*Gut, gut.* Did you buy some new trousers?" She put the can back.

"No, I hadn't even thought of it. I figured the money was probably to make sure I buy her a ring."

"*Ja*, that, too." She pulled a chair up next to the small table.

Ben's elbow sat heavily on the table, while his fingers rubbed his brows.

"You have worries, I can tell." She touched his shoulder. "I can ask Carl to help you, maybe some things man to man."

Ben shot her a small smile. "No, nothing, man to man. I suppose none of this is how I pictured. I would have liked to have my family here. But then, my brother Levi got married without any of us."

She wrapped her thick hand around the back of his neck. "It is hard to be away from family. I miss my sons every day. But can I say, Benjamin…" She cleared her throat. "You have been a joy to me. I smile every time I see you. You have a *gut*, light heart. You make the ordinary delightful, the way you help me in the kitchen. You've brought peace to that house that I don't think was ever here before. Getting Nadine away from here will be the best thing for her. She wasn't meant to be an underling. She was like a princess when she was little. She needs to have her own say. I couldn't think of a sweeter, stronger, young man for her. She is a very lucky girl to have you. You have the kindness and patience she needs."

Ben nodded thanks to Edda. He surely hoped he did.

An hour later, he took one of the dairy horses into town. He could have walked it, but something about being back in the saddle made him sit taller. The air was crisp, and it awakened his dulled spirit. He wondered if he should just keep going—back to Michigan, back to Ready Springs. He could easily get away from this place, but he couldn't get away from himself. He needed to stick this out, to do something right. Even Edda saw this marriage as a good thing.

He tied the horse in front of the mercantile and took a long look at the saloon. Part of him wanted a drink like he wanted his next breath, but another part wanted to find Marcus and bring him to the Von Kellers. One o'clock would be a good time for Marcus to reappear from wherever he was, tied and gagged if need be. He shook his thoughts back to what was needed. He never noticed before, but the little library front door was straight across from the saloon. Minna's comment about Nadine and the books now made sense. One good thing about his new bride, she could never point a finger at his mistakes.

Ben walked through the mercantile, wondering why he'd never been in here before. It was bigger than he thought as he walked past all the lady things back to where he saw the men's garments. He tried to find some trousers that were better than work clothes. He didn't want to spend the money on a whole suit.

"May I help you?" A woman with a crisp white apron stood near him.

"Maybe." Ben pulled off his hat and scratched his head. "Do you have any nice trousers in my size?"

She took a step back. "I do, but you have very long legs." She began to pull some from a stack. "Gray or brown?"

Ben scratched his head again. "I don't care, as long as they don't come up to my ankles."

She smiled. "These might work, they have quite a large hem. I have a gal that can let them out." She walked to the back of the store, nodding at a curtain. "Go behind the curtain and try them on. I can mark them, but she won't pick them up until Monday."

Ben took them and went behind the curtain. This was embarrassing. He'd never tried anything on in a store, and he couldn't wait three days for them to be hemmed. He tugged off his boots. Maybe Edda could do that. He made sure the curtain blocked him from anyone's sight and quickly pulled on the trousers like he was caught in a fire. The waist was fine. The fabric felt as if he could feel the wind through it. The cuffs hung only a few inches above his feet.

"Are you ready?"

Ben jumped at the store clerk's voice. He pulled back the curtain to see her standing near, holding a little metal ruler in her hand. "Hmm, let me check, to see what we can work with. Can you step out here for a moment?"

Ben looked left and right, gripping the curtain for protection. This felt ridiculous; he just couldn't cooperate. "I think I'll just buy these. A woman I work with will finish them. I need them by tomorrow."

"Oh, I see." She tucked her little metal ruler back in her apron pocket. "I'll meet you at the counter when you're ready."

Ben closed the curtain again. Pulling off the nice trousers, he left them in a pile while he dressed in his old clothes. Sitting on a little stool, shoving his boots back on, he looked down at the nice trousers crumpled in a pile on the floor. Why couldn't he make himself reach for them? Dropping his elbows to his knees, he let his head drop. *I need to put away childish things. Why is this so hard?* Rubbing his hands through his hair, he tried to straighten up. *Men wear nice clothes to their wedding.* Biting hard on the corner of his bottom lip, he grabbed the new trousers and went out.

"Will this be all?"

"Do you have any jewelry here?" Ben didn't see any on his way through the store.

"What kind of jewelry?" she asked.

"Rings. I'm looking for a wedding ring."

"Oh, of course." She bent under the large counter and pulled out a tray of rings. "New trousers and a ring. Are you about to be a groom?"

"Yes, ma'am." He shot her a quick smile. "Tomorrow."

"Oh, my." She pushed the tray toward him. "Do you know your betrothed's ring size?

He paused. "No, ma'am."

"Is your bride from around here?"

"Yes, she is the daughter of the Von Kellers."

"How wonderful! I know the family. Lovely Margaret. And she found the perfect tall young man." The woman smiled. "You'll be the most handsome couple."

"Actually, I'm marrying Nadine. The middle sister." Ben pulled out a small shiny gold ring from the tray. "How much is one like this?" He was starting to get a headache.

"Well, you can pay the ten dollars now and use it for the ceremony. If it doesn't fit well enough, you could bring it back for a better size. After your honeymoon would be fine."

"Thank you for all your help." Ben handed her the ring, and she put it in a small box with cotton.

After paying the woman, he took the things wrapped in brown paper, nodded and walked out.

"Honeymoon?" he said, looking out to the street. He opened the saddlebag and shoved his things inside. Grabbing the horse's reins, he walked toward the hotel. He wasn't staying in the big house in her room, just a few doors down from her parents, that was for sure, and she wasn't going to join him in his room. Oh Lord, now his stomach hurt, too. He tied up the horse and stared at the double glass-paned doors of the nice hotel. It brought back the gut wrench of the morning he couldn't find Henry and Margaret.

Pushing back his hat, he rubbed his temple. *This is a different hotel. It will be a different room.* He pressed his dry lips together. Would Nadine welcome his touch? After everything in these last weeks, he could not welcome hers. He'd rather be chaste until the baby was born. Maybe by then he could find some of the old feelings. Ben pulled his hat forward. Two ladies laughed as they walked by. Oh, how he needed a drink. An older gentleman walked out of the hotel door. Ben stepped forward and held the door. *Just walk in,* he told himself. He didn't want to spend his first night of married life hiding in a cow barn.

35

It really was the sisterly thing to do. Margaret exhaled, sitting on the corner of her bed that afternoon. She had offered to take over with Minna while Nadine prepared for Friday. Margaret had spent most her days avoiding Nadine at all costs. Minna was a welcome distraction until Ben had followed them outside next to the new swing Minna loved. She had vowed to herself she didn't want to know if Nadine was pregnant. But she had to be. All this wedding rush was as clear as the newspaper stories printed in Chicago. But then she surely didn't want to know if it was Ben's. She wanted to believe it wasn't. Why couldn't she just keep her mouth shut? Which would hurt less? Knowing they had a moment of immoral passion? Even though he said they didn't. Or knowing that he would defend Nadine's honor at the cost of deserting her?

Neither thought brought any relief to the pain that rose inside her. Ben had almost come out and called her a hypocrite. It was the godly thing to protect the innocent from vile alcohol. It was the right thing to do, to help widows and orphans. But how could Margaret slap his hand at his decision? He said he was just trying to do the right thing. If she hadn't left him in Black Falls, maybe this wouldn't have happened. She was reaping what she sowed. They had real feelings for one another. Maybe he would have chosen her. He asked her to wait, so why did she have to take things into her own hands? She rubbed her palms over her bedspread. She slipped slowly from sitting to kneeling next to her bed.

Father, forgive me. I'm feeling the pain of not waiting for You. I try too hard. She swallowed a lump in her throat. *I care too much. I think too highly of myself.* She dropped her head onto her sleeve, catching a few stray tears. *Please forgive me. I desire a simple life that pleases You. You are enough for me. Grant me the grace to get through these next days. Please bless Nadine and Ben tomorrow, and for all their years together. Amen.*

Margaret stood and dabbed her face dry. She looked around the room. Her mother had no business redecorating her room. As soon as all the spectacle of this wedding was over, she would sit down with her mother. She would promise to visit more, and promise not to run off onto the mission field. Maybe she would invite her parents and Minna to come for a visit. They would understand her more if they could see what was important to her. Ben's suggestion rang true. She caught her reflection in her vanity mirror. She had changed. Her chin quivered, and she squeezed it to stop. Her mission work didn't feel important anymore. Maybe one day it would, but for today, nothing felt important.

The next morning, Margaret awoke to Minna yelling something about her dress. She hated it, it sounded like. Margaret rolled over and smashed her pillow over her head—these next hours would be excruciating.

"Margaret." Nadine pounded on the door. "I'm coming in." Before Margaret could say yes, Nadine flung the door open. "Could you please get out of bed and help me? Mother and I specifically asked Minna to wear her yellow dress. It was lovely three months ago when she got it. Now she thinks it's as ugly as the outhouse. Who cares if it looks like spring?" Nadine stalked around. "No one is going to be here but us. It's only going to be the smallest wedding in Elbert County. Why does she get to rant and rave today? Certainly I've had my dreams collapse." Nadine quit pacing. "I don't care if she wears a feed sack. If you care at all, then you deal with her."

Margaret had pulled her robe on, standing up. "Why are your dreams collapsed?" She exhaled a heavy sigh.

Nadine stopped and made eye contact. "Do you think this was my dream? To wear my old cream frock for my wedding?"

"Then wait and get the dress you want. Order one from those fancy catalogs you love." Margaret pulled a brush through her hair, knowing she was antagonizing her sister.

"Did I tell you I'm wearing mother's veil? The German women do a splendid job with their lace patterns."

Looking at Nadine, Margaret felt her heart crushing. For this moment, she wanted to see her, really see her, little prim and proper Nadine. How had she been lured in by that terrible man? She just stared at her, feeling compassion for the first time. Nadine was trying so hard to hide her lie, like the little child who never liked any dirt to touch her.

"Why are you staring at me?" Nadine squinted.

Margaret took a few steps toward her, wrapping her little sister in her arms, something she had never done before. "I know we haven't been close, but I just want you to know that I love you." She squeezed Nadine. "I do want you to be happy." She pulled back and looked at Nadine's confused face. "I believe if you will love and care for Ben, he will love and care for you in return."

"I know that." Nadine stepped back. "That's why I'm marrying him."

Margaret gave her a weak smile. "I'll deal with Minna. Don't worry about anything. Take your time to get ready. One o'clock will be here before you know it."

There was no noon meal, and everyone agreed they would wait and feed the reverend and his wife with the family after the wedding. While putting a few touches of wedding décor around the house, Margaret had seen Ben come and go from the kitchen. He'd nodded at her as he filled the tinder box, but no smile was to be found.

"Carl can do this." She approached him. "You should be getting dressed. The reverend will be here any moment. My parents are ready, Minna is dressed, a small accolade to my abilities." Margaret wanted to reach out and touch his arm, but he continued stacking the wood.

"I just need to keep busy. It helps. I'll go get dressed now." He looked up, and she could see the moisture in his eyes.

"Ben, what...?" Before she could finish, he was through the back door.

The clock struck one, and the reverend and his wife were seated in the parlor. Mrs. Von Keller asked them about their travels to see family, to which they seemed confused.

"Mother, would you like to go check on our bride? I just saw Carl, Edda, and Ben walk in."

"*Ja, ja*, I just can't believe our Nadine is getting married." She trembled, looking to the reverend's wife. "Our children grow up so fast, *ja?*"

Her mother took the stairs slowly. Margaret took a moment to introduce Ben to the reverend and his wife. She felt herself breaking into a cold sweat, the irony of her being the hostess at Ben's wedding. She moved out into the hallway, looking for her mother. Any minute now, she would send her father halfway up the stairs so he could walk Nadine down.

Ben stared out the window as Nadine's father and the reverend talked. He looked so handsome. New pants and pressed shirt. His short brown hair damp with water, pressed back into place. He looked up at her, and she sucked in a quick breath, embarrassed to be caught gawking at him. She turned to the stairs—of course, Nadine would keep everyone waiting. Ben looked pale and serious, his lips cracked and dry. She wanted to be angry with him. For heaven's sake, what was taking so long? Minna bounced down the stairs. "How much longer?" Margaret asked.

"I don't know. Mother asked me to look down here. Nadine isn't in her room." Minna headed for the dining room.

"What?" Margaret followed her. "She isn't down here."

"That's strange," Minna said. "I already looked down the back stairs."

Minna headed past the parlor to the kitchen when Margaret saw her mother standing at the top of the stairs. She was holding a piece of paper to her chest, her face chalk white.

Margaret pulled up the layers of her best dress and started up the stairs. Her mother pulled back into the upstairs hallway, handing her the letter.

Mother and Father, I am so sorry for all this turmoil I've caused. I'm in love with a man named Marcus. I've gone away with him. We're to be married soon and I will write as soon as we're settled. Please forgive me. I know this is all a shock. Nadine

Margaret and her mother both clasped their hands over their mouths.

"What are we going to do?" her mother whispered. "The reverend and his wife...Oh, poor Benjamin. This is going to break his heart."

Margaret was still reeling. She looked at the letter again. That was it? She turns everyone's life upside down, then leaves a simple letter? She heard her mother mumbling something about the shame on this family. Wrapping an arm around her mother's shoulders, she leaned in. "Don't fret, mother. Let's call Ben and tell him. Then we'll just explain to the reverend that Nadine needs more time and isn't comfortable going through with the wedding today. He'll understand. No other information is necessary."

"Oh my, oh my," her mother moaned. "Why didn't I have just sons?"

36

"What?" Ben couldn't have heard right. Mrs. Von Keller was mumbling in German, rubbing her forehead. Standing in the corner of the upstairs hall, he tried to focus on Margaret's words. "She what?"

"Here, read it for yourself." Margaret handed him the letter.

Ben scanned it and tried to understand. "She's gone? Did anyone see her leave? Did anyone hear a horse or buggy or anything?"

"We've all been so busy this morning," Margaret sighed. "But I did talk to her earlier. It had to have been sudden. She was planning on marrying you."

"How do you know that?" Ben glared.

"I...asked her to be good to you." Margaret's shoulders dropped. "She believed you would be good to her. I know her, she was being honest."

"I'm going to find them." Ben turned and went down the back stairs. "I should have wrung his neck when I had the chance," he mumbled, running out.

He was halfway to the barn when Margaret's words finally registered. In all this mess, Margaret was the caretaker. She obviously didn't trust Nadine's character. Why in the world did he think this would work? He threw the saddle over the horse and let him out of the stall. Margaret had to ask Nadine to be good to him. Oh, Mags, beautiful, caring, loving. Why did he allow this to go on? Margaret was everything he ever wanted. His heart began beating for the first time in weeks, as he swung up in the saddle. "Hah!" He kicked the horse forward. If he hurried, he could find them both and drag them back in front of the minister before the minister had finished dessert. If they had any problem with that, he'd hog tie them and drag them.

The barkeep grabbed Ben by the collar. "Enough! You're disturbing the customers." He jerked Ben out the back door, facing him in an ally. "I let you look around. I told you they're not here. I saw them ride off over an hour ago. Now get!"

Ben jerked from his hold. "Tell me which way they went. Someone had to have seen them. Or I go back through each room again."

"He wouldn't tell me," the barrel-chested man bellowed. "All I know is his daddy is starting a saloon somewhere out west. Maybe Helena, I can't remember. They've been planning his move for weeks."

Ben's heart was pounding against his ribs, and he wanted to punch someone.

"Montana? Give me a place, Fred!" Ben found a two by four in the dirt and picked it up. "What about Madison? Chicago?" He swung it closer to the man. "Helena! You're such a liar." Where?" He lunged, about to swing at the barkeep. He felt someone grab his shoulder and heard a loud *thunk*. His body slammed into the dirt. Grasping at the thin air to get up, he couldn't make contact before everything went black.

"The young strapping ones usually have a hard head," Ben heard, as he felt his eyelid being pulled back. The bright light was painful, and he tried to close his eyes again. Instead, he rolled and found his stomach come up to his throat.

"Bucket," he croaked." Someone shoved a tin bowl under his chin as he lost his stomach contents into the bowl.

"Where am I?" he moaned. The room was spinning.

"I think he'll be fine now that he's awake. Find me if he can't stand or remember his name."

"Thanks, Doc."

The lantern faded away along with the voices. He recognized the steel bars from the last time he was in here. Jail. Why was he in jail? He remembered the saloon. Was he drinking? He felt for the source of the pain in his head and found a large lump.

"How long have I been in here?" he called to the deputy.

"Just a night and day." The deputy came up to the bars.

"What are the charges against me?" Ben tried to focus.

"Attempted murder."

"What! I didn't lay a hand on him! Are you his brother or something?" Ben swallowed the bile that threatened to come up. "I'm the one who got knocked out. I should be charging him with attempted murder." He wanted to stand, but the cell began to spin.

"Well, I've already been out to the dairy. I spoke to the man that came for you last time. He said he doesn't want you back, said you've been nothing but trouble. He figures a bit of time in behind bars might be good for you."

"Are you joking?" Ben knew Carl had something out for him. But was he that ruthless?

"Well, something like that. Maybe I can get Fred to come around." The deputy walked out.

Ben laid down and covered his eyes with his arm. His head was pounding, and he just wanted to get some sleep. This all had to be a bad nightmare. He would wake up tomorrow and find something that made sense.

The next morning, Ben thanked the deputy for his oatmeal. The deputy set his bowl down and handed him some dirt-stained canvas dungarees.

"Put these on. I'll keep your pretty duds for later."

Ben reached out for the stiff clothing and felt his mouth go dry. "What are these for?'

"Work duty," the deputy said.

"Where am I working? Who am I working for?" Ben said, frustrated.

"The great County of Elbert."

"How long is this work duty?"

"I suppose that depends on you. Cooperation might take off some of your time."

Ben gave a slight nod. "Great. It does get worse. Just great."

An hour later, his ankles shackled with chains, the jail wagon headed out of town. Ben fought the fear that he had no idea where they were taking him. The headache and humiliation were competing for his attention. Maybe Fred really was in with the deputy. Maybe he wouldn't get to talk to a judge. He watched the landscape carefully. He would find a way from these chains, escape if he had to.

"What did you do?" a salt-and-pepper bearded man asked. They hit a rut, and they both rocked back and forth, chains clanging.

Ben snorted, looking past the man. "I chased after a woman who didn't want me. In trying to do the right thing, I roughed up Fred at the saloon, and his goons knocked me out."

"No, what did you do to get locked up?"

Ben finally looked at the man. His scars and dents showed what a rough life he'd lived.

"Just wrong place and the wrong time, probably wrong life."

"Ha, I hear that," The man slapped his knee. "Don't worry, I've been at the mine before. There's so much rock to haul out, you don't even need a brain. At dark, after you get slop for dinner, you'll close your eyes and all you can see is rock and dirt. All those pretty gals you been chasing won't haunt you anymore. Rock and dirt, that's all you're gonna think of. Rock and dirt."

Day one of hauling wheelbarrows of rock, gravel, and dirt out of the mine looked just like day two and then day three. By day four, Ben was either going to run or go crazy. The work wasn't hard; he could push twice as much as the old guys. It was not knowing. Did the Von Kellers care at all? Did they think he'd run across the country after Nadine? Certainly rescuing one daughter was enough. Were his pack, his letter from his pa, the broken necklace, safe in the small house? More likely at the bottom of the burn barrel. Would Edda wonder what happened? One minute he was clean and dressed up, looking forward to a nice dinner, the next minute he was in filthy duds, a knot the size of his fist coming off his skull. He should never have come to this town, the dairy. He should have worked in the last rock quarry he was offered. That one included pay. Pay to get his own horse back and way to get back home.

Pushing another full wheelbarrow, he begrudged the day he'd followed that letter to the dairy. Just when Margaret had helped him put his faith back in God and faith back in himself, life turned into pure chaos. He groaned, and another blister popped on his hand. Even though he thought he could make himself honorable by marrying Nadine, he couldn't. So much effort—for what? His hopes were continually short-lived. Now, this deep hell pit happened because he had tried to be sacrificial. *Don't think of yourself, do something right for someone else.* He smirked. How could God kick him so far down?

It had been ten days of solid work. Hour after hour, with only a supper break. The dark clouds moved in, and Ben thought it felt like snow. He heard the guard whistle, but since he'd never spoken to any of them, he kept his nose to the grindstone. "You there." He looked up and shuffled to the guard waving him over.

"The deputy is waiting for you over there." He nodded to the road.

The deputy sat on the buckboard seat and pointed to the back. "Get in. You're done here."

"What?" Ben asked. "Where are you taking me?"

"Back to town."

Ben jumped in the back, chains dragging. "Then what?"

"Then get back to the dairy or whatever you want. I worked out a deal with Fred. I got ya out of those charges."

"You did?" Ben didn't believe him. What kind of scheme was this now, since their charges against him were phony? Ben gripped the side as they turned toward town. Every ounce of him was on alert. He wouldn't believe anything in this place. He was done with sticking things out, doing the right thing. The first moment he was free of these chains, he was getting out of here and never looking back. Small, wet flakes of snow began to fall.

37

The buckboard rolled to a stop in front of the jail. Carl was standing on the wooden sidewalk. Ben's anger spiked, and he wanted to confront Carl, but it didn't matter. More than anything, he just wanted to get out of there. He jumped down, chains hitting the walk with a clang, and followed the deputy inside.

"Here are your duds." The deputy handed him his nice clothes as he bent to unlock his chains. "There's a barrel of fresh water out that door. You can wash up and change."

Ben took his things and tried to walk toward the back door. He had gotten used to shuffling his feet. Now his legs felt like feathers without the heavy chains. He tucked himself behind a fence and dropped his stiff, grimy, foul dungarees. Grabbing the rag hanging from the barrel, he began to scrub his body with freezing water. Carl had a lot of nerve, coming after him. Standing there like he was the next prison guard. He snapped his clothes on over his damp body and tried to squeeze the water from his hair. Shivering, he looked around the fence. He didn't owe either of them the time of day. A light dusting of snow was covering the fence and buildings. The problem was, he needed a coat. If he stole one, he'd just end up back where he started.

Opening the back door, he noticed that Carl hadn't moved. He stepped closer, teeth clenched, body shaking and tense. "Now what?"

"You're free to go." The deputy nodded at the door.

Ben's nostrils flared. What kind of game had they been playing? The humiliation, standing here back in his wedding clothes. He strode toward the door, trying to breathe in the air of freedom. What a crazy, upside down road he'd traveled. Freedom was all he had ever wanted. He walked into the brisk air, heart beating like a drum, cursing the day he'd left Michigan.

"Wait," Carl said.

Ben stopped, but didn't turn.

"I have your things, your coat, your gun."

That gun had been in his family for years. He walked over to the dairy wagon.

"You can come back if you want." Carl cleared his throat. "The family thinks you have run after Nadine. They don't know about this."

"Because you forgot to mention it." Ben leveled him with a glare, slamming his hat on.

"I can tell them I just saw you in town."

"No, thanks. I know you told the deputy to keep me. I'm done with all the lies." Ben grabbed his things.

"I did it for Margaret," Carl said as Ben was about to leave.

Ben slightly tilted his head. "She's a grown woman, I can't imagine she needed your help."

"She is like a daughter to us. I don't expect you to understand." Carl looked at the ground. "I listened to the way she talked about you when we picked her up. I could tell she had feelings for you. Now that she has returned to Chicago, you are welcome to come back to the dairy."

Ben tried to decipher what he was saying. "You needed to get rid of me until Margaret gave up and moved back to Chicago?"

"*Ja*, that's true. First Nadine, then Margaret. You have no business playing with those girls' affections."

Ben ran a hand over his patchy beard. Carl thought him the wolf, coming to devour one of the innocent. Dare he defend himself? His mind flashed to pushing those wheelbarrows full of rock. It was no use. He'd tried to run from his waywardness, only to drown in it again. Carl wanted to teach him a lesson. Maybe he had. He shoved his coat on and jerked his pack and gun over his shoulder. "Goodbye, Carl. Please tell the Von Kellers and Edda thank you for everything." He turned and stalked away.

Ben followed the road a mile or so from town before he could quit looking over his shoulder. Let Carl deal with the Von Kellers. If he wanted to lie to their faces, let him. He didn't care. None of them would give a stack of cow patties for what happened to him.

Two teen brothers rolled by in a wagon and began to slow. "Want a ride?"

Ben nodded his thanks, put his foot on the back wagon wheel and jumped in. Leaning against the sideboard, he dropped his things between his knees.

"Where ya headed?" they asked.

"I don't know." Ben shoved his hands in his pockets. "Anywhere far from here."

Something hit his fingers as he shoved his freezing hands in his coat pocket. The wagon jerked forward, and he pulled out an envelope with money. Probably just his back pay. That would help. He looked at the other envelope, a letter from his mother. That would probably not help. He shoved them both back in.

"What's your names?" Ben called to the two on the seat.

"I'm Paul, this is my brother, Drew."

Ben tipped his hat. "I'm Ben. How far you going?"

"Johnsonville."

"Great. Thanks for picking me up."

He leaned back against a wooden box. For the first time in weeks, he felt the muscles in his back relax. He'd purposely held everything together. Held it together for Nadine, remembering her tears and her broken heart as she sat on the floor of her room. The way she clung to him, what a sap he was. He shook his head, what about everything he'd done for Margaret.

He almost believed he could be everything she saw in him. How could a Bible peddler like her have feelings for him? She most likely needed another cause to rescue. *If you could only see me now, Margaret. Only today-out of prison chains.* He leaned his head against the wood box. He could still feel the painful twinge where that knot had been. What was wrong with this family? Why did he get dropped into the only crazy family around? His parents would have never found common ground with these people today. Simple people like a simple life and there is nothing wrong with that. His oldest brother James had met Frieda. There was no crying. No production. He asked her to marry him, and they got married the next Saturday. His father and brothers had always worked the mines. They made a decent wage and took care of their families. Ben closed his eyes, still seeing rock and dirt. Should he head back to Ready Springs? He reached into his pocket and pulled out his ma's letter.

Dear Son,

I was so glad to hear that you have been helping the Von Kellers. I still remember you children playing hide and go seek after church. I pray that you will be a light to their family. Ben dropped the letter into his lap. His ma was a good soul, but she had no idea how menacing the Von Kellers really were. As soon as he could forget about all of them, the better. *Levi and Allison made it safely to Madison. Word is, there's a new baby on the way. I'm so fortunate to see my children marry and settle down. Madison isn't too far from you. I don't know if you can get away, but I'm sure they'd love to see you.* Ben looked up. Madison. Maybe that was his destination. He'd been wanting to talk to Levi, but all his reasoning had changed. He chewed on his bottom lip, finishing the letter.

I asked the Lord for a scripture for you. This one came to mind.

"These things I have spoken unto you, that in me ye might have peace. In the world ye shall have tribulation: but be of good cheer; I have overcome the world." John 16:33

Sending my love to you,

Your Ma

Peace. Ben tried to remember the last time he'd slept in peace. The last time he'd worked or done anything in peace.

"Can you do any carpentry?" One of the brothers broke into his thoughts.

Ben folded the letter. "I can. What are we talking about?"

"A barn. Our pa's running out of time, snow's coming." Paul said.

"We'd have to make sure it's okay with him. Maybe just help us for a few weeks?" Drew added. "We've been trying to help with the farm, but it's just taking forever."

Ben nodded his understanding.

"Room and board, our ma's a good cook."

"Yeah, take me home with you. I happen to be in-between jobs. Let's see what your pa says." Ben wanted to ask about their family. *Please, Lord, let there be no sisters. Not even one.* Working on a barn sounded good. Maybe even peaceful. Just as long as there were no pretty, dark-haired sisters.

38

Oh Lord, there were sisters. A bushel of them. The wagon didn't even come to a complete stop before two little blonde girls came skipping out. Ben smiled at them—thankfully, they were wee bitty things. Another one, probably a young teen, walked out of the door of the simple wood-sided farmhouse. He jumped down and nodded to her as she walked up to him.

"Hi, I'm Ben." He held his hand out, and she shook it, giggling.

"This is Sarah," Paul said, opening the back of the wagon. "We have an older sister." Ben held his breath. "Rebekah."

Ben decided to ignore that. He began to unload the lumber and boxes from the wagon.

"Did you get my fabric? My needles?" Sarah tried to wedge in where they were unloading.

"Hold up." Drew pushed past her. "Let us get this stuff out first. Sarah, go find Pa."

Ben watched her glance up at him as she ran off. So far there didn't seem to be a bunch of fuss from these siblings.

One of the little ones followed him back from where they stacked the lumber. "This is Kit." The little blonde held a cat up to Ben.

"Nice to meet you, Kit." Ben shook the little gray and black paw. "What is your name?

"Catherine."

"Hello, Catherine, I'm Ben Graham." He lifted a wooden box onto his shoulder.

"Why is Ben Graham here?" Catherine asked as Paul walked by.

"To help us with the barn. Go tell Ma one more for supper."

Ben wedged in next to the brothers on the long bench at their table. They all moved down, knocking the smallest blonde off at the other end.

"Come here, Livy." Their pa scooted his chair back. "I have just the place for you." He picked her up and sat her on his knee.

"Sorry, little Miss." Ben grinned. "Didn't mean to bump you off your spot."

"She usually ends up here, anyway," Mr. Nelson said. "Let's pray." The children bowed in unison. Ben closed his eyes on cue, thankful for the reprieve of this simple table. The little girls with their pigtails and calico dresses. The next sister and brother with sandy blonde hair. The oldest, Paul, and the parents with light brown hair. The smell of the fresh bread under his nose.

"Amen," they said together.

The front door creaked open, and a round faced young woman walked in. She pulled her coat from her shoulders and hung it on a peg. Tugging her bonnet off, Ben noticed the light sandy hair, soft eyes, and a few faded freckles across her nose.

"Sorry I'm late." She sat on the opposite bench.

"This is Rebekah." Mr. Nelson said, passing the potatoes.

Ben nodded and tried not to smile. She lingered a bit too long, looking at him. He kept his eyes on the food. She was obviously pretty, even with blotches of red from the cold.

"Nice to meet you," he said, quickly looking down and plopping potatoes off the spoon.

"Ben, tell us about your family. Are you from around here?" Mrs. Nelson asked.

"No, my home is in northern Michigan. But my brother and his family live in Madison. When I'm done helping here. I'll head that way to see them."

"I see." She nodded, smiling. "We appreciate your help with the barn. The house was newer when we bought it, but the old barn was almost to the ground. We had to get by until the crops came in." She poured Catherine a cup of milk. "What does your pa do in Michigan?"

"He used to work in the copper mines." Ben hesitated. "But he passed away several months ago."

"Oh, I'm so sorry," she said. "How does your ma get along?"

Ben felt his jaw twitch. Just like Mrs. Von Keller, womenfolk worrying about each other.

"We're all grown. I'm the youngest. My older brother James and his family live close." Ben glanced quickly down both sides of the table. The children ate their supper so quietly, you wouldn't even know they were there. Peaceful. That word from his ma's letter came to mind. Rebekah watched him and looked quickly away.

"Thank you for this fine supper. You have a wonderful family." If they only knew the skunk hole he had escaped from.

"While we have Ben here, Drew can do my chores, and I'll help him first thing on the barn." Paul looked to their pa. Ben wondered if Drew would be upset.

"Sarah, you can feed the horses and milk the cow for Drew, that way the boys can help on the barn." Mrs. Nelson said.

"Yes, ma'am." Sarah nodded.

Ben listened. Children obeying their parents? No whining? No convincing otherwise? This seemed so strange, yet so right. He hadn't thought of Minna in weeks. She had everything a child could want. He tried to imagine her being told she would pick up the care of the horses and milking the cow. That girl would be screaming and carrying on. What a difference this meal was!

Ben stoked the little potbelly stove in the small tool shed. The cot was old and under some horse tack, but he didn't mind. Even though the hospitality was a kind offer, he didn't want to bunk with the boys in the house. He rubbed his hands near the stove; this would keep him warm enough. Oh, just to be alone, without Von Kellers or dirty-smelling convicts. To enjoy the sound of only the wood crackling. He scratched his head, thinking. He'd left out his jail time when telling this family his recent travels. It wasn't like lying. They were good people, and as long as he could stay away from trouble, it should stay away from him. He grabbed his blanket and curled up on the cot. Just when he was about to snuff out the candle, he heard something. Every muscle alert, he sat up on one elbow. Sneaking out from the shadows, Kit jumped up onto him. "Okay, you I can handle." He blew out the light and listened to the cat purr next to him. *Peace. This is peace, Ma.*

39

During his first week of barn building, Ben was starting to feel as if he'd found his way home. Amidst the smell of the lumber and the pounding of the nails, his mind could relax. At night, sleep came easily, and his body didn't feel on alert anymore. Mr. Nelson gave him directions daily, then he'd check on his work and praise him for a job well done. Paul and Drew worked just as hard. If they ever pushed and prodded each other, Ben never saw it. The whole family had kind and even dispositions.

Each family meal was simple and hearty, no strange German food. He enjoyed just listening to the stories of the different children. And he learned that if he never spoke to, looked at, or touched a young woman, she would ignore him, too. Rebekah was pretty enough. He even liked listening to her talk around the table. But he had not even a hankering to know her.

Ben grabbed another board Paul handed him. The barn was looking good. The work felt worthy, and he felt an honest kind of tired. He straddled a beam and pulled more nails from his leather apron. Sometimes at night, right before his eyes closed for good, he could see Margaret. It was the two of them moving around their little shed. Talking, eating together, watching Henry play. Holding her in his arms as they danced around the tree in the candlelight. Would he ever forget the way she felt in his arms, sleeping next to her? The way she smelled like spring flowers? Would he ever not desire to hear her compassionate voice? Her laugh was like rich Sunday hymns, and he bit his lip in recollection. Did she think about him? Probably just to pray for his deliverance.

Paul handed another board up. "Last one. Looks like rain."

Ben pounded the last plank and looked up. It had been gray and cold all day. He glided his legs around the beam until they found the ladder. He carefully backed down and looked up to see the three little Nelson girls riding their horse back from school. Sarah held the reins while Livy held on. Catherine balanced over the swaying rear. A sudden crack of thunder rattled in the sky. Ben gripped the shaking ladder, and looked up just in time to see the horse's uprised hind legs hit the ground and Catherine flip off to the dirt. Sarah pulled the reins to keep the horse on all fours while it skittered back and forth. Ben's feet smacked the dirt hard as he ran to where the horse was about to bolt. In one smooth grasp, he pulled the bridle down and held the horse in place. He reached for Sarah as she slid off into his arms. Livy was hanging on her sister's back and reached out for Ben. He quickly set them on the ground and handed the flustered horse to Paul. Catherine lay on the ground, not moving. He bit hard into his lip as he scooped her up. Trying to be careful with her, he saw blood seeping from the back of her head.

"Hey, Catherine. Can you hear me? It's Ben." He walked quickly toward the house. "Can you open your eyes, honey?" She was limp as a sack of potatoes. Sarah flew by him, dragging Livy.

"Ma! Ma!"

Ben stepped up on to the porch as Mrs. Nelson met him.

"Oh Lord, Catherine." She pulled Ben into the dining room.

"Set her on the table." She grabbed a rag and put it under Catherine's head. "Sarah, get the old quilt and my medicine box."

Ben looked down at his blood-soaked sleeve. "Can I go for the doctor, ma'am?" Breathing hard, he wished Dr. Ketchum was near.

"Just… let's give her a minute." Mrs. Nelson took a wet rag to the gash. "Catherine, Catherine May, can you open your eyes?" She covered her with the quilt.

"She flipped off the back of the horse. We didn't hear any other thunder, Ma. We would have walked if we'd known."

"I know, dear." Mrs. Nelson gently touched Sarah's chin and quickly turned back to tend to Catherine.

Drew and Mr. Nelson walked into the dining area. "What can I do?" Mr. Nelson brushed the hair from Catherine's face. "Do you think anything is broken?" Ben moved back, feeling like an intruder. They spoke in soft whispers to each other, obviously keeping their fears between the two of them.

"Paul, take the girls in the other room and pray. Drew, maybe you should go and get Rebekah."

Ben glanced outside as the dark rain broke loose. "I can do it. Is she at the school?" Ben wanted to save the family from something.

"Yes," Mr. Larson said. "Take my horse. Drew, make sure all the animals are secure."

A bright flash lit up the room, and they all stilled, waiting. A few seconds later, a low roar rattled the walls and windows.

"I'll get to the school." Ben nodded at them. "I'll be careful," he said, reading their minds. He walked back to the front porch and untied the horse from the railing. By the time he reached the edge of their property, he was soaking wet. Giving the horse a kick, he bent into the gallop. The rain on his face was beginning to sting. "Lord, help her," escaped from his lips. He looked up to see that white clouds were breaking through the dark ones. "Please, Lord, you are the only one who can make good from bad. Please, heal her." The tin roofline of the school was ahead. He slowed the horse to a trot and approached. He'd prayed for Margaret, and she got well. Swinging his leg off the saddle, he dropped into the wet dirt. Ben wiped the water off his face and tied the horse to the hitching post. He took the steps two at a time and flung open the school door.

"Miss Rebekah."

She swung around so fast that she dropped the eraser.

"I need to take you home." He didn't want to step farther in and leave a puddle on the floor.

She quickly put the eraser on the big desk. "What's wrong?"

"Catherine took a tumble off the back of the horse. She's unconscious."

"Oh, no! I'm done here. Could you check the stove?"

The fire was almost out. She met him halfway down the row of desks.

"We should make sure the storm has moved a bit. I don't want you getting hit by lightning."

She looked up at him with worried green eyes. He swallowed a dry lump in his throat. They had never really spoken to each other. She looked like she might want to trust him. He looked toward the wall of windows. "It's still a bit dark."

"I guess you didn't bring the wagon." She pinched the sleeve of his drenched shirt. "Or a coat?"

"Just your pa's horse." Blast it, why hadn't he thought this through? He wished he could kick himself. "Maybe I could ask one of the townsfolk to bring you home?"

She shook her head, a calm strength on her face. "Let's go. I'll be fine."

They walked outside and she pulled a brass key from her pocket. After she locked the school, they stood under the eaves for a moment.

"I haven't heard any thunder. Let's try now." She pulled up her skirts and ran down the steps to her father's horse.

Ben stood close behind her. Wrapping his hands around her waist, he told her to jump. She popped up, and he easily lifted her onto the saddle. He grabbed the saddle horn, put his foot in the stirrup and swung up behind her. He had to reach around her to hold the reins. There was an instant warmth that penetrated his body. He felt bad to see that the rain was already soaking into her hair and dress. He tried to lead the horse forward without touching her, but it was impossible. The horse bolted, knocking her back against him. She tried to sit forward, but the bounce of the gallop knocked her into him.

"I've got you." He wrapped his free arm around her waist. He could feel her relax against him as they both tucked their heads against the pelting rain. Why hadn't he taken care of the stock? Mercy, this was a better job for a brother.

40

B en looked up as a crooked flash of light rent the sky. The storm seemed to be moving away. He grabbed the reins tighter as the rumble stirred the air. The horse never missed a beat as it slowed into the yard of the Nelson's home. He swung off quickly and reached up for Rebekah. She was soaked to the bone. Their eyes met, and he tried to offer her a small smile as she slid quickly into his arms and he returned her to the ground.

"Thank you for coming for me," she said, rain running down her face.

He nodded toward the house. "Go on in, your ma won't want me on her dry floor."

"No, please come in and get warm by the fire." Ben felt her hand pull at his elbow. He stepped back, surprising himself at how fast he could move away. "No, you go help. I can dry off by the little stove in the shed." He pulled on the reins and took the horse with him toward the barn. He rubbed his elbow against his side, trying to erase her innocent touch.

Ben jerked the saddle off the horse and flung it over the railing. Poor little Carolyn. He hoped she had awakened.

He stepped from the stall and stopped in his tracks. The child's name was Catherine, not Carolyn. Carolyn was from a hundred years ago. A character in a story he didn't want to keep remembering.

He grabbed the chain that kept the horse in and jerked it hard across the opening, slamming the hook over the eye. He entered the tool shed and started the fire in the little stove. Levi had a similar little stove for cooking in his cabin. Unbuttoning his shirt, he pulled it off, remembering that terrible day at Levi's cabin. The smoke came up from the back of Allison's skirt, burning her legs. He twisted and wrung the water out of his shirt into a bucket. Throwing the wad of a shirt into the hay in the corner, he remembered how upset she had been. Sitting down, he roughly pulled his boots off. Allison, a beautiful woman who seemed to enjoy his company.

His arms strained to pull off the wet denims. Just like Nadine. He pulled one trouser leg so hard his fist hit the shed wall. Wincing at the pain, he shook his hand for relief. She smiled at him for what, just long enough to use him for her own gain? He grabbed his blanket and tried to dry off his cold skin. Pulling the water from his soaked head, he smoothed his hair flat. Having feelings for Margaret had landed him in work camp. The Von Kellers found a sure-fire way to get rid of him. *She probably thinks I'm still wandering around looking for Nadine.* He dropped his head into his hands with the disgust of it all. He didn't need this sweet young woman squeezing his arm, pulling on him. No sir, no thanks. How much pain and confusion could one body take?

Just when the dry clothes and warm shed were working, Ben noticed something soft and warm, not enough to remove the rock in his stomach but maybe for little Catherine. Kit, her cat, wandered in to curl around his ankles. He scooped the cat up under his arm and grabbed his jacket off a nail. "Let's go see how your friend is doing."

The rain was only a drizzle as Ben dodged the puddles and ran to the porch. He knocked softly, and the door creaked open.

"How's she doing?" he asked, as Drew opened the door.

"She woke up for a bit. Ma got a couple stiches in to close up her head. But she doesn't want to stay awake."

Ben took off his jacket and hung it with the family's coats. Kit straightened up under his arm, as if to greet everyone.

"I want Kitty." Little Liv reached up for the cat. Ben got down on one knee in front of the tyke. "Can you wait just a minute? Can you help me see if sister wants to wake up and hold her?" He looked up at Mr. Nelson to ask for permission. "She's in the room on the right." Mr. Nelson stood from his rocking chair. "She loves that cat. It's a good idea, Ben." Ben took Liv's hand and walked with her to the bedroom. Mrs. Nelson sat on the end of the bed with her hand on Catherine's leg. Rebekah sat on the floor near her pillow. Both women looked up as he entered, and Rebekah quickly looked down.

"Can I see if she responds to Kit?" Ben asked Mrs. Nelson.

"Yes, let's see if we can get her to stay awake." Mrs. Nelson reached for Liv and Rebekah stood up, moving back.

"Hey, Catherine." Ben gently tapped her shoulder. "I have a visitor for you." He waited. She didn't move. "It's Kit. She wants to say hi. Can you open your eyes and say hi, just for a moment?" They all waited in silence.

"Hi," Catherine said, without opening her eyes. Rebekah and Mrs. Nelson smiled at each other.

"I'm going to take your hand. Here's Kit." Ben reached for the child's hand and brought it down on the cat's soft fur.

"Can you tell Kit I can't play right now?" Catherine said slowly, eyes still shut. "I have a headache."

"Sure, honey. Kit understands." Ben smiled.

Rebekah stood up next to Ben, lightly touching the cat tucked into his arm. "Can you remember what story we read in school today?"

"The old lizard had a hat." Catherine's face twitched with pain.

"That's right. What part did you like?" Rebekah was standing uncomfortably close to Ben.

"I don't know, Bek, do I have to do school now? I'm tired," she said, never opening her eyes.

"If you'll take a sip of water, then we'll let you get back to sleep." Mrs. Nelson sat on the edge of the bed and held the cup to her daughter's lips.

Ben looked around and bent down to give the cat to Liv. "Here, sweetie, Kit is all yours."

"Don't put any ribbons around her neck, Livy, she doesn't like it." Catherine cracked her eye at her little sister.

Ben, Rebekah, and Mrs. Nelson all smiled with relief. "I think she's going to be fine. Come on, Livy, let's get some supper on the table," Mrs. Nelson said as they walked out.

Ben turned to follow them. "That was a great idea, Ben," Rebekah said. He ran his hand down the back of his head, feeling the small tender skin that remained from weeks ago. Finally, he turned his eyes on her.

"Bringing in the cat. You must understand children. I work with them every day and never thought of it."

"Well, Kit and I are like this." He brought up his crossed fingers. "It was really Kit's idea." Rebekah's face warmed with sweet approval.

"We live together in the shed, tell stories each night, you know." Teasing her, Ben almost felt like his old self.

"Well, you're good with children." She smiled.

Ben grinned, wondering what he should do next.

"You can go eat with the family." She nodded to the door. "I'm staying in here with her."

"Sure." Ben felt as stupid as his legs were long. Of course, he needed to leave.

He sat at the end of the bench as the family served up a simple meat pie with corn bread. It was happening again. He couldn't get attached here. This was a hard-working family. He only caused trouble wherever he went. He needed to finish with the barn and move on. He sat with head down and listened to the children talk. Maybe one day, the Lord would forgive him his folly. Maybe one day, he could settle down in one place, be stable, be content, have a family of his own.

"Kit!" The family moaned.

Ben's chin flew up to see that the cat had jumped up on the dinner table. His long arms were able to snatch the cat first. He tucked it under his arm and stood. "I see why you're not welcome in the house. We'll take our leave now. Thank you, Mrs. Nelson, for another warm meal. I'm so glad your Catherine is doing better."

"There's more supper, Ben. You only had one helping," she offered.

He raised his hand. "No, thank you, I'm full."

"Thank you for your help today, son. Very much appreciated by the wife and me." Mr. Nelson smiled.

Ben nodded back and lifted his jacket off the peg and threw it around his shoulders. As he said goodbye, he looked past the table and saw Rebekah in the shadows, leaning against the hall wall. She was watching him, kindness and thankfulness in her expression. She slowly raised her hand to wave goodbye. He swallowed hard and went to tip the hat that wasn't on his head. He nervously rubbed his forehead instead. He cleared his throat and made a hasty exit.

"Hey, Kit, ranch cat, want to trade places?" He strode across the yard into the barn and set the cat down. "I'd like catching mice to be my only worry."

41

Margaret shook the rain water off her umbrella before she crossed the threshold.

"How was school today?" Her roommate Eugena looked up from her book.

"Oh fine." She hung her coat on the hall tree. "When the children can't get outdoors for their running and play, they can't seem to concentrate." Walking to the large bay window, Margaret looked out, breathing out a long sigh. "It's probably not just them. Oh, I don't know." The rain hitting the window seemed to dull her mind even further. "I can't seem to concentrate, either."

"Are you looking forward to the holiday? Goodness knows, after the sickness you've been through, maybe you just need to get back home and rest." Eugena rose, pouring her a cup of tea.

Margaret took the cup and saucer, attempting a weary smile. "Thank you." Her friend was trying to help. "I know I haven't been myself, and being with my family was challenging."

"Still no word from your sister? I can't believe what she did to your family. I do pray for her."

Margaret took a sip of the hot tea. She really hadn't even spent any time praying for Nadine. She was still angry at her selfish sister. When would God help her to move on? Even if she mouthed the right words in prayer, she couldn't imagine it could cover the raw sting. What had happened to Ben? Her mother said something vague in her letters. He had met up with Carl and Carl said he'd moved on. Her parents didn't really blame him. They were still reeling from Nadine's foolish departure.

Margaret glanced over at Eugena, who had resumed her reading. She tried every distraction. Reading didn't help. Even her writing had suffered. She attended the temperance meetings, but her heart didn't stir for it anymore. When they spouted the injustice of what alcohol was doing to society, she still believed they were right, only now 'those people' had a face. A warm, caring, and handsome face. A beautiful smile that would melt snow. A glint of pain in his brown eyes. She sighed, supposing that temporarily alcohol could cover that kind of pain. Her passion for the cause had gone somewhere. She was a hypocrite. If her temperance sisters ever knew she was in love with a man who drank, they'd snub her in a moment.

"Did you see Henry today?" Eugena broke in.

"Mmm, yes." Margaret turned from the window. "He's one of those who has a hard time with his studies." Ben was smart enough to question how Henry would fare in a school setting. Of course, she thought he'd be grateful to be rescued from poverty and attend school. So many of her convictions she questioned now. Was God trying to knock her off her high horse? She closed her eyes, feeling the truth. "I tried to talk to him, I know it's difficult for him to sit still." She let out a long sigh.

"But you've said he improves every day," Eugena said, hopefully.

"One step forward, sometimes two steps back. He's back to taking food and hiding it under his pillow. I've asked the commissary staff, and they said he eats all his meals. It's funny, he never did that with me. He could eat too fast and had some strange sleeping patterns, but I never saw him hide food."

"So something about going to bed maybe upsets him. Might the food under his pillow be a comfort?" Eugena offered. "Where did he sleep on your travels?"

"Next to me." Margaret saw the obvious for the first time. "Usually like a little piece of meat sandwiched between…" She pulled her thoughts up quickly. Her sweet Eugena would faint away if she knew she had shared her nights with Henry *and* Ben. "I think you're right, dear friend." She massaged her forehead. Oh, how she had tried to block those tender memories. "I'll talk to him more about it. Maybe he's scared."

Margaret pulled her tangled nightgown from around her legs and rolled onto her side. She had tried miserably to get comfortable and allow her mind to drift to sleep. Maybe she should try some comfort items, the security of bread and cheese under her pillow? How could she be so daft? Henry suffered from the same malady she did. They missed the old life.

She squeezed her eyes shut and tried to bury her face with her arm. She had a comfortable, warm bed. *Thank you, Lord.* Her parents, in their distraction over Nadine's behavior, had agreed to allow to go her back to Chicago. *Thank you, Lord.* She seemed to be a rare survivor of the dreaded typhoid. *Thank you, Lord.* Henry had some little friends his age. *Thank you, Lord.* She could see him and care for him with her time at the school. *Yes, thank you, Lord.* She had spent weeks with a fun-loving, tall, strong friend, who danced with her by candlelight, celebrating a birthday she didn't think she would live to see. *Thank you, loving Lord.* She blew out a flustered breath and pushed off with her elbow, flopping to her other side. "The Lord is my shepherd, I shall not want, He maketh me to lie down in green pastures…"

The next day, Margaret grabbed two special buns from the bakery on the corner. She held her wrapped goodies and made her way to the school. She finished up her first class and asked the children to line up.

"Stay out of the puddles, boys and girls." She gave them each a stern look as they passed by. She followed her line to the back door and called out for Henry. He ran over to her.

"Can I have you for a minute? I brought you a surprise." She grabbed his hand and walked him back into her classroom.

"What is it?" He looked hopeful.

She unwrapped the two sweet buns and put them on her desk. "This is our secret, okay?" She tapped her finger on his nose as he nodded. "If you want to save this for your room or maybe tonight, you can."

"No," he grabbed the bun and took a large bite. "Can I take it outside?" he said, mouth full.

"No, I wanted a chance to talk to you. Does your tummy feel likes it gets enough food here? Here at the school?" She waited, but he took another mouthful of the bun and nodded again. She rubbed the back of her neck. "I wish Ben were here," she mumbled.

"Can he come?" Henry's eyes shot wide.

Margaret groaned slightly, feeling they were off track. "No. I don't know where he is." She noticed that Henry had stopped chewing.

"I miss him too, Henry." She stroked his dark silky hair. Would he welcome a hug? They were the only two people on the planet who shared the same heartache. She gave his shoulder a small squeeze. "Are you okay here? Do you miss the reservation? Are you scared at night?"

He took another bite and shrugged.

She bent down on a knee and looked him in the eye, gently bringing her hands up and down his plaid shirt sleeves. "I will do whatever I can to help you. You know that, right?"

"Can I have the other one for later?" He reached for the bun.

"Yes." Margaret rose and wrapped it up.

"Mrs. Middleton calls me a rascal. What's a rascal?" Henry piped in.

Margaret smiled. At least he was talking with her. "It's just a name for boys with lots of energy and big ideas."

"Was Ben a rascal?" He shoved the bun in his small coat pocket.

Margaret bent down again, attempting to button his overflowing jacket. "Yes, Ben was a rascal. I would guess he still is."

42

Ben set the stack of planks next to the barn where he was working. He came back around to the barn door and almost ran Rebekah over.

"Sorry, I didn't see you there." He dropped his hands quickly where he had reached out to steady her. "Are you looking for your brothers?" Stepping back, he gripped his hands together nervously.

"No, not really. I thought I would saddle Brownie myself." They stood in an awkward silence. "I have to be at the school in a bit."

Ben finally realized why she wasn't moving. "I'd be happy to help you. Do you want to take Brownie? I can do that." He moved to where the saddles sat. He lifted it up as she placed the bridle in the horse's mouth. She undid the chain and led the horse out to the middle of the barn.

Ben dropped the thick blanket on the horse's back and threw the saddle over. She stood near him as he cinched up the buckle.

"I'm glad you're staying for Thanksgiving. You've been such a help here. Between the barn and Catherine, my family thinks a lot of you."

Ben brought the horse forward out of the barn, feeling his throat close up.

"I'm thankful for the work," he said, barely looking at her. "I'll be heading to Madison to see my family soon." That sounded safe enough.

"Oh, I didn't know."

Ben clearly heard the disappointment in her voice.

"Well, you're welcome to stay. You're a very hard worker." He made the mistake of looking up to see the appreciation in her eyes.

"Here you go." He handed her the reins, thankful that sweet round face didn't see his many faults. "I've enjoyed my time here." He began to back up. "Have a great day at the school."

The slack in her jaw was obvious, and he stopped.

"Would you mind giving me a lift?" She nodded toward Brownie.

"Of course, sorry." He shook his head, embarrassed, and walked up beside her. He put his hands around her waist, noticing for the first time the plain, dark blue dress she wore and the simple gray cape around her back and shoulders. Before he could tell her to jump, she spun around. "Would it make a difference if I said I hoped you would stay?" A little dimple appeared with her soft smile.

Ben's face flushed. Why was he standing so close, his hands still on her waist?

"Umm...I..." He sucked in a breath and willed his feet to back up a bit. He ran his hand over his face, searching for any words that would not pain this innocent young lady.

"Anyone with eyes can see that you're sweet and caring and smart and…"

"I feel a but coming on." She squinted mischievously.

"…and intuitive," he continued, smiling.

"Do you have someone special? Someone waiting for you at home?" she asked softly, leaning into Brownie.

"No." Ben shook his head, looking at the ground. "But I did, not too long ago." She didn't look hurt, but understanding, almost like a friend. "I was left at the altar." He wondered what that had to do with anything.

"Oh." She grimaced. "That must have hurt. I'm so sorry." That sweet smile appeared again. "But I'm curious to know what happened. Can you tell me?"

He shook his head. "Not right now…you'll be late to school." He pushed her back around and grabbed her waist. "Jump."

Firm in the saddle, she pulled Brownie around to where he walked.

"Soon though, okay?"

"All right. Sometime."

"I can't wait." She smiled. "I'll have my hankie ready." She gave Brownie a little kick and headed out of the yard.

Hankie ready? Was that a glimmer of tease in her eyes? She could make a man believe that life with a woman could be effortless and enjoyable. He exhaled as he picked up another stack of planks. No crying, no manipulating, no giant slivers to the heart.

That night, Ben lay on his cot and pulled out two shiny items. One was a wedding ring that cost a pretty penny. He didn't even know if it would have fit Nadine. Obviously, he had never even had a chance to show it to her. He moved the ring back and forth between his finger and thumb. Holding it close to the candle's flame, he wrinkled his nose. He would never give this to anyone. It would be a constant reminder of his stupidity. Like dropping his trousers behind a thin curtain in a store, he just wanted to gather what was left of his pride and move on.

The other was a broken gold chain with a small gold cross. This he needed to toss into the hot coals of the little stove. He had stolen it from a store front. He looked at where the chain had broken apart when Margaret yanked it off her neck.

The ring he had bought with his own money. He wrapped it back up and put it in his bag. Might as well sell it and put it toward a horse. What a crazy path to get what he wanted all along, just a horse and some money to get home. He sat up, grabbed a rag and opened the front door of the hot stove. With just a toss, the broken, useless chain would be gone. He hesitated, feeling the heat against his fingers. The air going still, he prayed. *Lord, please forgive me. For the times I have hurt You. For the times I have hurt others. I am just like this broken chain, not worth…*

Paid for.

The words interrupted his prayer. He pulled his hand back from tossing the necklace into the stove. He'd heard his whole life that his sins were paid for on the cross. Did he believe that? Could a lifetime of poor choices still qualify? Could it be that simple? He sat back and looked at the gold chain lying in his palm. Paid for. A trinket or a life. What meaning would they carry if they were truly paid for?

Time to believe it. I forgive you. I've already paid the price owed. I love you.

Sounds in the stillness, warming every part of his being. There was a contentment rising in his soul. Isn't that what his ma was praying for? Peace for him. Accepting that God wanted to give him a clean slate, he closed his eyes and breathed it in. After a minute of serenity, he rested his elbows on his knees and watched the chain and gold cross dangle between his fingers. *Dear Lord, thank you for forgiving me. For not leaving me but always pulling me up to You. I want to accept this new day, this fresh start. Please guide me with your love.*

Amen.

43

After work the following Friday, Ben borrowed a horse and rode into the small Johnsonville community near the Larson farm. Glancing over to the school house, he saw a few ladies were in there talking, but he couldn't make out Rebekah. She had once told him the usual teacher suffered from gout and she often filled in for her. Seeing Brownie tied next to the building, he quickly turned toward the small town. He wasn't avoiding her, he just didn't want her to see him. Oh, if he could just stay focused. He jumped down from the Larson's horse and tied it in front of the small mercantile. Pulling off his hat, he rubbed his head before replacing it. Time to come out of hiding. The store was half the size of the one in Elbert County, but not as rustic as Crockers in Ready Springs. He entered, nodding to the man behind the counter and praying for favor.

"I'd like to see about selling this ring." He pulled it from his pocket. "It's never been used."

"I see." The man took it from his fingers and held it up to the glass window. "I don't give out cash for items, but I could give you some store trade." He gave it back to Ben.

Ben chewed his bottom lip as he looked around at the general goods. "I need the cash for a horse, a saddle." Two ladies entered the store, and he felt flustered. "Thanks, anyway." He began to walk away, tipping his hat at the ladies.

"Wait, I still might be able to help you." The man came out from behind the counter. "My nephew has a decent horse he's been trying to sell. He lives with me. I'll settle up with him for the ring. Go down two blocks past the school. The horse is brown with white legs. Ask for Richard."

"Richard, yes sir, thank you for your help." Ben left the store and grabbed the Larson's horse. He walked a few feet down the street and looked up to see Rebekah watching him from the front steps of the white school house. She smiled and turned to finish locking up. Descending the steps, she met him as he was about to pass by.

"What brings you to town this late afternoon?" She walked in step with him.

He bit down on his tongue. It would be so easy to say *to see you. Because you're pretty and uncomplicated and…no.*

"Trying to buy a horse."

"Ahh, yes, the trip back to the family. When will you be leaving?" Her tone was even, without guile.

"Don't know, don't have the horse yet." He sounded a bit curt. She looked at the ground and fell a step behind.

In that split second of seeing her expression, something jabbed him in the gut. He pulled up on the reins and stopped. "Rebekah, that didn't come out right. Do you want to help me find someone named Richard? I guess he has a horse for sale. You know people here, I don't." That offer still held no warmth; she'd be smart to turn around and ignore him.

"Yes, I know Richard. He lives with his uncle and aunt, right up here." They continued to walk ahead. Ben offered her a nod of thanks.

"This must be the horse." They walked up to a large white fence behind a white clapboard house. Ben handed the reins to Rebekah and bent down to go through the opening between the fencing. The brown horse approached, and Ben ran his hands along its back. Bending down, he grabbed a hoof and brought it up on his knee. After inspection of the horse's legs, he checked its teeth, then looked back at Rebekah. "Seems healthy, calm enough."

"Hi, Rebekah." They both turned to see a young man approach. Ben noticed his slick hair and nice clothes. A very thin mustache sat on his upper lip.

"Hello, Richard. This is Ben. He's been working for my father and is interested in your horse."

"Nice to meet you." Richard stuck his hand out while Ben cut back under the fence.

"Nice to meet you, too." Ben pumped the limp hand up and down, fighting the urge to wipe the damp feeling off his hand. He noticed Richard was watching Rebekah.

"How have you been, Rebekah? I was sorry not to see you at the social after church on Sunday. My aunt had made two of her cherry pies. Canned cherries from the store, of course. But her crust is the best I know of."

Rebekah's face remained stoic. Ben found their interchange somewhat amusing.

"My family needed me at home. You heard my sister took a bad fall from our horse last week?"

"Yes, yes." He grabbed her hand and patted the top. "We prayed for her at church."

She pulled her hand from Richard's grasp. Ben wondered if she thought it was clammy, too. Maybe the boy broke out in a sweat every time he saw her. A small snort escaped as Ben looked down, kicking the dirt.

"How about the horse? Is he for sale?"

Richard finally looked back at Ben. "I'd have to talk to my uncle. He gave it to me years ago, and now that I'm going to college, he thinks it would be a good idea." His gaze went right back to Rebekah. "Your frock brings out your eyes. You have very nice eyelashes, Rebekah."

Hating to interrupt Richards's efforts, Ben said, "I already spoke to your uncle. He's the one that sent me over."

"Oh," Richard said, never taking his eyes off Rebekah.

"I'd like to ride him around your pen here." Ben started back under the fence, giving up on conversing with Richard.

Moments later, satisfied, Ben jumped off and headed back under the fence. "I'll take him."

"Well, thank you, Richard, for that kind offer." Rebekah practically pushed the reins into Ben's hand. "We have to be going. My mother will worry."

"May I come by tomorrow, then? I'll bring the buggy. Should it rain, maybe you could just invite me in for lunch or time with your father?" Richard was trailing after them.

"I think I'll be helping my mother with canning tomorrow. Maybe another time." Rebekah hastened her steps.

"Soon," Ben heard Richard's weak voice after them.

"Someone has a large feather in their cap for you Rebekah." Pulling the Larson's horse along, Ben noticed his long legs had a hard time keeping up with her. "Too bad you'll be busy canning tomorrow. Especially since there aren't any fruit or vegetables to can."

She muttered something, rolling her eyes.

"What was that? I couldn't hear you."

She pivoted quickly, and Ben stopped in time, but the horse knocked him forward into her.

"Sorry," they both said.

"I didn't mean to step on you," Ben said.

She rolled her tongue around the inside of her cheek, fighting what she wanted to say.

"You really do have pretty eyelashes. Though I think I prefer your eyebrows." He bit his bottom lip, holding back his snickers.

She took a step forward, rising onto her toes. Ben stiffened, all teasing gone. Slow as molasses on a cold morning, she moved upward, never wavering from eyeing him intensely. Her eyes closed just as Ben felt the whisper of her breath on his lips. Frozen solid as ice, he closed his eyes and felt the soft pressure of her lips on his. Before he could respond, she moved back, drawing her hand down his shirt.

"Nice to know you like something about me."

Standing in the middle of the road, he stared, stunned silent. Watching her as she headed for the school house, untied Brownie and rode out.

44

What kind of game was this girl playing? Ben stood frozen on the street, dumbfounded. *Maybe I shouldn't have teased her.* But kissing him in the middle of the street... good night, he never saw that coming, not for a hundred miles. He swiped the back of his sleeve across his mouth. It wasn't unpleasant, it just wasn't right. *What if someone had seen us? She's a school teacher, for goodness sake. What if it got back to her parents?* He imagined her brothers with both guns on him and his things tossed out by the pigpen. His mind flashed to Carl standing outside the jail, and a shiver ran up his spine. Pulling the Larson's horse forward, he wanted to settle up over the new horse and get moving on.

With what seemed like a good trade for the ring, Ben was able to purchase horse, saddle, and tack. Richard stood on the porch and waved as Ben pulled the new horse from their gate. Suddenly this pleasant community was closing in around him. He just wanted to get his things and move on. He spied the saloon as he was mounting the Larson's horse. Something for the cold nights on the road. He gave the horse a kick and jerked the rope forward, holding the other animal. *Just get back to the Larson's place,* he thought, gripping the rope. *Do one thing right, don't get distracted.*

It was dark when Ben rode into the Larson's farm. Paul came out from the barn. "We missed you at supper." Paul smiled. "This must be the new horse Rebekah said you were thinking on."

Ben smiled back, relieved there was no gun pointed at him. "Yes, it is."

Paul opened the gate and reached for the rope holding the new horse. Ben released it as Paul led the horse into the corral.

"Come in when you're done." Paul hollered as Ben took the Larson's horse into the barn. Taking in a clear breath, he unsaddled the horse. The barn still smelled like new wood. He stopped and looked around. They had done good work. This place had been a good reprieve, except for that show Rebekah had put on in the street. He headed for the house.

Entering the front door quietly, Ben decided to keep his coat on and make an excuse as soon as he could. Catherine was sitting in the rocking chair with Kit. "Hey, Missy. How's the head?"

"Still working." She went back to dangling yarn in front of Kit.

"Ben, come on over," Mr. Larson said from the table.

Ben approached slowly. He nodded at Drew and Paul as he slid his long legs onto the bench.

"Rebekah said you were seeing about a horse in town."

"Yes, sir." Ben lost track as Rebekah approached with a bowl of chicken soup. "Thank you." He nodded, never looking her way. He looked back to Mr. Larson, trying to remember the question. A spoon was held out in front of his face. Eyes down, he tried to take it from her, but she held it fast. He finally had to look her in the face, and she suddenly let it go.

"I bought a horse. Yes, sir." He began to scoop the warm broth into his mouth, willing himself to ignore her. "I'm planning on moving on."

"I see." Mr. Larson nodded. "You've done a fine job on the barn roof. We'd spent five months doing what you finished in one. You're a skilled tradesman."

Ben nodded his thanks, still chewing. "I can't thank you enough for the warm bunk and wonderful meals."

Mrs. Larson approached, Livy balanced on her hip. "Rebekah and I were just saying, you look like you have more meat on your bones than when you got here."

Ben smiled, looking away as Rebekah came to sit next to Drew. "I'm sure I do, I've missed home-style food." He remembered the gruel at the labor camp.

"Well, then you're going to love Thanksgiving," Rebekah said. "Drew and Paul are hunting in the morning."

"That so?" Ben took another bite, wishing they would all quit making him the center of conversation.

"We'll wake you up at dawn," Paul said. "I know just the place."

"I'll be ready." Ben sat up straighter.

"What's your plan, son?" Mr. Larson asked.

Ben swallowed, but the food seemed to jam in his throat. "For the future?" He wished both the parents weren't looking at him. What did they want to hear? "I think as long as the weather holds, I'll head on to Madison." Why was his heart racing? "Got family there I haven't seen in a while."

Rebekah stood and reached for his bowl. "Another bowl?"

"No." He shifted in the chair. "Thank you, I'm fine."

"Well, you've been a great help, Ben." Mr. Larson slapped him on the shoulder. "We'll miss your company. You know you'll always be welcome at our table."

"Yes sir, your hospitality has been the best thing. And your cooking, ma'am."

"Oh, well now." Mrs. Larson set Livy down and reached out for him as he stood. "Maybe we'll pray for some snow." She hugged him.

He hugged her back and couldn't avoid seeing Rebekah. She had crossed her hands, bowed her head and closed her eyes. She even moved her lips. Praying. Ben felt his head swim and quickly released Mrs. Larson. He cleared his throat and moved back from the table. Was he hexed when it came to parents and daughters? Rebekah smiled and quickly looked to the floor. Trouble. Always the same trouble, following him wherever he went. Trapping him, like a beaver in one of Levi's traps. But hunting was something he would always make time for. He looked up at Paul and Drew. "I'll be out front at dawn." He turned to the front room. "Bye, girly girls." He waved to the little ones as he went out the door.

Enjoying the cold night air, he walked up to the fence where his new horse grazed. "You doing okay here?" He put his hand out flat as the horse walked forward and sniffed it. "You okay if we stay till Thanksgiving? I can get ya some pie," he said, rubbing the horse's velvety ears. "You need a good name." He took the horse's jaw in his hands, looking closer. "How about Jordan?" The horse moved from his grasp and headed back out to graze.

Ben leaned into the fence. *I'm interested in crossing over. Lord knows this is a good family.* He stretched his arms out, hanging onto the fence, and looked up to the sky. But he didn't want to be here. It was beginning to feel too much like the dairy. He wasn't playing with a girl's affections, he'd learned his lesson. *Thank you, Lord,* he said to the sky. Even the desire to get a bottle before heading out didn't appeal to him. He turned toward his little tool shed. The mister and missus showing appreciation, that was nice. Good-hearted people.

45

Paul held his free hand in the air. "Quiet, we're almost there." All three of them slowed their steps. Watching for any movement, Ben couldn't help but smile. He hadn't had this much fun in a long time. Hunting with his brothers seemed like years and years ago, yet it pulsed in his blood like nothing else.

They all crouched lower, Paul and Drew hiding easily behind a barren bush. Ben squatted down, back against an old fallen pine. Nothing was strenuous, but he liked how the air pulled in and out of his lungs. Life felt anew in the crisp morning; there was a familiar excitement in the anticipation.

He hunched lower and placed his gun on his knee. He'd already told himself this would be Paul or Drew's kill. He remembered what the thrill was like to bring home the game for the family. His own brothers excelled at it, making his kills rare. But when he did, it felt like he could run up the highest mountain. A bit like what today felt like, hearty and satisfying down in his bones. Paul's turkey call brought his thoughts back. Waiting patiently, he heard the faint rustle somewhere in the distance. He smiled again, watching the brothers stare ahead like a couple of bird dogs, both of them raising their rifles to their cheeks, fingers poised over the trigger. Paul's eyes quickly darted to Drew. A tiny nod was the signal between them; Drew could take the shot. Ben felt himself holding his breath. If he missed, they might be out a delicious meal

There was a shot, and Ben looked over to see Drew smiling from ear to ear. He did it. It would be turkey for dinner! Now they just had to go make sure that thing wasn't a six or seven-pound bird. He could eat that alone.

Ben sat cross-legged on the braided living room rug, the fire crackling and the little Larson girls watching him. Teaching little hands to play jacks was harder than he thought. But he was warm, and the smells from the kitchen were flooding his senses. All three little Larson girls sat in a circle with him, bodies wiggling.

"Livy is too young," Sarah piped in. "She can't figure it out."

"Watch. I'll bounce the ball, Miss Liv, and you pick up a jack." Ben said to the little blonde, trying to give her a chance. He gave it a good bounce and reached up to catch it. She jumped up and tried to catch the ball in unison with Ben. She stepped on him, but he caught her and rolled on his back, lifting the tyke in the air. "No, I was getting the ball, you were getting the jack." He laughed, spinning her above him. Catherine jumped up and pounced on Ben's chest. "Oh no, two against one isn't fair." Ben lowered Livy on top of Catherine, tickling them both. He flipped the girls around, and they landed on the old braided rug. They giggled and squirmed until he had them both trapped between his arms. "Now you're both going to get it." He tickled them and pulled them back as they tried to get away.

"Sarah!" Catherine reached out as Ben pulled her back. She came to help Catherine, and Ben easily pulled her in with the sisters. All three were giggling and rolling back and forth, trying to get past his grasp.

"Time to wash up, girls."

Ben stopped suddenly, hearing Rebekah's voice above him. Winded, he sat back on his heels, the girls escaping like little mice.

"They find you very entertaining," she said, looking down on him. "In fact, we all do." She smiled coyly.

Ben squinted at her. She thought she was so clever. Little did she know, he knew all the tricks to get someone's attention. Reaching his hand out for help to stand, he purposely missed her outreached hand and stood. "Let's eat."

Ben pushed around his fourth helping of mashed potatoes and turkey gravy. His belly was about to burst.

"Sarah." Rebekah sat back down on the bench with the family, handing a paper to Sarah. "Everyone's done. Would you mind sharing what you wrote for your report on Thanksgiving?"

Sarah came to stand next to her father at the head of the table.

She looked down to her paper. "My report is on Sarah, of course…" she smiled to the family. "Sarah Josepha Hale. She was an editor of the Ladies Magazine and Godey's Lady's book."

"Catherine, do you remember what an editor is? We talked about it in class." Rebekah asked.

"Umm, is that a person who looks at what people write and makes sure everything is spelled right and such?"

"Yes, I'm glad you were listening. Go ahead, Sarah."

"In 1827, she began to agitate…" Sarah looked up to Rebekah. "That was one of our vocabulary words. Agitate means to stir up or make a fuss." Rebekah nodded her teacher approval as Sarah continued. "…for a Thanksgiving holiday. She began to write articles for the magazine. They were often stories or recipes. Then she began to write letters to governors and senators…" Ben felt his eyes begin to droop. *Just like Margaret.* He yawned, trying to straighten up as Sarah continued. "She even wrote to the president. After thirty-six years of crusading…another vocabulary word. It means to wage any vigorous, aggressive movement for the advancement of a cause or ideal." He knew that word firsthand.

"She won the battle. And on October 3rd, 1863, President Lincoln proclaimed November 26 would be a national Thanksgiving Day, to be observed every year on the fourth Thursday of November." Her chin bobbed up with a smile.

The family clapped, and Mr. Nelson patted her on the back. "Wonderful report, Sarah." Ben clapped late, realizing he was barely listening. She was a woman who was on a crusade. Hadn't he said those exact words to Margaret? He wondered if she had gone back to protesting. He hated how she would lay down her life for her causes. He pictured her sunken face and motionless body in that foul-smelling wigwam. To die in a forsaken state—for a belief, a conviction. He wanted to be angry, but it wouldn't come. He would have fought a dozen Indians to get her out of there. He would have died to save her. She was the most amazing person he'd ever met. His heart seized up with longing for her. If he just hadn't agreed to assist Nadine in her sad plight... someone slid a piece of pumpkin pie in front of him, and thoughts of Margaret were diverted.

Mrs. Nelson and the little girls had long gone to bed, Drew and Paul said good night, and Ben stood and walked to the door. Mr. Nelson was snoring with his head back against the wooden rocker. Rebekah looked up from her sewing and smiled. She stood and met him at the door.

"Can we sit on the porch for a moment?" She pulled on the door latch. They walked out and sat on the porch step.

"Here." Ben draped his jacket around her shoulders. For some reason, he didn't feel nervous around her.

"You promised to tell me a story," she said softly. Ben narrowed his eyes in confusion.

"About being left at the altar. Is that really what happened?"

"Yes. It's just a long, confusing story." He scratched his head, looking out into the darkness. "Before coming here, I worked on a dairy farm in Elbert County." He was at a loss himself as to how this would make any sense. "Because the family was friends with my family years ago, I was treated better than a just a worker. I ate with the family, helped out more than expected."

"That sounds familiar." She lightly bumped her shoulder into his arm.

"I was very interested in their daughter. Her name is Nadine. She was…oh, I don't know…whatever is the runt of the family? She was the opposite."

"Hmm." Rebekah sounded intrigued. "Go on."

"Well, I thought I knew her well enough. But once again, I lack clear judgment." Ben stretched his legs out. "So by the time we were about to stand up before the reverend, she was out the back door."

"What? Why? What are you not saying?"

"She'd been seeing someone else."

"No!" Rebekah said, shocked.

Ben was ready to get up and leave. Guilt assailed him for leaving out the middle part. Why not tell her he was also falling for Margaret, a beautiful woman he still couldn't go an hour without thinking about?

"I'd better be going." He stood quickly.

She jumped up and handed him his coat. "I'm sorry. I can see you're in pain over your fiancée. I find her decision completely irrational. I'm sorry she caused you such heartbreak."

"Here's the thing." Ben's conscience was pounding in his ears. "I've not been the steady Freddy every gal is looking for. I've made plenty of mistakes." He took a step back away from the porch. "I certainly feel another coming on, I mean, what you did in the street. People talk and I don't, well, I mean, you are beautiful and obviously a…great teacher." Her face dropped a bit. "I mean a really good young woman." She winced in the soft moonlight. "See, I need to shut up." He scratched his jaw. "Rebekah, I need to get home. It's been too long." Did that just come out of his mouth? Why did he sound like a lost school boy? He shuffled his feet, not caring how it sounded. It had been brewing so close to the surface, just waiting for the bravery to be said. "Your brothers, your parents, especially you have been so good to me. Good for me. I can't explain it. I usually stay too long."

"But you haven't."

"I'm leaving tomorrow." He took in a deep breath. "I'll say my goodbyes to the family in the morning."

Even in the darkness, Ben saw her blink rapidly. *Please, Lord, if she cries, I'll be feeling worse.*

"I understand," she said, sighing. She turned toward the door and looked back over her shoulder. Flashing a crooked frown, she went in.

46

Levi Graham was humming a favorite hymn. He'd wondered for months how he could survive living in Madison. Surprisingly, it wasn't half as bad as he'd imagined. After all Allison had been through and all he had gone through to win her heart, living in Madison was small potatoes. Pressing harder, he worked the oil onto the soft deerskin. *"On Christ the solid rock I stand...all other ground is..."* He never was good with all the words. Thankfully, Pastor Johnson had only asked him to preach; his singing would never get him anywhere. Humming the tune again, he looked up to see a large shadow in the doorway of his workshop. The sun was harsh through the gray winter clouds. "Can I help you?" Levi squinted.

"I think it's something about sinking sand."

"Ben!" Levi took two long strides, leaping into his younger brother's arms, slapping his back and squeezing him hard. He pulled back and grabbed his brother's face. "Look at all this." He tugged on Ben's beard. "No wonder I didn't recognize you. You went and turned into a man. Geez, Ben, your arms are like solid tree trunks or something."

"Want to arm wrestle?" Ben gripped Levi's coat, smiling.

"Yes, of course. But not this minute." Levi pulled back, still looking him over. "I can't believe it. Ma said you were working at the Von Keller's dairy farm. Are you still?"

"No." Ben grimaced. "Haven't been there in a while."

"Ma probably told you we had moved here. I'm just so glad to see you." He grabbed Ben and gave him a shake. "I can't believe it. Allison is going to be shocked. Let's go find her."

Allison heard the ruckus at the door before it even opened. Surely not? Could it be? "Is that Ben?" she said as soon as they entered. "For pity sakes." She embraced him. "You've changed, Ben." She eyeballed him, beaming.

"You've changed a bit yourself." He looked down at her large belly, then back to Levi. "I knew you two had it bad for each other. You didn't waste much time, Levi."

Levi grabbed him and gave him a push into their living room. "Come in and take your coat off. Tell us where you've been."

"Ben, I had no idea. You certainly didn't tell Ma all these details. I wish you would have written me. Something. The Von Keller's man had you put away for a simple alley fight? That's crazy." Levi got up and paced the room. He'd listened for over an hour as his brother poured out the details of his time with the Von Kellers. Margaret running out before he could get her home...Nadine leaving him at the altar...being thrown in a prison camp. This made Levi see red. "What if he'd left you there? I can't abide by that. I can't see how any man that shared his home would be so callous." Ben reached out as Levi stalked by him.

"Levi, I know why he did it," Ben said, resigned. "He thought I was just playing with the Von Keller girls' hearts. He just wanted to teach me a lesson." Ben stood and joined Levi at the hearth. "And it worked, I hightailed it out so fast that I never looked back."

Allison rolled back in the rocking chair, hands rubbing her belly. "I don't know, Ben. Everything you did for Margaret was heroic. Even what you offered to do for Nadine." She paused. "But I'm not one to talk. Levi was doing everything within himself to help me, and I still misjudged him." She shook her head.

Levi rubbed his face. "I would never want to go through that again."

"Love does conquer all," Allison whispered.

"Honestly," Ben turned to look at them. "I've had enough time away from the Von Keller dairy to think. Even in my short time living with the Larsons, I can see the things God was wanting to do. Even getting away from your shadow." He raised an eyebrow at Levi. "Taking some long hard looks at myself."

Levi sat back down and reached over to hold Allison's hand.

"I've been angry." Ben tightened his lips. "Angry about a lot of things. Angry Pa wasn't a man who could give any praise. Angry I wasn't there when he passed. Angry you kept me on your string. Angry that my older brothers do everything right."

Levi choked. "What?"

"Angry that I knew I was never good enough for Nadine. Angry that Margaret would live and die for her convictions and I didn't possess a drop of that kind of strength. But mostly, angry at myself. For waking up in jail cells. For saying I would only have one drink when I knew it was a lie. God was always calling me, deep in here." He pounded on his chest. "But like a coward, I ran to the next thing to just get away from myself." He ran his fingers through his hair. "But I can't get away from myself."

"Ben, you said now you can see the lessons. What do you mean?" Levi asked.

Ben stared out the window, where it was already dusk. He wondered if he had the words to explain. "You know how when we went fishing as kids? We'd get upset when the wind would come up and blow our lines back to the bank?"

Levi nodded.

"Then we got smart and clamped some weights on?"

"Yep."

"I've had no weights on my line. Anything and everything just blows me around. I haven't found anything important to me. Until I was with Margaret, I didn't know people lived with such purpose." He glanced at Allison. "She told me she thought I was close to finding my purpose."

"She always was a caring, sweet girl." Levi broke in. "Maybe you should go see her? Make amends."

"No." Ben shook his head. "I think it would cause her more pain."

"Do you care about her, Ben? Your face turned red, just now." Allison said.

"Of course. I care deeply about her."

"She's four or five years older than Ben," Levi said to Allison.

"I don't care about that," Ben piped in.

Levi and Allison looked at each other.

"She's also smarter and kinder and a lot better dancer." Ben turned and tossed a log on the hot coals.

"Dancer?" Levi asked. "I thought you said she had typhoid?"

"She did. This was weeks later, on her birthday."

"Before she left on the train with the little boy?" Allison asked.

Ben nodded, his brow crinkled. He'd said too much. "I can tell Ma's been praying. She asked me to follow after peace. I had peace at the Larsons. I had peace when it was time to leave. I have some money in my pocket, a decent horse, and my kindred in front of me. I just want to live from a new place. Stop looking over my shoulder. I want to find what God had intended for me all along."

47

By the end of the week, Levi knew he had to say some-thing to Ben. He'd weighed it out in his mind and prayed over it. It was just the two of them, working on some taxidermy one afternoon.

"I appreciate your help with these foxes. This one was starting to decompose." Levi added some stuffing to his animal.

"People pay you for these?" Ben shook his head.

"Here in the city, they do. This fox a gentleman wants mounted, like a trophy, I guess." Levi cleared his throat. "I've been wanting to tell you something. But it hasn't been easy. I keep thinking about when you said that you were angry at Pa. I understand why and I've hesitated because I don't know if what I tell you will help you have peace or make it worse."

Ben stopped what he was doing and eyed Levi.

"Remember when I told you about going to Ready Springs, running into the folks, the first time I took Allison and how we ended up getting married?"

Ben nodded.

"Pa said something that I don't think I'll ever forget. He'd had a dream. Not just any dream, he believed God spoke to him."

"Our pa? You're talking about our 'religion is for woman and children,' pa?'"

"That's right." Levi nodded. "He dreamed he was outside the cabin and we were all inside. A fierce wind came up, and he was trying to pull on the door to get in. He could see us all inside and no matter how hard he tried, he couldn't get in. Suddenly the wind took us all up into the air, and he was left alone. Now I can't say what the Lord uses, but something about his dream made him want to give his life to the Lord."

Ben scratched his neck, expressionless. "Hmm." The air grew still. "I'd had a letter from him, I wouldn't open it for the longest time. I didn't want to hear his voice of disapproval. Now it makes more sense. He actually wrote some very kind things."

"Because he really had changed. When we came to him before he died, he wept and apologized for being so hard on us. He was tender and caring to Ma, like I'd never seen before. You should have watched him love on little Miranda. I didn't know he even had an affectionate side. He wanted to read the Bible every day. He joked and smiled, like he was a different person."

"That's great," Ben said flatly. "What hurts is picturing you all around. James and Frieda. Levi and Allison. Little Miranda, Ma. But where is Ben? Who tried to find me? Did everyone just figure I wouldn't want to be there?" He jabbed his hands in his pockets, rocking back on his heels. "He still was the only father I've ever known. Would have been nice to be invited to the funeral."

"Of course you were invited. We just didn't know where to send word. I would have taken horse, stage, boat to get you there. That's something I deeply regret."

"Not your fault, Levi. You need to quit being my keeper." Ben let out a tired huff. "I was on the road, a couple weeks out from Ray and Thelma's. It's hard to write when you don't know where you're going."

Levi grabbed Ben's flannel shirt. "I'm sorry," he said, eyes piercing. "We love you. Pa loved you. I just wish you could have seen that side of him."

Ben nodded and put his hand over his brother's. "I'm not angry. I've been learning my choices have penalties attached to them. This was just one of the hard ones to swallow."

Levi released his grip and rubbed his hand up and down Ben's stiff arm.

Ben gave him a crooked smile and went back to stuffing his fox. "We have a good ma. She's faithful and strong. I guess every family has their troubles. You should have heard Mrs. Von Keller when she was riled. I think I was more scared of her than I was of Pa."

"That so?" Levi squinted at him. "I just remember her sad and crying. Ma trying to comfort her after their son died. Never paid enough attention, I guess."

"That's what Margaret would say about you. She remembers how handsome you were." He rolled his eyes. "Just 'cause you were quieter, all the girls took it as rejection." He laughed.

"I was dumbfounded by girls. If they didn't want to talk about hunting or fishing, I knew I had nothing to say." Levi remembered clearly why he never entered in the school-yard mischief. "All they wanted to giggle about was their clothes and ribbons. Margaret was different, though. She seemed to be a gentle soul, always looking out for others." Levi paused. "I noticed you never said much about missing the chance to marry Nadine."

"No." Ben swallowed hard. "She's certainly beautiful, but I think God spared me from a lot of heartache. She's a handful. I was just trying to do the right thing."

"I can understand that. It's a big step. I know God's guiding you." Levi tried to stand the fox on its feet.

"Was that how it was with Allison? At least in the beginning?"

"No, that girl just snuck right up to my heart. For some reason, I had myself convinced that God and I were good enough. But you were there, you know I was over my head. I didn't know if I was coming or going around her. I think I was unsure if I could let myself love like that. That real, hopeful, future kind of love. So I tried to just be a Good Samaritan." Levi shook his head, remembering his confu-sion. "It was the desire of my heart to be married, I was completely head to toe wanting her for my wife. I wish I'd had the good sense to admit it."

"What made you wake up?"

Levi laughed and felt the heat rising up his neck. "First off, it was *after* we said our vows."

"I think I know where this is going. Don't say anymore. She'll always be my sister-in-law and, well, you know…" They both snickered.

"What's so funny?" Allison walked in with two mugs of hot coffee. Levi squinted and looked to the back wall. "Nothing." He reached out for a mug. "Thanks for the coffee."

"Stuffed fox." She gave a lopsided grin, gazing at their work. "If Levi isn't shooting something, or trapping something, he can stuff something."

"Yes, he can." Ben glanced at her belly, fighting the smile that was curving upward.

"I feel like I've walked in on something."

Levi tried carefully to read her expression. "I was just telling Ben how I fell in love with you, but was too stupid to admit it."

She gave him a forgiving wink.

"If you hadn't fallen off a cliff right in his path, he probably would still be up in the cabin at Sault Creek, preaching to Patch and the four walls," Ben said. "God does work in interesting ways."

"I'd never thought of that, Ben." Allison nodded. "Levi was just being who he is. A trapper. Seems to speak to the fact that what God has for us, He'll put right into our path. He said He's concerned with all our ways. What do you think, Levi?"

His head flew up. "I don't think God caused your uncle to push you off a cliff just so I could have a wife." He looked to Allison and back to Ben for some agreement. "I think

He does watch over us, but also gives us free will with our choices. I do believe we can find His grace and strength, even when it looks bleak. And in the depths of our own stupidity, He will bless us." Allison dropped her chin, smiling. Snuggling up to Levi, she gazed into his eyes. Levi let go of the fox and wrapped his arms around her, slowly kissing her forehead, cheek, and lips.

"I thought we were talking about God," Ben complained. "This marital display is a bit much for me. I'm thinking I should leave you two alone." He headed for the open door.

"No, no." Levi chuckled, still holding Allison close. "Don't go."

Ben was already out in the small yard between the house and the workshop. "Take your time, I'll be back," he called back to them. Rounding to the back of the shop, he watched his horse nibble the grass by the fence.

"Hey, Jordan." He scratched behind the horse's ears. "You ever been plumb stupid for a pretty filly?" His mind drifted to all the young woman he had been near these last months. Each one had their sweet moments. Moments that made him want to hold them close. Moments he couldn't wait to forget. He rubbed the soft velvet hair under the horse's chin. One face smiled back at him in his thoughts. One young woman he'd be stupid forward and backward to win her love. He'd do anything to have her back in his life. He appreciated Levi saying love is risky and making a personal declaration is a tough thing.

So do it scared.

That was a strange thought. *Do it scared. Tell her what you think and feel.* His heart started to pound. What if she showed him the door?

But what if it's wonderful?

48

Ladies of Mercy School, Chicago. Six months later.

"Margaret, your last article was amazing. So different from your other writings," Mr. Frank said to her. "As the chaplain here, I might ask you to speak at the next chapel. Your words were very touching, finding the love of God not based on what we do, but who we belong to. So many of us falter on the side of works and not much faith." Margaret stood in the teachers' refreshment room, nodding her appreciation.

"All your articles have changed," Mrs. Canby said, "since you returned from your mission trip last fall. The article on finding our approval from God is my favorite. It changes our service when we do things from approval, not for approval. I'm helping my second graders look at what they do well. Society has already cast them aside, yet they can learn to see the good things God sees in them. It's so important, at any age." She smiled.

Margaret took the kettle and poured hot water over her tea steeper. "Thank you. God has had me on the potter's wheel." She sighed.

Mrs. Chamberlin, the school director, walked in. "Wonderful, I was hoping to catch some of our staff. I wanted to introduce you all to our new math and woodshop teacher."

Margaret removed the tea ball from her teacup and lifted the cup to her lips. She looked up and saw a familiar, tall, handsome man.

"Oh, dear!" Her hot cup and tea suddenly spattered all over the floor.

"Miss Von Keller, are you all right?" someone said. She didn't remember the cup falling from her grasp. The other teachers bustled around, looking for a cloth to help her with.

"Did you burn yourself, dear?" Mrs. Chamberlin said.

"No, I don't think so." She carefully leaned around Mrs. Chamberlin. Could it really be?

"Bens, what are you doing here?"

Ben smiled at Mrs. Chamberlin, who looked confused. "Mar...Miss Von Keller and I are acquaintances."

"Actually, our parents were friends when we were children." Margaret tried to wipe the tea off her skirt.

"Are you sure you didn't get burned?" Ben asked. "Your face is very red."

Margaret let out a small whimper. "Woodshop? Really?"

"Mr. Graham had a wonderful proposal. He was aware of the joblessness of the young men from the slums. He felt he could start a woodshop program for them where they would learn a useful trade." Mrs. Chamberlin beamed. "Not just building homes and such, but furniture, maybe pews for churches. Some of the things the boys could sell, helping keep the woodshop running."

Speechless, Margaret tugged at her collar. The other staff introduced themselves, excited for the new program. "He'll be staying in the B building and helping Mr. Frank with the some of the night shifts."

Margaret felt herself swaying. "So you are not married yet, Mr. Graham?" Suddenly, she realized how unfitting the question was.

He grinned, never taking an eye off her. "No. And you? Have you walked the aisle?"

"No," she whispered, staring back.

Ben shook hands with the others as they told him how nice it was to meet him. Margaret had to tell herself to breathe. She couldn't believe he was standing here. He looked wonderful, more wonderful than any human on the planet.

"Margaret, since you and Mr. Graham are acquaintances, would you mind finishing the tour? I have a meeting in a few minutes."

"Of course, I'd be happy to." She couldn't look at Ben. Surely the staff saw her unusual reaction. The two walked out to the hallway.

"Perfect timing." He grinned ear to ear. "I can't wait to see Henry."

Margaret was still in shock. She couldn't for the life of her follow him. She willed her feet to move. *What's this about? He's not a teacher. Had he lied?* "Henry." The boy's name burst into her thoughts.

"I can't wait to see him. When is his lunch? Will he be out in the play area?"

She turned and faced him. "Henry, of course. Yes, yes, you can see him. He'll be so delighted to see you." Something in her gut dropped. He was here to be near Henry.

"Are you really going to work here? I didn't think you could ever live in the city." They walked down the steps of the C building.

He smiled at her and looked up. "Spring is trying to break through. It's been a long winter." He sounded sorrowful.

"What happened?" Margaret touched his arm, and they stopped at the bottom of the steps. He looked over his shoulder where a line of little ones walked to the next building. He looked back at her, close yet distant. What was in those warm brown eyes? Pain? Longing? Hope?

"I needed a swift kick from God, and His timing is never late in that." He shook his head. "I knew this could be uncomfortable for you. I didn't know what your life was like and I didn't want to disrupt anything here. You don't have to give me the time of day, really, I'll be fine. I had to find myself and find my purpose, as you told me to." His face softened. "I realize I love children, I love building things. I think I'm fairly good at it. You know I'm not a math teacher. But my proposal for the woodshop has so much to do with measuring and math, I think your director overlooked my lack of formal education."

"It is a brilliant idea, Ben. Really."

"Your director never asked me how I knew of the conditions in the city, or the needs of the children." He smiled.

"It was all from you, but I never mentioned anything about you. I wasn't even sure you'd be here, until ten minutes ago. I really don't want to complicate...you know..." He looked to the ground.

"I was so shocked to see you. I've tried a thousand times to put you out of my mind, and then I look up and there you are." Her laugh dipped, and there was the sweetest agonizing silence. She shouldn't have said that, but stared at him anyway. He looked so healthy, his face fuller, body thicker. All those weeks he made sure she and Henry had plenty to eat, taking whatever was left. She broke the heart-stirring recollection. "The children should be coming out for lunch soon. Let's walk and see if we can catch our Henry."

"Mags! Oh, wait a minute. I've got to call you 'Miss Von Keller.' I'll have to work on that. Hey, is that him?" Ben's voice boomed. "That boy over there?' He pointed across the patio. "He's grown six inches!"

"That's him, Mr. Graham." She emphasized his name. "And he's only grown two or three inches." She noticed one of the other teachers watching them.

"Ben, how are you going to greet him? The staff here knows I brought him back from the reservation, but they don't know about us." She looked down quickly, wondering if she had just romanticized it all in her mind. Her face turned red with embarrassment.

He finally took his eyes off Henry. "Oh, I never thought of that. What do you want to do?"

"I think I'll say my goodbyes now. I need to prepare for my next class. When he sees you, he'll probably want to jump on you. Maybe whisper in his ear that you work here now and have to show some distance."

"That doesn't feel right," Ben scoffed.

"Or we go to my director and explain everything."

Ben straightened up. "That's what I don't want. I don't want to cause you any more pain than I already have."

She blinked, stunned by the sudden honesty of his words. "I have to go." She turned, wiping her damp eyes.

"Can I go to church with you Sunday?"

"I suppose so. Meet me on the corner of South and Sixth Street. Say, nine o'clock."

She wondered if Ben had even heard her. He had already moved swiftly toward Henry.

*   *   *

Henry looked older. The haircut, the new clothes—he wasn't the same ragged child who had helped him care for Margaret. Ben waited until most of the children left the outside table. Henry was working on his second bowl of soup, and Ben looped his long legs around the bench and sat next to him.

"Hey, buddy." Ben nudged him.

Henry looked shocked and then cracked a large smile. "What are you doing here?" He stood and wrapped his arms around Ben's neck.

"I am 'Mr. Graham' to you, bud, and I'm here at the school to teach woodshop and building things."

"Can I be in your class?" Henry lifted the bowl and drank the last of the broth.

"Of course you can. I mean, it'll take me a few days to get some wood and tools together." He looked around and cleared his throat. "Miss Margaret is worried that all the people here don't know we all lived together. It would cause a problem with her job." Ben wondered if Henry would grasp the implications. "So we aren't going to talk about it with the people here. Okay?"

"Okay." He wiggled his nose. "They took my slingshot away. They said I could have it back if I didn't use it on the other kids."

"Do you like the other kids?" Ben wondered how he'd be accepted.

"Yeah, they're my friends. I still have the cup and ball game you gave me."

"I felt bad I didn't get to say goodbye to you." Ben wanted to somehow say he was sorry.

"Miss Von Keller told me you had to get back to your old job."

Miss Von Keller. Henry had already adapted to his new culture. Well, he had prayed long and hard. Hadn't he felt this is what God wanted him to do, even if Margaret had moved on? He hadn't thought he would have to keep his relationship with Henry a secret.

"I know how hard it must have been to start over. I mean...come here. Maybe you can help me learn the ropes?"

"Okay." Henry got up from the bench, gathering his napkin and bowl. "We don't have any jump ropes. But we can play tag."

49

"You've been wearing your hair down this week."

"Oh, have I?" Margaret sat on the small chair in front of her mirror. She smiled at her roommate, putting the brush down. "I'll wear it up for church."

"It looks lovely down, too. You look younger, or something. I keep thinking something's wrong, though. You've been distracted. I can hear you tossing and turning all night. Is it the next temperance meeting? You haven't protested in months."

"No, no." Margaret nervously pushed the pins around on her table. "Just some changes at the school, nothing serious." She caught her reflection. What a liar. The stress of avoiding Ben, then looking for him, then hiding, then looking, was taking a toll. She wondered if he would even remember where to meet her this morning. What about the staff from Ladies of Mercy— some of them attend the church. They were bound to be seen together. She took a deep breath and grabbed her shawl.

"See you later." Margaret reached for the door.

"Can you wait a bit? I'll only be a few more minutes."

Margaret squinted. "I'm meeting someone."

"What kind of someone?"

Margaret shook her head, still facing the door. "He's a new teacher at the school. He asked about attending church."

"Oh, why didn't you say so! Now everything makes sense." Eugena laughed. "Some changes at the school all right. Is he handsome?"

"I don't know." Margaret opened the door flustered, "Maybe I'll have something to tell after church."

"Oh, you better," Margaret heard Eugena say, as she closed the door.

Making her way to the bottom of the stairs, Margaret froze. She couldn't get her heart to stop pounding. All these friends and colleagues didn't understand. How could they understand? What would she say? That Ben has the strongest arms she's ever felt? That his care and kindness takes over every part of her heart? That she only rehearsed every laugh, every late night talk? That his kisses have yet to leave her mind and body? That she had spent months trying to forget him? She yanked the door open and ran down the stone steps. It was only a few blocks, so why was she running? How ridiculous she must look. She recognized his perfect backside and willed herself to slow to a walk. A crisp white shirt pulled on the thickness of his shoulders, and his soft brown hair lightly touched his collar.

He turned around and smiled.

Margaret panicked and walked past him.

"What's wrong, Mags?" He followed her.

"Down here, there is a wash room in the basement of this building," she said. They stepped down five or six stairs, sunlit through the small low windows.

"Are we going to church?" Ben asked.

Heaven help her, he looked so innocent, yet it was now or never.

"Ben, here's the truth. Straight out. I know that's how you like things."

He nodded.

Why couldn't she get a full breath? "I love you. You know this." Her voice faltered. "I told you months ago." She sucked in new air. "I admire your desire to be here. I see it as one of the best ideas for the problems in the city. I do. I just don't know what to do. I can't figure it out." She swallowed hard. "I couldn't bury my feelings when you weren't here, and now that you are here, even my roommate knows there's something wrong with me." She closed her eyes and felt his hands begin to rise up her arms. They were warm, and she swayed forward, but she needed to stay strong.

"Mags, come here." He pulled her against him, holding her. It felt so familiar, so warm, so right. He lightly kissed her temple. "I love you, too. Can you forgive me for being young and stupid?"

"Of course," she murmured. His words were sweet, but she couldn't survive another heartbreak with him.

"I've been in the darkest valley." He broke in. "I had almost convinced myself I could never get out. I've made so many mistakes, and you've seen most of them." He pulled back, gripping her elbows. "I had one of the most valuable things in my pack, and I wouldn't even read it. My father had written me a letter before he died. I don't know how to explain it, but it began to change me, what I believed about myself. I needed to go back home to Ready Springs. I knew there was nothing there for me, but it pulled me back. I watched my ma living a new life and realized all my family has changed. I somehow convinced myself they were all like a tightly sewed hem and I was the only loose thread. But everyone has moved on, so maybe I just needed their permission to be my own self. And then you..." he bit the corner of his lip, fighting emotion. "...you loved me, like God loves me. Thank you for your faith in me. I can't say it right, but it revived my faith in myself and that God is for me." He paused, enjoying the sweet silence. Placing a soft kiss on her cheek, he said, "But I don't want to be your younger brother."

He smiled, gently kissing her cheek again. "I want to marry you. I want to love you with everything in me." Closer and closer to her lips he came, until she moved her chin up, meeting him. It was everything she remembered and more, so tender and full of desire.

He pulled back, breathing hard, resting his head on her forehead. "I don't want to take over the dairy...ever." His voice was raspy and he quickly tasted her lips again. "I promise to support your causes," he said, eyes locked on hers. Arms wrapped around her body, he slowly lifted her off her feet. "I promise to always be taller than you." She threaded her hands through his hair as she slowly inched down his body. When her feet touched again, he reached into his pocket. He pulled out the gold chain with the little cross.

"You broke this chain, that day at the dairy. It wasn't easy to fix." His eyes dropped as he opened the clasp. "Nothing worthwhile ever is." He looked back at her, remorse and hope mixed in his eyes. "Will you take it back?"

"Yes," she whispered.

"I guess I should mention I stole this, about a year ago."

"Oh, Ben…"

"It was laying on the ground." He rubbed the gold cross between his fingers. "But God spoke to me. He showed me His grace and forgiveness. I know it was God, because I haven't wanted a drink since."

She put her hands over his and stared into his eyes. "Amazing. Some chains need to be broken off, others only He can repair."

Reaching up, she traced her fingers across his cheek. "This repaired necklace will always be precious to me. Just…just as long as I don't get Nadine's ring."

He brushed his nose gently across hers. "The ring is now a horse named Jordan."

"Perfect," she whispered. "Oh, I've missed you."

"And I missed you. Your voice was always in my head. Almost leading me. The part about being close to my purpose, do you remember that?"

She nodded.

"I didn't know I even had a purpose, or needed one. One day Allison was talking about the things God puts in our path. Suddenly things became clear. It's not that hard.

I just had to look at the things I love. I love children. I love wood and enjoy making things. How could I put it together? And you, lying on that old rug in the Ketchum's storage shed, reading me your articles about the conditions in the city. The children left to their own. Thinking about what future Henry would have. God used all of it. I wish you would have been there when your administrator gave me the job. I just about jumped through the roof. I know it sounds silly." He pressed his lips together, eyes tender. "But I knew for the first time that this is my purpose. This is why I'm on this earth."

"Oh, Bens, I believe it, too." Her eyes welled up. "There was this day…" she lightly touched the hair behind his ear. "…that I was waiting to go to heaven." She wiped a loose tear. "And I looked up and there you were. The goodness in your eyes moved me beyond words. I could feel it bringing life back to me. Purpose has never been about greatness, it's always been about goodness. You have goodness in wagon loads. And so many others will feel your goodness, too." Tears rolling free, she closed her eyes and breathed in the moment. Quickly opening them, she said, "You said something about marrying me?" She waited with a sweet smile.

"Yes. I did." Clutching her hands, he got down on one knee. "Margaret Von Keller, I promise to spend every day being worthy of your love and devotion. To love you in the grace of God. Will you be my…" He stopped, a twinkle twitching in his eye, "…just a few years older, but nonetheless, my wife?"

"Oh, Bens!" She pulled him back up to stand. "Yes, and I will love you in spite of *your* age, and grow old and sassy with you." She grasped his face in her hands. "God will guide us."

"Amen, then!" He grabbed her and dipped her back, watching the gold chain gather against her beautiful skin.

"The final burden of remembrance does not rest on us; if it did, we should all despair. Jesus is called the author and perfecter of our faith" (Rom. 12:2). He is the One who put the romance in our hearts and the One who first opened our eyes to see that our deepest desire is fulfilled in Him. He started us on the journey, even though we may for long seasons forget Him, He does not forget us." *The Sacred Romance*

Brent Curtis, John Eldredge

Julia David

Break every chain   *Inspired me-*

There is power in the name of Jesus
There is power in the name of Jesus
There is power in the name of Jesus
To break every chain
Break every chain
Break every chain

You're the all sufficient sacrifice
So freely given such a price
Bought our redemption
Heaven's gates swing wide

There's an army rising up
There's an army rising up
There's an army rising up
To break every chain
Break every chain
Break every chain

To break every chain
Break every chain
Break every chain

Publishing: United Pursuit Music (ASCAP) (admin. by info@unitedpursuit.com)
Writer(s): William Andrew Reagan

Listen/Watch: https://www.youtube.com/watch?v=EN6 w2JX1p8g

Listen/Watch: If you need to get movin' (like your house clean) listen to Kim Walker and Jesus Culture, Break Every Chain

Julia David

Lift Your Head Weary Sinner   *Inspired me-*

Lift your head weary sinner, the river's just ahead
Down the path of forgiveness, salvation's waiting there
You built a mighty fortress 10,000 burdens high
Love is here to lift you up, here to lift you high

If you're lost and wandering
Come stumbling in like a prodigal child
See the walls start crumbling
Let the gates of glory open wide

All who've strayed and walked away, unspeakable things
you've done
Fix your eyes on the mountain, let the past be dead and gone
Come all saints and sinners, you can't outrun God
Whatever you've done can't overcome the power of the blood

If you're lost and wandering
Come stumbling in like a prodigal child
See the walls start crumbling
Let the gates of glory open wide

If you're lost and wrecked again
Come stumbling in like a prodigal child
See the walls start crumbling
Let the gates of glory be open wide

(Oh, oh, oh, oh, oh, oh, oh, oh,)
(Oh, oh, oh, oh, oh, oh, oh, oh,)
(Let the chains fall)
(Let the chains fall)

Written by: David Crowder, Ed Cash, Seth Philpott
Lyrics © CAPITOL CHRISTIAN MUSIC GROUP
Lyrics Licensed & Provided by LyricFind

Listen/Watch: https://www.youtube.com/watch?v=PgEAh
VTjV44

Author's note:

One of our well-intensioned professors in Bible College, said to my husband and I, "ministry is find a need and meet it." Not too complicated- got it. Here we go!

Now, twenty-five years later, I think, Holy Cow, there are A LOT of needs in the world! Neighbors, family, work, and church are the obvious things in our path, and so we narrowed down the great commission to doable pieces. I need a nap just thinking about *those* areas.

Then we hit ministry burnout.

How can God allow burnout with such kindly Christian servants? Revealed a bit later—our hearts for service were coming from a twisted place. Somehow "more was better" and "fatigue wasn't Godly," had slipped in. "The only goal was excellence" and "die to self" rang out our tired ears. <u>From crashing came clarity.</u> One area that became clear was every area of ministry is not ours to meet. We *do* have the Godhead Trinity still in control. (Can I get a Halleluiah!) The other was the revelation Margaret got while sitting on a *bench with Ben. Why are we striving for things we already have? If someone had stopped me (and some tried) and asked, why are you going so hard? I would have said, 'it's all for God. Pleasing Him.' Which would beg another question, so if you stopped the hamster wheel life, would God still be pleased with you, approve and accept you? Had I been a martyr servant without realizing I already have all the love, grace and approval I could ever want? (Like the cross didn't confirm that?) It was a **huge** belief shift for me. Never serve

God because you have to, but because your well-tended soul just graciously wants to.

Better yet, just be His daughter. It's so fun.

<u>Read more on this-</u>
Simple Tuesday, Emily P. Freeman. She taught me how to be a *bench sitter.
Present-over-Perfect, Shawn Niequist. She taught me, God loves (and approves) of rested, content souls. (And now I do too.)

Kickn' those broken chains to the curb-
Freedom and Grace-
Julia

Come visit at: Juliadwrites.com

What about runaway Nadine? Abandon and alone, her riveting story picks up in Black Coat. Mighty Ones, Book 3, Out 1/18.

www.ingramcontent.com/pod-product-compliance
Lightning Source LLC
Chambersburg PA
CBHW030556180626
46816CB00005B/1567